The Lost Girl from Belzec
Ravit Raufman

Producer & International Distributor
eBookPro Publishing
www.ebook-pro.com

The Lost Girl From Belzec
Ravit Raufman

Translation: Yael Schonfeld Abel

Contact: raufman1@013net.net
ISBN 9798409923518

In memory of Julia Pepiak, Righteous Among the Nations.

THE LOST GIRL FROM BELZEC

RAVIT RAUFMAN

～

Imagine your horror movie: the phone rings and the screen displays Ariella Appel's name. "Hello," you answer, and are told that Adva, her daughter whom she loved, has cut herself again, but deeper this time, and more severely. You rush off to Tel HaShomer Hospital, Intensive Care, and ask at the desk for Adva Appel.

"Are you her mother?" the nurse inquires, and you reply that you aren't. *Her sister?* No. Not family at all. *Well, then, who are you?*

"Her therapist?"

The nurse assesses you with a gaze. They cannot share any information with you at the moment.

And imagine it's not a horror movie, but it's actually happening. And while you're wandering the hospital corridors, as the doctors fight for your patient's life (who knows, maybe she can still be saved?), the phone rings again, and Amnon's number appears on the screen.

"Noga," he tells you. "I understand you didn't end up making it to Mom's."

"No," you reply, debating whether to tell him where you are now. There's obviously no point, but you still hope for one. You would like to tell your brother you were already on your way to Mom, until you had to do an abrupt about-face. And you would like to tell him many more things. But he speaks up first. While you were gone, it turns out, your mother slipped in the shower. Imagine your mother waiting for you, and waiting for you, until she feels conditions are right for a final collapse, for spreading out on the shower floor tiles, like an indictment. Imagine the caps of the shampoo and the conditioner raised, gaping, as if caught in mid-query. *Where are you?* And imagine Ariella Appel appearing at the end of the corridor, collapsing, pale, into Israel Appel's arms.

"It's over," she tells him. "They can't save her."

You assume your therapeutic expression, the one covering your skin like a mask protecting you from all the years roiling beneath it. *I had to come here,* you'll think. Or that's what you'll imagine yourself thinking, although you know. It's not like anyone is actually waiting for you here. It's not like caring for this girl, who, in any case, had never thought life was such a blast, can relieve you of the memory of another girl, the one you once were. The one who once loved someone down to her very bones, down to the last cell in her body. It's a different force that once again propelled you from your parents' home, meaning your mother's. This mother who, one day, with a ravishing *abracadabra*, made the one you love disappear. And you thrust the cell phone, whose screen remembers the number of your living brother, deep into the pocket of your coat, and for a moment, you think he really does want to talk to you.

Noga, he might want to tell you, meaning his screen does. *Noga, I'm sorry. Lily and Iris are sorry too. Maybe even Dad.* The two screens can conduct a family conversation of sorts, and you and Amnon wouldn't even know what it was about.

"We can't share any information with you," the nurse had said earlier, and in the disturbing light of the fluorescent bulbs, you wonder what she knows. What she knows about all the information that could never be shared with you. And there, your mother is spread across the bathroom tiles, like an indictment, and what's going to happen now?

1.

The prettiest pipe in Dad's collection was from Egypt. It was big and black, and we called it "the peace pipe," even though there was no peace between Israel and Egypt yet. And the prettiest postcard from the collection of postcards Dad would send was from Japan. It showed the face of a woman with almond eyes. When I moved the postcard, one of her eyes would wink. On the back of the postcard, he had written out, in printed letters: *To Noga my big girl, who can already read, hello from faraway Japan. Say hi to Mom, too.* In the afternoon, I'd sort out the postcards and the pipes by country, trying to match a postcard to every pipe until eight p.m. arrived, and then Mom would take me back to the children's house,[1] to put me to bed.

Our house was in the kibbutz's old people's neighborhood. On our right was Clara, who worked in the laundry. Across from us lived Hilda and Shmul, the only old people in the neighborhood who were still a couple. Next to them was Kalman; I have no idea what he looked like; he hadn't left his house ever since Sarah passed away. There was a loquat tree in his yard, and the bats would spit out the peels of the fruit on the walls. "Ew," Mom would say when she saw the spitting through the window. "Ew," she also said about the many cats that Clara raised. Hilda's Shmul was "ew" as well, and Mom said Hilda knew why. Other than those neighbors, the neighborhood also included a little old cabin in which no one lived.

---

1   The kibbutz (plural kibbutzim) is a form of collective community in Israel that was traditionally based on agriculture. Communal child rearing was the standard in most kibbutzim, from their establishment in the early twentieth century until the 1980s. The children lived in the children's house, under the supervision of a *metapelet* (caretaker), and had communal sleeping arrangements with their peers, visiting their parents at "the parents' house" only for several hours a day.

My preschool teacher was named Sigal, and her cat was called Blackie. Sometimes, in the afternoon, I'd go with Carmel and Einav to visit Blackie. We would give her milk in a bowl, and when Blackie was a year old, Sigal allowed us to tie a red ribbon with a bell around her neck. We would walk Blackie along the paths of the kibbutz and the bell would ring. We took her on strolls to the dining hall, to the club, to Nahum's shoemaking workshop, and one time, she even went with us to the pool, on the jacaranda lane, where a bee had once stung me. We couldn't bring her to Mom's house since Mom was allergic to animals. But when I told her about Blackie, she said it was good to have something to love: "It's mentally healthy." Mom was a social worker who knew about things that were mentally healthy. For example, raising me was mentally healthy. Being away from Dad was also mentally healthy, because that way, they missed each other and were always happy to meet once every few months, when he returned home from conventions abroad and brought fancy things that were new to the kibbutz: a device that extracted pomegranate seeds, a special hard cheese slicer that could be used on the holiday of Shavuot, when the kibbutz received hard cheese, as well as a contraption that extracted the core of an apple. Some things were not so mentally healthy, but were unavoidable, for example when Nadav died. Mom said you couldn't choose everything in life, but they had me, and they were very happy. And they also had Iris and Lily and Amnon, all of whom sometimes came home on weekends.

Other than Blackie, who was mentally healthy, I also liked Billie Goat, who was raised in our petting zoo, as well as Polynesia, the parrot I was in charge of in preschool. When Polynesia grew ill, I could already write, and I sent a letter to Dr. Dolittle on behalf of all the kids in Palm Tree Preschool. We explained to the doctor that our preschool was in big trouble. That Polynesia was feeling very bad. He was limping, coughing, and he was feeling downcast, too. Sigal was the one who suggested the word "downcast" and it seemed appropriate. We explained to Dolittle that we knew he was very busy, that there were plenty of animals to take care of. But we truly (and Sigal suggested adding "and emphatically") requested that he find the time to visit us at Palm Tree Preschool as soon as he could, if possible. On a separate page, we included the entire class's signatures. Those who couldn't write yet were allowed to scribble or draw instead of signing. We gave the envelope, addressed, "To: Dr. Dolittle, England," to Aviva who worked in the post office, and she promised to send it. After Polynesia died, we buried him behind the sandbox, and Mom said it was okay to cry and express feelings.

There were other animals that died in our preschool. The ants from the ant farm, the fish from the aquarium, and also our rabbit, who, because I asked nicely, got to be called Nadav, but when Carmel yelled really loudly because a bee stung her, Nadav died of a heart attack.

In our talks before afternoon nap, Sigal would tell us about interesting things happening in the world. Before our trip to the sea, she told us that if we looked far, we could see how the water blended into the sky. I asked if, during the talks, I could show the class the postcards my dad sent from a bunch of interesting countries, even from Africa, and Sigal said I could do it sometimes, but not every time, since we had to give other kids a chance, too. Before bedtime, she said that if we looked at the moon, we would see it had a face. And one time, after we were already in our PJs, she took us all out of class, arranged us in a line, and we walked in the dark to Wheat Preschool to see how the night-blooming jasmine, which was climbing up the preschool wall, bloomed in white.

At night, we'd sometimes have the same dream, about the old man who kidnapped us and tossed us into the deep end of the pool. In the dream, he'd walk among us like an ordinary guy, and even smile at our parents and talk to us around them like he was our buddy. We couldn't explain to our parents who he really was, since every time we tried to explain, we lost our voice. We would wake up sweaty and it was easy to see who else had the dream that night.

When Lily and Iris were discharged from the army[2], they worked for a month in the kibbutz's preschool classes. Lily worked at our class, Palm Tree Preschool, and Iris worked in Wheat Preschool. Lily would tell me, "At home, I'm your sister only, but at preschool, I'm everyone's caregiver."

When we graduated to the first grade, there was a big celebration on the lawn next to the club. We wore white shirts with a red flower embroidered at the edge of the collar, and sang "'A' is for Apple, 'B' is for Butter." The best part of the song was the chorus, when the six- and seven-year-olds, who were our age, drew with chalk and crayons. And best of all was when all the letters

---

2   In Israel, military service is mandatory both for men (three years) and women (two years) at the age of eighteen.

danced together. All the parents came to the ceremony, including my mother, who put a little note in my new pencil case, which said: *Best of luck, with much love. Mom and Dad.*

Anyone who was sick could sleep at their parents' house. There were lots of ways to be sick: a thermometer in the tea usually got the job done immediately. There was a rumor that so did swallowing chalk, but I never tried. You could also make lots of visits to anyone who was actually sick with a real fever. And you could also go out in the wind with your hair wet after washing it on Friday. But one time, after we'd already gone to bed, I was really and truly sick. They brought Dr. Ginat, the kibbutz doctor, to my bed at night, and when he woke me up and I accidentally called him "Dad," my mom got really upset. She said: *I knew it, I knew at once that something was wrong.* She also said: *Why does this always happen to me, of all people?* Then she wrapped me up in two blankets. One made of wool, which was called "the prickly blanket," and another flannel blanket, and asked one of the dads to help her carry me home. I stayed in bed for two weeks, in my parents' bed, and Mom lay down next to me on the rug. When she gave me the medicine, she let out a strange sort of whistle, a kind of *foo-foo-foo* sound reserved for such occasions, and said: *Don't worry, Nogi, you'll bounce back. It's just the flu.*

Every day, she made me tea, placed a damp towel on my forehead, and told me stories about the strange deaths of previous generations in the family. The most disturbing was the story of the *baba-koyna*, Grandfather's grandmother, who got pregnant when she was fourteen years old; no one knew who the father was. She was terribly tired when she had the baby, and grew even more tired when it didn't sleep at night. One night, the *baba-koyna* fell asleep holding the baby and dreamt that she was baking bread. At least that's what she said when they found her baby in the oven. When I asked Mom if it was a true story, she said she didn't know, and I asked to watch TV.

After a week of being laid up in my parents' bed, I knew the order of the TV shows by heart for every day of the week. In the morning, there were educational shows, and also a lady who made handicrafts, which she "happened to have prepared in advance." You could prepare the projects "for your little brother, or little sister." And those who didn't have little brothers or sisters, or whose siblings had died or left home, could just make them for themselves, or for their mother. Until six in the evening, there were cartoons and other good kids' shows like "Zipper." Then, there was programming in Arabic and a newscaster with plenty of makeup would say *Sadati wasadati*, before the show "Innovations and Inventions." At eight, after the news, the programs in Hebrew began again, but Mom insisted I go to bed so that I would get better, and also to maintain the same bedtime as the one at the children's house. It was mentally healthy. She lay down on the rug and closed her eyes, and that was the sign that I needed to fall asleep, too. I closed my eyes and planned which poem I'd send to the poetry corner on "Zipper." One day I wrote a poem called "I Had a Dream." I asked Mom to send it to "Zipper," Television Broadcast, Romema, Jerusalem, reciting the address to the tune the kids on "Zipper" always sang.

After she sent it off, I wondered to whom else I could send letters from home. I found addresses of girls my age from the Pen Pal column in *Baby Elephant* magazine, which had already published one of my poems, and in *Warbler* magazine, and in the newspaper *Davar for Children*, and even invited one girl from Kfar Yona to come visit me at my kibbutz. I invited her to come on Tuesday at five-thirty.

One evening, Mom was called over to the secretary's house since there was a phone call from Dad. She began to rush around between the walls of the house and stood in front of the mirror, dressing up, then changing her dress and putting on jewelry in honor of the phone call. She had a big copper broach that was a family heirloom, and I hoped it hadn't belonged to the *baba-koyna*. After the door slammed shut, I quickly followed her out without her noticing. I followed her in my bare feet all the way to the secretary's house, and when she picked up the receiver, I stood by the window. She was sitting in the armchair in the secretary's house in her dress with the copper broach, and I heard her say: *Ari, you haven't heard what happened? She's awfully sick. Her fever's sky-high.* And also: *You're staying in Tel Aviv? I told her you were at a conference in France. Send an appropriate postcard, maybe with a photo of the Eiffel Tower, if you can find one.* And she ended with "Kisses," and also with "I love you too," and "Good night," and "Yes, I know, missing each other is the best."

I managed to beat her home. By the time she arrived, I was already "fast asleep," like she told me later. I conducted an experiment to see whether when you closed your eyes, you still kept breathing, and I saw that you did, that breathing isn't related to the eyes. I heard her brushing her teeth, washing her face, and flushing the toilet, and also telling herself all kinds of things, like,

Ruthie, you're strong. Ruthie, you're pretty, before she lay down on the rug next to me.

In the next few days, she didn't believe me that I was healthy. I didn't know how to prove it to her. I did a backflip and a handstand. I sang the song about the ten little monkeys. I told her the joke about Billie Goat, that the olives we ate were actually her poop, and also the joke about Nadav. And when that didn't make her laugh, I explained that it wasn't our Nadav, it was Nadav the rabbit. Finally, she broke down and said, *okay, that's enough, Noga, you can go to class.*

***

The two letters arrived together: the letter from the producers of "Zipper" and the postcard from France, with a photo of the Eiffel Tower. I found them in the parents' mailbox at the dining hall, where it said: Aaron and Ruthie Glover. All of the kibbutz members were arranged in pairs inside the mailboxes, with the man's name first, and the woman's name next to him, and only once in a while was there the name of one member, man or woman, who had never gotten married. "Poor thing," Mom would say about a woman like that.

The letter from "Zipper" read, *Dear Noga, we received your nice poem. Way to go! We hope we'll find a place for it on one of our upcoming episodes.* The post-card from France was colorful: *My sweet Noga*, the letters in Dad's handwriting flickered on the back. *I heard you were sick, and I wish you a rapid recovery. All is well here in France, and I hope to come home soon. In the meantime, be good to Mom. Love you, Dad.*

Other than those two letters, not a single letter arrived from the girl in Kfar Yona, and I thought that was really not okay. After all, we had agreed to write to each other. I cried the whole day, and the next day too, during school. Leah, the teacher, asked what happened and I told her I was really sick. That I had a serious, fatal disease that sometimes kills people, and that there was one girl, from Kfar Yona, who was supposed to come visit me at five-thirty because I was sick, and she didn't, and if I died, she wouldn't even know.

2.

In the winter
The darkness of five in the evening gathers in the earth as if
it had never been illuminated
I like five p.m. in the winter. Perhaps I too was once
earth.

"Pretty and sad," I told Adva, who raised her eyes from her cell phone, on which she writes her poems. And when she said I was just saying it because I was her shrink, I told her she was right. And yet it was still pretty and sad.

We were sitting and staring into space in the room I had recently finished redecorating, staking a claim upon it that could never be taken for granted. See-through curtains, cream-colored walls except for the bluish wall with my diplomas. We listened to the murmur of the water purifier, from which I poured water for both of us every time, but while I would empty my glass in every session, Adva's glass would remain full. Sometimes we'd joke about the fact that Adva always left the glass full, but as time went by and the cuts on her arms multiplied, we stopped joking.

The session had already come to an end, and Adva asked that I at least do one little thing for her, and wouldn't pretend I was sorry when our time was up. If I really was sorry, I'd sit with her a bit longer.

"I know, there's no way to make it easy," I said, wondering if I believed myself, if there really was no way to make it easy, and if we truly did always have to end on time, and what was this constant negotiation over time. Then the door floated a little back and forth, never slamming all the way; Adva always left something of herself before leaving the room, walking out a five-foot-seven adolescent body that was misleading in its freshness, in a cheerfully colored tracksuit, its sleeves concealing five pink and red lines—some of them already fading since they were etched in with a box cutter, and one, relatively new, actually done with a pencil.

The meeting with Jonathan had been pushed back for two and a half hours due to unexpected prep for a matriculation exam, and I agreed to the unexpected delay although I had been supposed to show up early to be with my mother at the kibbutz, since Jenny was leaving for her Christmas vacation. Once again, I converted one time into another. Time with Jonathan instead of time with Mom, and I thought about how Jonathan was also converting time with his mother into time with me, and how in two and a half hours, we'd be sitting together, each of us fleeing from his or her mother, and imagining each other, putting together somewhat-new, somewhat-old characters out of the puzzle of life, finding temporary sanctuary in each other, the way I always rented out the rooms of my heart by the hour, vacating myself for a bit. And once again, I called my mother. Ruthie Glover. The one sitting in front of the TV on an eternal couch, with coffee and bread and jam, waiting for me.

"Hi, Nogi, sweetie, my pretty girl," Mom answered in an eighty-three-year-old voice. "Are you on your way?"

"No, Mom, I'm held up at the clinic. Did Jenny already leave?"

"She's leaving at one. Aren't you coming at one?"

"I'll come at four. Will you be okay?"

"At four, you say? Okay, four is fine."

"Will you manage?"

"I've managed so far, haven't I?"

The cell phone dropped to the armchair. Adva's breaths were still in the room; I envisioned the image of the red lines on her arm, like five Do Not Enter traffic signs, while wondering how I would talk about it with her parents, how I would tell them about a daughter they didn't know, in an action signaling a return of things to their natural formation, the one that could have been. And soon Jonathan would arrive, and my form would shift in front of his eyes, and his own form, and the room, with the purple orchid on the corner table, the one that had been a gift from a group of students, with detailed instructions on how to take care of it, it was a sensitive plant, and the silk curtains shielding the window, which looked out on Shimon HaTarsi Street, and on Tel Aviv, which was sweating even in winter, and on the cafés, and on the Filipinos gathering to celebrate Christmas Eve before they were deported, and on the Sudanese and the Eritreans, who, like Jonathan and Adva, were also finding temporary sanctuary here to convert one time into another, one place into another, one exile into the next.

The road from Tel Aviv to the kibbutz advanced like a saga I had learned to recite by heart, but whose meaning I had never truly figured out, and I rushed down it in the blue Opel in order to minimize my lateness. In the tricky light of the winter sun, Ariella's number flashed on the phone screen, and I thought about the gift of always calling at the wrong time, when things were hectic, and although two mothers in one trip was an overdose, I answered. The session with Adva was still fresh, the poem she had written about five in the evening was still echoing, although I couldn't remember what, exactly, gathered the earth in—winter or darkness.

"Noga," Ariella's voice broke into the receiver. The blue Opel stopped on the shoulder and made a U-turn.

***

In second grade, I moved into a room with Liat, Tamir, and Ram. Before bedtime, we liked to sing "Every Wave Bears a Memory,"[3] mostly the line "If I could only kiss those lips," which cracked us up. I told them that Tova Hershkovitz, the children's book author who wrote *From the Notebook of Storio the Elf*, was actually just a pen name of mine, and that I had written all the books in the series. Every night, before we went to sleep, they asked me to read them new chapters that hadn't been published yet, and that way, they would know what was happening before anyone else did. Every evening at eight, when Mom walked me to bed at the children's house, I planned out the next chapters in Storio the Elf's notebook, but one time, Liat told her father that Tova Hershkovitz was actually Noga, and he said that was poppycock, that Tova Hershkovitz was Tova Hershkovitz and Noga was Noga, who one day might be a writer, but in the meantime, was just a second-grader. They planned to give me the

---

3   "Ruthie," also known by its first line, "Every Wave Bears a Memory," is a song composed by poet and lyricist Haim Hefer based on a Russian song called "The Mail Trio Gallops." The lyrics deal with yearning for a distant beloved.

silent treatment, but I explained that he simply didn't know, that no one in the world knew that it was me and that if they were patient, they'd see that every night, until the end of the year, I would have a new chapter in the notebook.

During recess, we played with the guinea pigs. Each of us chose a guinea pig and we'd race them to see which one made it to the line next to the big swing first. Only Tamir was allowed to pick Juantorena, who was the fastest guinea pig, since if someone slow picked Juantorena and won the race, it wouldn't make sense. I always picked Golda, who was old, and no one expected anything from her anyway when it came to running. Sometimes Golda would take a rest in the middle of the course, just as Juantorena and Sebastian passed her by, vigorously competing for first place. No one noticed she was resting, and I'd whisper in her ear: *It's okay, Golda, you're a lot smarter than them. When you grow up, you'll be a great writer.*

In the shower, the boys liked to hide their weenie between their legs and say, "Girl peepee, girl peepee." After we toweled off and got dressed to the sound of the words, "I see London, I see France, I see someone's underpants," we had to go rest in our rooms with a book. We hated resting and got mad at the fifth graders, who didn't need to rest and pretended they were dying to do it but weren't allowed. Wake-up was at three-thirty. We ate bread with jam and played "Who's missing in our little house?" until it got to be four o'clock, and the first of us to notice, for example, Liat, who could read time, would yell: "G-o-ing to the pa-rents."

One day, Dad returned from France for a short visit. He came to Israel for a week before leaving for a conference in another country. I didn't know which one since he hadn't sent a postcard yet. Leah the teacher invited him to class to tell us about his research in the Gamla excavations, and he came. He brought all the kids sugar-coated almonds, and Carmel said they had those in Israel too, but the ones from France were yummier. Other than the coated almonds he also brought his research assistant, Nili, a tall woman with brown hair and a city-lady haircut, with a city-lady skirt and blouse, and high heels, and a necklace and earrings. Gamla was a Jewish city in the Golan Heights that was destroyed during the Great Revolt[4] at the end of the Second Temple period. Leah explained that a temple was a house of worship. Ram, the only kid in class whose parents were divorced, raised his hand and asked what 'the Second Temple' meant, whether it was like having two houses after your parents got divorced. And if so, how you decided which parent had the first house, and which had the second. Dad smiled and explained patiently that although a temple was a house of worship, it was still different than a house, and Neallie smiled too.

Gamla was a city surrounded by a wall in the days of Joshua bin Nun, an important leader whom Leah promised we would learn all about in fourth grade. And a lot earlier, in a period called "the Early Bronze Age," there had been a settlement there that was destroyed. Leah explained that "destroyed" was another word for "ruined." She handed out colored pages and everyone had to draw Gamla. I walked over to Leah and explained that because I knew Gamla really well, and had even taken part in the excavations there and found coins and all kinds of treasures, I wanted to draw something else, and she agreed that I could draw France. I tried to think what France looked like, and decided to draw France after it was destroyed. I took all the crayons that were on the table and smeared them all over each other, but it didn't look like anything, not even something that had been destroyed. I asked Neallie if she knew what France looked like, and she said she did, but that everyone had to draw from their imagination, that there were no rules here. Then my belly really started to ache from all the sugar-coated almonds and I asked Dad to go home with him, but he said he couldn't, that he had work to do, and that he'd be with me in the afternoon and would also tuck me in himself at eight.

On the way to bed, I told him I was working on a new chapter in Storio the Elf's notebook for Liat and Ram and Tamir. He asked who Storio the Elf was, and I explained that he was both an elf and a magician, that he had a magic pencil and a little notebook, and that he flew around among the children and wrote down stories. Dad said it was a great idea, and that if I looked around, I

---

4   The Great Revolt or First Jewish–Roman War took place between 66 and 73 CE. It was the first of three major rebellions by the Jews against the Roman Empire fought in Roman-controlled Judea, resulting in the destruction of Jewish towns, the displacement of residents, the appropriation of land for Roman military use, and the destruction of the Jewish Temple.

would see how there's a story in everything. He didn't need to say it, I already knew, but I still looked around, and I saw him and decided to find a place for him in the story. I told Liat and Ram and Tamir about a man who roamed between the different countries and, in each country, he had a research assistant dressed according to the tradition of that country. In Holland he had a research assistant with wooden clogs, in Japan he has a research assistant in a kimono, and in Africa he has a Black research assistant in a raffia skirt.

3.

Just three days after Mom slipped in the shower, I went back to work at the clinic, although Lily and Amnon had dismissed me back on the day it happened. "It would be a waste," they said. "There's no point in you staying."

When I opened the door, I discovered my orchid had wilted. Its purple head was drooping and its petals lay still at its feet. "I'm so sorry," I was mumbling at it when the phone rang and I saw Eli's number on the screen.

"Don't ask," I whimpered into the device. "Don't ask."

And he asked, "Is her condition worse again?"

I crossed out the session I'd scheduled with Adva for next Wednesday from my weekly planner. I took the red pen from the box of pens on my dresser and drew one short line over her name. That's it. All gone. Like all things in life that would arrive and then suddenly disappear.

"Who's missing in our little house?" I could ask my clinic next Wednesday, at one p.m. "Who's missing in our little house, and where and why has he disappeared?" I could continue asking my mother, although I knew in advance I would never get an answer.

I also crossed out the parental guidance session I had scheduled with Ariella and Israel Appel. Another red line slotted itself within the pages of the weekly planner, preparing me for the empty interval awaiting within my schedule. There were plenty of things to do within the empty interval. I could, for example, go to the unit to visit Mom, even if Lily and Amnon claimed it wasn't necessary. Now I could drive in a leisurely manner. No need to rush. Mom's spill was already history. And history, as we all know, cannot be changed. Now it was just Amnon asking, "It was your turn, right? I didn't get mixed up, right?" Now it was just Lily suggesting not to include me in the shift rotation anymore. "Come when you can. In the meantime, apparently, you've got other things to deal with. All kinds of patients you think you can save." Now it was just Iris calling from Houston. Not calling me; Lily was the one she called. "What happened?" she asked Lily. "What happened?" she asked Amnon, too. "Is it true, what I heard? Noga didn't show up?"

***

During autumn in third grade, something new happened. It happened when we started going to afterschool classes at four without going through the parents' house first. We had a different class every day. There was a cooking class, where we learned to make poached eggs and chocolate cake with sprinkles. There was a birding class, where we were given heavy binoculars and went with Yehuda to the area behind the fish pools, where we learned to distinguish between herons, ibises, storks, and flamingos, all belonging to the Ardea family. Yehuda told us that in Leviticus, the heron is mentioned as a bird that's an abomination and shouldn't be eaten, and asked for a volunteer to read the quote he had written down on an index card. I volunteered and read out loud: "*And these are they which ye shall have in abomination among the fowls; they shall not be eaten, they are an abomination... And the stork, the heron after her kind.*"[5]

Other than cooking and birding classes, there was a handicraft class with Hagit where we learned to weave baskets and embroider on a napkin. Those who had a hard time threading a needle, like me for example, could weave all through class without embroidering. There was a board game class and a ballgame class. Those who really didn't get along with the ball, like me for example, could play board games twice. And those who really didn't get along with the boards, like Ram for example, could play ball twice.

I don't remember which class I was returning from that day when I saw a light on in the little cabin in our neighborhood, which had stood empty all those years. I approached the window and saw a man in blue work pants, like the pants worn by the fathers of the rest of the kids who worked in agriculture and not in research. His shirt was tossed on the sofa, and next to it were lots of other clothes and a big bag. I took a look from up close because it was

---

5   Leviticus 11: 13, 19

something new in our neighborhood. His hair was pretty brown and a little curly. Other than the hair on his head, he also had hair on his chest, curlier than the hair on his head, and black, with a silver necklace dangling over it. I drew even closer to the window, but immediately ducked, since I heard him calling out loudly, in a strange accent: "Ro-nnie!" I didn't answer, because my name wasn't Ronnie, and also because I didn't want him to know I was there. He called out "Ro-nnie" again and I sprinted to the parents' house. I came in huffing and puffing and found Mom sitting in the kitchen, drinking coffee and eating a slice of bread with jam, really focused. It was always important to her to focus while she was eating, so as not to miss even a crumb of bread and jam. She would narrow her eyes into a really thin slit so that the food wouldn't run away anywhere, and always offered me some food too, but I never wanted bread and jam. In the summer, she would offer me "ice *cream*," emphasizing the second word, so that it sounded like "I scream." That's how she said it "*I scream*," not like everyone else said it, and when I couldn't refuse and surrendered to the ice cream, even with the wrong pronunciation, Mom would serve it to me in a glass and say, "There you are." For anything she gave me, she said, "There you are." And also: "You deserve it," but not the way we'd say it to one another in class, when it meant, "You had it coming." She meant that I "deserved" something good, even if it didn't sound good.

Usually, our house looked pretty small, but when Mom sat in the kitchen with her coffee and bread and jam, it looked small and empty and full. Empty of people and full of all kinds of noises, like invisible ants were walking around in there. I stood across from her, breathing heavily, and she stopped eating and told me she had a surprise for me: she had bought a wooden recorder for me, which I had wanted for a long time, so I could play "Mary Had a Little Lamb," which we had learned in recorder class, and also a little book in English about Greek mythology.

She said, "Are you happy?" and I said I was. I couldn't tell her what had happened in the cabin, and didn't dare ask how come someone was living there, or who it was. She asked how class had been, and I said it was fine, and also asked how Clara and all the neighbors were doing, since it had been a while since I'd asked about them, and it wasn't nice not to ask after old people. They might die soon, like the ants in the ant farm. Mom asked if I wanted bread and jam. I asked her whether she knew the Book of Leviticus said we shouldn't eat herons, and she said she didn't. Then, she suggested we read Greek mythology in English.

The Greek gods resembled people, but they were stronger and immortal. Immortals are the ones who would never die. They could get hurt, like Polynesia, but they had physical vigor and they always healed. When they were injured, their blood would turn into gold. They could feel all the emotions we feel. For example, they could be sad, and they could be happy. They could be bored, and they could miss people or animals. It said they could also commit immoral acts, meaning do things they shouldn't do, and you couldn't get mad at them. Sometimes they'd pick up people to do the things our parents did with each other—hug and kiss, and the children they'd have would be half-people and half-gods. The most important god was Zeus, who was the father of all the gods. He married his sister, whose name was Hera, and ever since she was both his sister and his wife. I asked Mom how that could be, and she said it couldn't, it was just in mythology, but she didn't say "ew," maybe because it wasn't real. Then it was eight o'clock and she walked me to the children's house to put me to bed.

The new chapter in Storio the Elf's notebook was about a woman named Ronnie. Ronnie married a guy who was actually a god, and she would do immoral things with him, until one day they had a girl who was half-woman and half-god and also half-girl. When their half-girl would get hurt, half of her blood would turn into gold, and half would stay blood. That's why they called her Red Goldie, since she was both hurt and not hurt.

The next day, I asked Ram whether he knew that in the Book of Leviticus, you couldn't eat herons, and he didn't, since he went to ballgame class every day. He said that even if you could, he didn't think he'd want to eat a heron. I asked him what he thought about me coming to ballgame class with him, and he said, "I'm thinking okay."

I was the only girl with all the boys. When we played mini-basketball and we split up into two groups. I was picked last, which is the same as not getting picked at all, but everyone understood why and I didn't have any reason to feel offended. Everyone understood my fast was the boys' slow, and that "there's no need to compare," like Mom said when I asked her who she loved more—me or Nadav, although once Amnon used to say that you actually do need to compare, and it's too bad he had a bunch of sisters and not even one brother.

After class, Ram asked whether I wanted to come with him to his dad's house, to put rocks in his dad's bed, but I told him I had other plans.

When I got to our neighborhood, it was already dark, and at the exact second when I was looking, the light came on in the cabin, like it was because of me. The lights in Clara's, Kalman's, and Shmul and Hilda's houses came on too. I decided that in the next chapter of Storio the Elf, Storio's eyes would be like an electric switch, and wherever he looked, the light would come on. There were two bicycles on the deck, and next to them was an electrical tool that looked like a gun, like the kind I'd seen once on "Kojak" when they let me stay up late only because Dad was coming back from Australia at night. The blinds were half-tilted and I couldn't see what was going on inside. Just as I was trying to get a better look, the door opened, and a man came out of the cabin, but not the one I'd seen yesterday. I thought about pretending I didn't see him, but he said, "Hi, nice to meet you. Who are you?"

"I live here." I pointed at the parents' house and added that it was nice to meet him too. "And who are you?"

"I live here." He pointed at the cabin and smiled. He had white teeth and a dimple, and his accent was like those people talking on "Kojak."

"Oh," I said, and after a few seconds of silence, I asked, "And what's this device?"

"That's a drill. Do you want to see what it does?"

I shrugged and said that if he wanted to show me, I didn't mind.

He plugged it in, held the handle, and pressed a button that made tons of noise until the entire neighborhood was shaking and it seemed like even Kalman would step out of his house in a second. I covered my ears with my hands and he brought the tip of the drill up against the wall and made a hole there.

"Noisy, huh?"

"Yeah, noisy. What's it for?"

"There'll be a peg here to hang things on. Want to try and operate the drill?"

The drill was heavy. I pushed the button that made a really loud noise until my mom stepped out of the house. She was wearing tight turquoise pants and a tight shirt in a similar color that clung to the folds of her stomach, and I told the man with the drill that I had to go.

"Is that your mom?" he asked, and I said no and ran away.

I didn't talk to her the whole evening. She asked how class was and I said it was fine. She asked if I wanted to play "Mary Had a Little Lamb" on the recorder and I told her that if I wanted to, I would. She asked if I wanted to read Greek mythology in English and I didn't answer, until she said, "Okay, Nogi, you don't have to talk to me if you don't want to," and I told her not to call me Nogi. I also asked her to show me proof that I wasn't adopted. By the time it was bedtime, I noticed that almost everything in the house had a shadow. The books in the bookcase cast a shadow on the wall. The vase with the gerbera daisies cast a very strange shadow on the tablecloth, and the edges of the tablecloth cast a shadow on the tiles. My mother had a shadow too, a really big one, that walked everywhere in the house along with her, and sat when she sat. And I had a shadow too.

Around eight, my mother walked me to bed at the children's house. The whole way, we kept a large enough space between us, without exchanging a word, and in the light of the kibbutz streetlights, our shadow was long and strange.

4.

"I'm entrusting her to you," Ariella said when she brought Adva to therapy for the first time, and a girl Julie's age sat down on the couch and asked whether she could smoke. I replied, "No smoking, no chewing tobacco, and no littering," and Adva said no problem, she would smoke on the street, and left the room for Shimon HaTarsi Street, stood in front of the crosswalk next to a group of Sudanese refugees, produced a cigarette and a lighter, and asked the Sudanese if anyone needed a light. I watched her through the window, and only when I saw her heading off beyond the trees with one of them, a tall young man, did I exit the clinic, huffing and puffing, and said I needed a light, urgently.

"Come on, then, sis," Adva grinned at me. "Come sit with us."

"You don't have to come here, you know," I said, and Adva reminded me that she actually did, that she was here under a court order, in case I'd forgotten.

"But you don't need to see me specifically," I replied, and when Adva said it really didn't matter whom she saw, I answered, "Well, then, only inside the clinic. We're not having a session on the street."

"Did you hear that?" Adva asked the Sudanese fellow next to her. "We're not having a session on the street," and he nodded at her with a smile, and the two of us went into the clinic. Not before she left her cigarette with him, and asked me, "Do you have something against Sudanese guys?"

"I have to admit I don't know them well enough," I replied, and she cracked up: *They're here, right outside your window*, adding, "Want to see the cuts on my arms?" I said I did. Fifty minutes later, Ariella arrived and asked how it went, and both of us said it was pretty bad. Adva arrived for the next meeting alone, cigarette in hand, exhaled a last puff in front of my face, and stubbed it out with her foot on the doorstep. "Don't worry, I don't chew tobacco, either."

It was my birthday. Eli and the kids had some kind of plan and after the last session, I started organizing the clinic in preparation for closing. I watered the orchid, closed the blinds, and just before leaving, I stood looking at the room that had emptied of all the teenagers visiting it. Of Jonathan, who was scared to come out to his family. Of Romy and her affair with her geography teacher ("How does something like that happen?"). Of Adva, with the red cuts on her arms, which had somehow managed to injure my insulation as well. Sweet sixteen. In a moment, the clinic would also empty of me. I would lock it and hear myself heaving a sigh of relief as if something really had been left behind. I would drive home and leave the clinic waiting for me, an island within my life, an island to which the teenagers' parents entrusted their burdens, what they could not bear on their own. "Here," they told me.

I thrust my cell phone into my purse, and while I was locking the door, it rang from the depths of the purse, like a child asking for one last thing before being tucked in.

"Yes, Mom."

"Nogilee, my pretty girl. It's your birthday today."

"I know, Mom. Can I call you back later?"

"Okay. Are you done with chemotherapy for today?"

"Psychotherapy, Mom, not chemotherapy. Psychotherapy."

"Okay, Nogilee, don't get mad."

And I hung up since Eli was on the line. "Are you on your way?"

I walked toward my parking spot. Spring was everywhere, indiscriminate. When nature receives a command to rejoice, it rejoices, even in Tel Aviv. Or at least, that was how it looked. I thought about the balloons and cake waiting for me at home, about the mandatory family rite that we would soon all conduct as if carrying out a collective punishment with obedient joy, Happy Birthday, and I was already replacing one self with another, donning the mother, the one who preferred to be with her own children and not with other people's children, the one who wasn't anxious about the encounter with home, or about the effort of spending time there.

The phone rang again, and once again I had to stop and retrieve it from the depths of my purse.

"Mom, I told you I'd call you back later."

"Right, my Nogi, but I wanted to say congratulations. You're a year older. I wish you good health and a happy life. Call when you're done with chemotherapy."

"Okay."

"Did Lily already call to say happy birthday?"

"Not yet."

"Well, I'm sure she'll call later. And Iris?"

"She hasn't either."

"And Amnon?" she continued asking as if the conversation was a chance to count off the names of her children.

"Amnon too."

"Amnon too what? Did call or didn't call?"

"Amnon hasn't called either; he might call later. Mom, I'll call you back in a bit?"

"Sure, right, he might call later. And remember that Dad must be thinking of you right now from above."

"Right. He might send a postcard."

"What did you say, Nogilee, sweetie?"

"I said I have to go. Thanks for the good wishes."

When I called home, Julie was barricaded in her room and Tomer was hanging out in the TV nook, playing on the PlayStation. Eli was standing in the kitchen making pancakes, and an intrusive smell of frying was disturbing the house. A few inflated balloons were hanging in the living room.

"Welcome, congratulations." Eli smiled at me while frying, inviting me in for a hug, and I thought how, within a second, my clothes would smell of pancakes.

"Did you take my charger?" Julie yelled from her room, and Tomer replied that he would return it in a second.

"I'm going up to change," I told Eli.

I went up to the bedroom, closed the door, and stood in front of the mirror to see what a woman my age looked like.

***

In the next few days, I didn't get a chance to see the people from the cabin. All kinds of things were happening at the kibbutz at the time. The sweetsop tree next to the club filled up with fruit with funny shapes. On the bulletin board in the dining hall was a diagram of what the new dining hall would look like, and next to the board was a cardboard model, too. The president of Egypt came for a visit to Israel and we all went to the old dining hall to watch the visit on TV. Dad came for a visit to Israel, too. Mom polished the pipe collection and tidied up the garden nicely. For three days, she cleaned for him, defrosted the freezer in the fridge, which never contained anything but ice anyway, beat the rugs, and sprayed water on the window screens. She ran a rag over everything in the house, first a wet one and then a dry one, while constantly whistling that *foo-foo-foo* sound and also saying she was in a race against time. That's how she said it: "I'm in a race against time."

He arrived on Saturday, and they sat in the garden, outside the clean house, drinking coffee and listening to the sports show on the Voice of Peace, with Saul Eisenberg. Dad enjoyed listening to it and Mom enjoyed watching him listen. It was mentally healthy.

She asked him, "Are you having a pleasant time? Isn't it fun to be home?"

And he smoked the peace pipe and said Mom's garden was the prettiest place in the world and that there's no place like home and the three of us were happy. Lily and Iris and Amnon came to Mom's deck, too. They liked to come when Dad came and agreed with him that Mom's garden was the prettiest in the world, even though they hardly got to spend time there since the three of them left the kibbutz. We all sat together, a family, and there was plenty of talking and laughing, especially about how Mom distorted words, creating a kind of language of her own, "a Mom tongue."

"Who can tell me how you say 'jazz music' in Mom?" Amnon asked, and Lily and Iris had to hold on to their bellies, they were laughing so hard when they answered: "Gas music." *And how do you say 'dog' in Mom?* They were cracking up when they answered, "Cat!" They were right. Suddenly I realized it was true. Mom didn't distinguish between dogs and cats; they were all "ew" to her.

The conversation fascinated me. I started to understand they were imitating our mother's language, and that sometimes, we all had the same mother.

They went on: "How do you say 'cigarette' in Mom?" and suddenly, I knew the answer myself.

"Pipe," I said, pretty quietly, but they heard me. All at once, they went quiet and looked at me. And then they cracked up again. It was true, 'cigarette' in Mom was 'pipe.' That was how I discovered I knew more words in the Mom tongue. I knew "there you are," (*that's right, Nogi, that's right*) as well as "you deserve it." And "kibbutz" in Mom was "camp," "dirty" was "dirtful," Lily was Iris, Iris was Lily, France was Tel Aviv and Tel Aviv was Gamla.

In the evening, everyone left, Dad too, since he had research to do. Mom cleared the glasses and the plates from the deck table. She raked the leaves and organized the chairs on the deck while constantly making the *foo-foo-foo* sound. I remained sitting outside a bit longer, thinking about my mother tongue, which was always there, even when you couldn't speak it, but I had only noticed it when Amnon and Lily and Iris came. I wanted them to come back, to show them that I knew more words, and I thought how, whereas their shadow had been cast on the deck earlier, now there was the shadow of the vines, the oleander, and the taros growing in Mom's garden.

***

At the time, people were having all kinds of accidents and catching all kinds of diseases. Liat had chickenpox. When we were all standing in line for the shower, Liat was sitting all alone in a bath with Permasol solution. Tamir broke his arm, and we all drew on the cast with colored markers. Ram told us that while he was slicing bread in the bread machine, a cat jumped into the machine. Half the class believed him and the other half didn't. We went around asking each other: *Are you in the half that believes or the half that doesn't?*

The kibbutz bees stung Einav this time, and Carmel went to Tel Aviv with her parents to have a wart removed. Storio the Elf came down with polio but recuperated after a while. In Nahum's shoemaking workshop, we received "Yona" brand shoes (black for the boys and red for the girls) and the clothes depot[6] did a winter inventory and we received the clothes that the fourth-graders had returned. That was how the days went by until the first serious rain arrived, and after we celebrated and sang "It's Raining, It's Pouring," we took turns giving each other the flu, and then sore throats, and later pneumonia, too.

I'd already gone through three illnesses when I saw the light on in the cabin

---

6   The clothes depot was the kibbutz institution in charge of purchasing clothes and distributing them to kibbutz members.

again. It was a sunny day with rain, and in the old people's neighborhood, a six-colored rainbow stretched and curved. I stood in the middle of the path between Shmul and Hilda's house and Kalman's house. The parents' house was lit up with a kind of light that, though it came in from the outside, managed to somehow cling to the house, as if it was stuck inside. The man with the drill, only without the drill, emerged from the cabin.

"Oh, hello there," he said with a smile, with his white teeth and the dimple and the Kojak accent.

"Look at the rainbow." I pointed proudly at the half-circle, which, out of all the houses, was above my parents' house, which had grown suddenly colorful.

"I see it. You can't miss something like that."

"Leah says a rainbow is formed when rays of light are refracted in raindrops."

"Who's Leah? She sounds smart."

"She's my teacher."

"And what grade are you in?"

"I'm in third grade. In three months, I'm going to be nine years old."

"Ah, so you're already a big girl," he said.

"I learned how to read back when I was four."

"Wow, that's a lot of years of reading. I bet you've read lots of stuff."

"A bunch, lots of postcards my dad sent me from all over the world. Do you want me to bring them over to show you?"

But I didn't wait for an answer. In two seconds, I ran to the parents' house, to Mom, who was drinking coffee and eating bread and jam. I told her I was only popping in for a minute to take the bag with the postcards and going out to show them to the new neighbor who lived in the old cabin.

When I got back to him, I heard a voice from inside the cabin: "Ro-nnie," and the man with the drill, only without the drill, yelled back, "What?"

"So, you're Ronnie?"

"I am. And what's your name?"

"I'm Noga."

"Noga is a pretty name."

"I had a brother named Nadav, but he died."

"What happened to him?"

"He had a disease. Isn't Ronnie a girl's name?"

"It's both. But 'Noga' is just for girls, right?"

"Just for girls. And who's that inside the cabin?"

"That's Eli. Come in."

They gave me apple juice in a glass that was half-full and half-empty, and I drank from the full half while they told me they came to Israel to enlist in the army. Ronnie's parents lived in Canada, and Eli's parents lived in a place called Seattle. Now they were taking a seminar for soldiers who had made Aliyah, and they would enlist in the summer. 'Aliyah' meant 'going up,' but that didn't mean that Israel was higher up than other countries. It was like in the Bible, in the Book of Numbers, when Caleb says about our country, *Let us go up at once, and possess it; for we are well able to overcome it.*[7] I asked Eli and Ronnie whether when you left Israel, it was called 'going down,' and they were impressed and said I really got it. I told them that my father went down from Israel all the time, but then he came back up again.

I told them that I slept in a room with Liat and Tamir and Ram. That my favorite cat was Blackie and my favorite parrot was Polynesia, but he also died of a disease. And the ants in the ant farm died, too. And so did Nadav the rabbit.

"That's how it goes," I told them. "Not everything is mentally healthy."

I opened the bag and took out all the postcards. There were postcards from Australia, with pictures of koala bears, postcards from Thailand, with pictures of women with long necks, postcards from China with a photo of the Forbidden City in a view from above, postcards from Japan, from England, from Africa, and from France. They were in color, and in some of them, the color had already faded a bit, and the Japanese woman's eye didn't always manage to wink, maybe because I'd used it a bunch of times. I showed them a handstand and a backflip and said I had to go home before my mother came looking for me.

"So that *is* your mother?" Ronnie asked.

And I left.

***

Months of anticipation for my birthday. Mom bought a calendar so I could mark the days going by. I asked her if you could be in a race for time, and not

---

7   Numbers 13: 30

just against time, and she said it was a great idea. That was a race where all the sides win. In the afternoons, I prepared games and quizzes for the party. I cut and pasted and colored and wrote questions about the Greek gods and about kinds of cranes and about cities that had been destroyed and about kinds of diseases and about what blooms in the springtime. Lots of trees were blooming in our kibbutz. The Judas-tree and the tipu tree, and the blue jacaranda and the flame tree and the coral tree. There were also two almond trees in bloom in the kibbutz, and the most intoxicating was the scent of the citrus trees.

Every evening, I took a break from my preparations and popped over to visit my friends from the cabin to ask how their Aliyah seminar went. Mom allowed me to go. She smiled and asked me to tell them they could come to her with anything they needed from the kibbutz, and every evening, as I crossed out another square on the calendar she had bought, we were both for time and time was for us. I asked if Dad would make Aliyah for my birthday, and she said that of course he would, that went without saying. Maybe not on the exact date, but he definitely intended to show up.

Before the party, a few more things happened in the kibbutz. There was a general assembly where they voted for or against color TV in the members' homes, and about what to do with the families who already had a color TV. That was the first time that Einav and Carmel had a serious fight. Einav said that obviously, you shouldn't give a color TV to people who already had one, but Carmel, whose parents did have a color TV, said they should be given something else instead.

In the afternoon we went to the clothes depot to pick out a Purim costume and I wanted to dress up as a research assistant, but they didn't have that costume. There were queens and clowns and animals and Mickey Mouse and cowboys and native costumes, but I didn't want any of those things. Only a research assistant. My mom begged me to pick something since it was already dark and all the other kids had picked out costumes a while ago. What was the big deal? And it was only once I understood she was really upset, and that if she could, she would cry, with tears, that I agreed to be a Japanese lady. I walked around the kibbutz and tried to wink with one eye, but usually, it came out as a kind of blink, and Leah told Mom she thought there was something wrong with me, that she should have it checked out.

Two babies on the kibbutz were diagnosed with meningitis, and they started building a new neighborhood on the lot next to the soccer field. Other than that, there were a lot of regular days, days that switched between sun and rain, and the afternoons smelled like cotton. And garbage.

But on the day of my birthday, something scary happened. I came to the parents' house before the party to get ready, and every cabinet door or drawer I opened gave out an old smell, like stale breath, like someone being woken from a deep sleep, and I immediately slammed them all shut again. It started with the drawer in the dresser next to the parents' bed, where Mom keeps pens and pencils and all kinds of documents and certificates. I looked at her ID card. It said the card had been issued in Israel, that her name was Ruthie, and her last name was Glover. Her maiden name was Posner, her nationality was Jewish, and she was born in Poland in the year 1935. There was a terrible smell of pajamas coming from the drawer, and I immediately slammed it hard until I crushed my finger. I yelled "Ow," and Mom yelled, "Ow" after me, even louder, like the echo of another shout, and sent me to get iodine. But the medicine drawer let out old breath too, and I slammed it as well, and the same thing happened with the kitchen cabinets when I wanted to take out napkins and disposable cups.

Worst of all was the closet. I don't even know why I opened it. Maybe to check whether the epidemic had spread all over the house, or just in certain places. It replied with a mingled smell of sleep and mothballs, as if I had awakened the closet and all its contents from an eternal sleep. The whole house was like a colony of sleeping people, and it seemed like Clara's cats were about to leap out of the closet. Mom sat down in the kitchen with her coffee and bread and jam, as if she had nothing to do with everything that was going on, as if she didn't see and didn't know everything that I knew, like in that dream about the old man who threw us into the deep end of the pool. She didn't see that there was a sleeping beast lurking in the middle of the house, and I was the only one who heard it breathing and smelled its breath.

***

Happy birthday to me. Dad couldn't come to the party, and Lily and Iris and Amnon couldn't either, but while all the kids in the class stood in a circle, I ran to the cabin and called out loudly: *Ronnie! Eli! I'm nine years old! Come to my birthday party!*

When they came out of the cabin, I saw that their hair was wet, like they'd just washed it. Ronnie was wearing a button-down shirt and Eli was wearing Adidas shoes, real ones, not like the imitation ones Ram had, and was holding a wrapped present with a ribbon. They asked what had happened to my finger, and I told them I was "mortally wounded." That Mom's drawer had bitten me, and they laughed and said I was really cute. That's what they said: *you're really cute.* We walked into the circle in a daring threesome: me first, Ronnie next, Eli after him. The entire class was looking at us.

Riddles. Songs. Cake with sprinkles. Apple juice in glasses. All the usual materials that birthday parties are made of. Who could tell me who Hercules was? And what bird is an abomination according to the Book of Numbers? And what's the capital of France? And of Japan? And of Australia? And who could tell me how the Jews died in Gamla? Who knew another name for scarlet fever? And what was another word for 'cancerous'? And what was an auto-immune disease?

Eli and Ronnie lifted me up in my chair ten times, with the boys from class helping a little too, and Mom was happy and clapped. Teacher Leah bought me a blank notebook so I could write stories in it. Mom bought me the book *Family Party.* Eli and Ronnie bought me the book *Emil and the Detectives.* I realized they had consulted Mom on what to buy, and I was glad they had taken her seriously when she said they could come to her with anything they needed.

What was left of spring after my birthday went by very quickly. Loquat season, the fruit peels on Kalman's wall ("ew"). Mulberry season and the silkworms hatching from their cocoons. Roller skating and hopscotch season. Trying on sandals at Nahum's workshop: brown sandals for the boys and red ones for the girls. Color TV season (only for those who didn't have one!). After Israel's Yizhar Cohen won the Eurovision song competition with "Abanibi," it was fun to say: *Did you see what a pretty color Yizhar Cohen's shirt was? And weren't the backup dancers' dresses a pretty color?* And only Liat had the courage to say that both Yizhar Cohen's shirt and the backup dancers' dresses were white. No color at all!

***

Eli and Ronnie enlisted in the summer, a week after fourth grade started, the week when Blackie "passed away." Osnat agreed to put me in charge of the burial ceremony, and I eulogized and read out King David's Lament: "*The beauty of Israel is slain upon thy high places: how are the mighty fallen,*"[8] and wished that she rest in peace, said there weren't many cats like her and swore to remember her always, along with Polynesia and the ants from the ant farm and Nadav the rabbit.

Eli and Ronnie returned to the kibbutz on leave once a month, and time had a rhythm of its own. Some weeks, it went by slowly. Sometimes, it split up into tiny particles and could be found in the forty-five minutes of lessons, the thirty minutes of recess, the hour-and-a-half of afternoon naptime, not like before when things would arrive suddenly. Most of the time, I didn't notice its presence, but occasionally, I noticed that some things repeated themselves.

In English class, we watched lessons on TV with Dan and Edna. They asked, "What's your name?" lots of times, and after they answered, "My name is Dan," "My name is Edna," they nodded and said, "Good morning." We liked them and made fun of them.

The first rain still caught us by surprise, even though we knew it was coming. When Israel's Gali Atari won first place in the Eurovision, with the pink dress we saw on color TV, it was no longer the first time we had won. We found out we had a history. We also learned what history was: a study of the events of the past. The smell of autumn reminded us of the smell of autumn last year, and the same thing happened with the smell of Passover cleaning, of the *tabun* oven on which we baked pita bread, and of spiny broom and sticky fleabane flowers. We knew the scents so well that when the holiday of Shavuot arrived, we knew it ahead of time by the smell. Everything was reminiscent of something else, and it was impossible to know whether we liked the scent of challah bread on Friday because of what it was, or because of what it reminded us.

The parents' house still smelled like mothballs and pajamas, but the garden smelled like freesias, and when Mom looked at me, it seemed like I reminded her of something too, maybe something that hadn't happened yet.

Teacher Leah was replaced by Becky, and we moved into a children's house with two floors. On the bottom floor were the classes, the kitchen, the dining

---

8 2 Samuel 1: 19: King David's lament for King Saul and his son Jonathan.

tables, the showers, the bathrooms, and the storage rooms. On the top floor were the bedrooms and more bathrooms. When we stood downstairs, we could look up and see how high the bedrooms were. When we stood upstairs, we could look down and see how low the dining tables were. When Becky wasn't looking, we liked to jump down from the second floor.

Life gained height, volume, and weight. We, too, had height, volume, and weight. We knew how much we weighed and how tall we were. Last year's clothes got too small and we passed them on to the third graders. In the showers, we'd compare. We were more and less than each other. Constantly more and less than each other. Sometimes it was unbearable. Carmel sprouted pubic hair long before the rest of us. In the shower, she had an apologetic smile, as if it was wrong to get ahead of time, and we, too, didn't know what to do about it. It was only in the middle of the year that they separated the showers: girls in one, boys in another.

Our fights became troubling, vindictive, not the kind you bounce back from immediately the next day. Our games were always a competition with other girls: hopscotch, double Dutch, and jacks. We tracked which of us was the first one out. I was never willing to be the first one out. No matter what. If necessary, I'd cheat, and Einav said that if I kept doing that, no one would want to play with me. We kept tabs on each other. Our relationship accumulated a history. We had a future, too: we wanted all kinds of things to happen to us. We wanted to be in the Olympics. We wanted to perform on stage. We wanted to win lotteries.

Mom recognized that change. I felt she could see the wind blowing on my face and my body, leaving its mark on me. Sometimes it seemed like I also left my mark on the places I passed through, that something about me and around me was constantly shifting. When I arrived at the parents' house in the afternoon, she was no longer always sitting with the bread and jam. Instead, I frequently found her sleeping in bed. There was something frightening about her sleep as if the primordial beast that would sprawl, sleeping in the house's living room, had taken over the bed as well. As if someone had cast a spell over the house. I'd turn on the lights, shift the curtains aside, open the windows, and she would wake up and suggest we play Go Fish, or Rummikub, or Spit. I played with her a little and then went over to Liat's, or Einav's, or Carmel's. Their mothers had friends, and they would drink coffee together, and eat ice cream pronounced the regular way, not like "*I scream*," and they also had little brothers and sisters or big ones, and the doors in their houses would open and close and open. I'd sit in their living rooms and feel that I had something that couldn't be talked about, but I didn't know what it was.

Once a month, on a Friday, Eli and Ronnie would arrive. Sometimes only one of them did—Ronnie or Eli. They would get there around noon with their uniforms and weapons, and when I'd arrive at the parents' place, they were still sleeping. We all went together to Friday dinner in the dining hall: Mom, me, and Eli, or Ronnie, or both. When they both arrived together, I'd divide my speech equally, so no one would be jealous, since they didn't have family in Israel. We decided we'd be their family: Mom, and me, and Dad too, and maybe Amnon and Iris and Lily would be in the family too, and they gave me their military address so that I could send them drawings and poems. One Saturday, Lily and Iris and Amnon visited the kibbutz and also dropped by the parents' house. I told them about Eli and Ronnie. Lily told Iris, "Nogi has soldier boyfriends," and they both cracked up.

***

Hello Ronnie,

As I begin my letter, I'll ask how you are. How are you?

Our class is doing a research project. My topic is mime. Did you know you can talk without words? I sent a letter to the mime Hanoch Rosen, but he hasn't answered me yet. I read in the encyclopedia that mime is an action that creates a physical illusion. In our vegetable garden, we're growing strawberries and chard and we have a new mare. Her name is Breeze (drawing enclosed).

How are things in the army?

Bye, and see you soon,

Noga, "Oleander" fourth grade

***

Hello Eli,

As I begin my letter, I'll ask how you are. How are you?

Today in math class they showed us two parts of a poster board and both of them were called "quarter." Esther the teacher asked how they could both be a quarter if each of them was a different size. Liat knew the answer: each one of them was taken from a different-sized whole.

I borrowed Anne of Green Gables by Lucy Maud Montgomery from the library, and I read a chapter every day.

How are things in the army?

Bye, and see you soon,

Noga, "Oleander" fourth grade

P.S.

Enclosed is a drawing of our new mare, Breeze.

P.P.S.

Iris and Lily don't believe I have friends who are soldiers. Next time they come over, come see me in the garden. And I also wanted to ask you if you happened to know what Belzec is. I saw that word on a brown envelope in the drawer next to Mom's bed, which smells like pajamas.

***

"A letter arrived," Mom said with a smile as she was standing outside the house, next to the garden with the freesias. She opened her arms wide so I would come to hug her, and I agreed to a short hug and ran to the kitchen table to see what had arrived. On the table was the coffee cup, which was already cold, with a white stripe, a kind of crust, at its edges. Next to it, on the plate, was still half a slice of the bread with jam, and I realized Mom had left it all to come meet me when I came in. I tried to guess who has answered first—Eli? Maybe Ronnie? It was probably Ronnie since I sent his a few minutes before I sent Eli's, or maybe it was actually Eli?

Mom was standing right next to me, and I asked her if she could step back a little. She smiled and was excited while she handed me the postcard. It was from Dad. A postcard from Canada with a drawing of waterfalls, sent with a greeting for sweet Noga. She asked, "Are you happy? Are you pleased?" and I said I was.

"Is it fun to get a postcard from Dad?"

"Yeah."

Later I asked her if anything else had come and she said no, and it wasn't clear if she actually understood the difference between a letter and a postcard.

**

The years of fifth and sixth grade passed by mostly on the lawn. We played Capture the Flag, and jacks, and Red Rover, and Dog and Bone, and we rode our bikes all day. If it rained, we went into a classroom and played the shell game. On sports day we screamed out loud, straining our throats as we sang our favorite youth-movement songs such as "A Camp Is a Useful Thing," "The Trophy Is Ours," "The Blue Shirt," and "We Won't Forget How the Palmach Was Dismantled,"[9] while skipping the lines, "*We are the youth, the communists, seeking our fortunes / Russia is our mother, Stalin is our father, if only we were orphans.*" We were particularly fond of the rhythmic song about the fried chick:

Boiled chick, fried chick,
went for a walk, real quick.
But they got him
and they caught him
and they almost went and shot him.
I'm not a Soviet and not a cadet,

---

9   These songs originated in the youth movements that were active both before and after the establishment of the State of Israel. The blue shirt is associated with socialist-Zionist youth movements, particularly HaNoar HaOved (Working Youth) and HaShomer HaTzair (The Young Guard), its color intended to evoke blue-collar workers. The Palmach, a Hebrew acronym meaning "strike force," was the elite fighting force of the Haganah, the Jewish community's underground army during the period of the British Palestine Mandate.

I stay away from politics, you bet.
Don't arrest me, don't you shoot me,
'cause even a chick wants to live.

We moved to a one-story structure, and we didn't need two floors to know that life had height and volume and weight. We knew how much each of us girls weighed and wanted to be skinny and tall. The kibbutz held a cornerstone ceremony for the new dining hall. We stood in a big C shape, and every member, man or woman, was invited to add one scoop of mortar and say a few words, until Nehama Zinger lost her patience and put in a few scoops, one after the other, and everyone said, "At last, a girl who takes care of business!"

They finished building the new neighborhood behind the soccer field, and plenty of new babies were born in the kibbutz. We didn't know all of them. Clara and Kalman and Hilda and Shmul stayed old, and the bats kept on spitting loquat peels at Kalman's house. Clara's cats kept hanging out on her balcony, and Mom kept on saying "ew," and sometimes "disgusting" as well. Eli and Ronnie came back to the kibbutz every two or three weeks, and on one of the visits, I found out Eli had started officer training. *And what about Ronnie?* I asked Mom, and she told me that Ronnie hadn't. We'd solve the crossword puzzle in *Ma'ariv LaNoar* magazine, and fill out the "Test Yourself" questionnaire. Mom became a background photo for the kibbutz lawn. Occasionally, she would offer juice or bread and jam, and say in the mother tongue, "There you are."

Seventh grade was when we did our family history project. We worked for an entire month with Irit, the art teacher, on finding a special, artistic design for the binder, which stated, in stylish letters, "My Parents' Home." The boys asked the girls to draw for them and we all became good friends once more. We even decided that one night, after we went to bed, we would get up and shower together again, boys and girls, but we didn't really dare. In kibbutz meetings, they talked about transitioning from communal sleeping arrangements to familial sleeping arrangements, and some people said, "In ten years, ten, no more than that, I'm telling you, we won't even understand how we kept the kids there."

One day Carmel took me aside and told me she had gotten her period. She told me Einav had too, but she didn't want to tell anyone. On days when I was left alone in the shower, I'd stand in front of the mirror and survey the changes in my body. I was still very skinny but I could feel that the mirror reflecting my image back at me already had all kinds of plans and schemes in mind for me; I just didn't know when, and exactly how.

We would talk too loudly and crack up over all kinds of things. Some of us had Levi's and Wrangler jeans and we wore noisy wooden flip-flops that managed to be heard over all kinds of other noises. As birthday presents for our bar mitzvah and bat mitzvah years, we asked for a radio-tape and would record songs in English that were played on the radio. We listened to "Eye of the Tiger," and "Beat It," and "Mad World." We also listened to the Beatles and Simon and Garfunkel, Bob Marley and Foreigner, singing everything too loudly, fluent in the lyrics. Those with older brothers or sisters had a better grasp of the lyrics and knew more about clothes and music. It was then that I realized how elusive my brother and sisters were. They would reveal themselves sometimes, on weekends, like the headlights of a car in the rain, blinding bright, and then fading away.

Other than designing the binder, we had to interview the parents and draw a family tree. I went to the payphone by the secretariat and called Amnon, who had already left the standing army.

"It's Noga," I told him.

"Right, I can hear that it's Noga."

I asked whether he happened to have kept his family history project, and he didn't understand what I was talking about. Did I expect him to remember what had become of some school paper from twelve years ago? Iris was already married, and lived with Yossi in Meyerland, in Houston, and when I called Lily, who lived with Ilan in the Golan Heights, she said, "Nogi, this is an opportunity. Interview Mom and Dad yourself." That's what she said, *this is an opportunity, interview Mom and Dad*, which was a reminder that in certain situations, there was such a thing as "Mom and Dad." Mom and Dad who were a couple, and had other children besides me, and that they were the sort of thing that could be interviewed, and that this was an opportunity.

And this was how it went down:

Mom was born in 1935 in Lviv, Poland. "Here, I'll show you where it is on the map." How come all the other mothers got to be born in Jerusalem, or Tel

Aviv, or on the kibbutz?

In any case, Mom was born in 1935 in Lviv, Poland.

Not a good place to be born in at the time, but who gets to choose when and where they're born?

She was four years old when the war broke out, and unfortunately for her, she witnessed her father's murder with her own two eyes ("No way." "Yes, that's what happened."). All of Lviv's Jews were assembled in the park at the center of the town, next to the carousel and the Ferris wheel. Those who could play an instrument were lined up to form an orchestra, which played a Polish children's song. The young men who couldn't play an instrument were ordered to lie down on the carousel floor, where the Nazi soldiers rode over them with motorcycles.

"No one ran away?"

You couldn't run away.

"And no one screamed?"

Maybe they did, but the engines thundered so loudly that no other sound was heard. Even the orchestra was barely audible. Grandma covered Mom's eyes and ears, but the soldiers said everyone had to watch and clap in time with the rhythm.

"Did you clap too?"

Everyone clapped.

That was how the war in Lviv began. And when one day, a nice man walked over to Mom and told her all the neighborhood kids were invited to the Goldna Roisa (Golden Rose) Synagogue, since they were handing out candy there, she knew not to go. And that was a lucky thing since one Nazi soldier was personally waiting for each Jewish child, to smash him or her against the streetlights at the entrance to the synagogue. Mom was barely five years old, and she knew to stay away.

"How did you know? How do you know something like that?"

"I just knew."

Break. Bread and jam. *Foo-foo-foo.*

Some time later, Mom and Grandma moved to the ghetto in Lviv, and Grandma still had some jewelry that she managed to sell in return for potatoes and cabbage, and even bread. But it was clear to Grandma that they couldn't stay in the ghetto. She was a seamstress, and she had some fabrics. Mom was a pretty blonde girl ("like you") and Grandma sewed her a new dress, made her a nice pair of shoes, and one day they escaped the ghetto and boarded a train to Belzec, Grandma's childhood home, where there were people who knew her. "The people, where they were born, that's where they'll find help," Grandma used to say. It sounded better in Yiddish.

"Well, did it work?"

Not so much. On the way to Belzec, a Polish woman walked over to Mom and told her to get away from that woman with the black hair because she was Jewish. Mom didn't understand why she had to get away from Grandma. She took care of her, didn't she? She chose to stay with Grandma until they were both taken off the train mid-route and locked up in jail in Rava-Ruska. Later, Mom understood they actually had it good in jail, since there was food there, but while she was in jail, she didn't know it was a good thing. And those words, that she needed to get away from Grandma, troubled her.

5.

"Don't ask," Adva told me in one of our sessions. "Don't even ask how unbelievable my mother is."

"How unbelievable is she?" I asked.

"Seriously? I told you not to ask. Kiiiiding. To make a long story short, now she has a new idea. If I get good grades, she'll consider letting me get a motorcycle license."

"So, what do you think?"

"What I think is that my mother needs to find a different outlet for her frustrations. How about if she comes to see you? Instead of sending me to this lame appointment every time, she can come herself. And besides, if she saw what was going on under my sleeves, my grades would be the last thing on her mind. And besides, let's say she agrees, let's just say she agrees. In any case, there's no chance that my dad would agree."

"Wow," I said.

"Wow what?"

"Wow what you're telling me. Both about what's going on under your sleeves, and about your dad, and about your mom, too."

"So, what do you say? How about if she comes to see you instead of me?"

"Let me remind you that you're here under a court order, but regardless, I understand you'd really like to see your mother in therapy."

"Damn, you're a genius. How'd you come to that conclusion?"

"And if your mother came to me for therapy, what would you want to happen here?"

"That's it? We're playing 'let's pretend'? Cool. Then I'd like my mom to have a life. That's what I'd like. So that when someone calls to tell her I stole a motorcycle, which, by the way, I didn't even mean to steal it, I just wanted to take a little joyride and bring it back, then she won't cry on my dad's shoulder like a baby and ask why I'm ruining her life."

I leaned back on the couch and sighed.

"You're sick of it too, admit it. Why don't we wrap it up early today and you can go on with your life? Unless you don't have a life either."

***

Eli didn't go back to the kibbutz after his discharge from the army. In his battalion, he met an NCO in charge of education named Hila and moved in with her to a village in the south. Ronnie left the standing army for a short period, for unclear reasons, and all kinds of rumors about getting in trouble and insubordination spread through the kibbutz. One day, in the spring of my junior year of high school, I met him on the path leading to the dining hall.

"Nogi." He was happy to see me, and I ran to him and he lifted me up as if I was still the same girl he had met on the day I saw him with the drill. He had already moved from the cabin to a neighborhood of bungalows. In his place, an old woman named Katya moved in, and it seemed as if he had been spared from something by leaving the neighborhood in time. He told me he was transitioning to a different role, and in the meantime, had been granted a long leave. He invited me for coffee in his bungalow and asked how I was doing and how high school and my matriculation exams were going. I told him I was writing a paper on the concept of hubris in Greek mythology and classic literature.

"Wow, sounds serious, Nogi."

"Well, guess what, I'm a serious girl. Did you know the first volume of Hitler's biography is called *Hubris*, too?"

"No. I didn't know that. And I didn't know you were that serious."

"Most serious."

"Serious enough to agree to cuddle with me here under the blanket?"

I took off my shoes and snuck under his blanket. I didn't have to sneak in; he'd invited me. But I did.

***

The next days had a dense scent of jasmine. And honeycomb. And Adam aftershave. Every day after school, I rushed to Ronnie's cinder-block bungalow. We attended a regional school at the time, along with other kibbutzim, where I met Lior and Nitzan and Arbel. I didn't tell them about the bungalow, but I stopped focusing on what they told me, and perhaps I stopped focusing at all. Something about school became entirely irrelevant, and sometimes, in the middle of Bible class or history or biology, I left the classroom and walked along the road to hitch a ride to the kibbutz. Every passing car driving toward the kibbutz looked like something going in the right direction. Life at the time had only one direction. My hair was disheveled, my skin was freckled, my clothes were bohemian, cut at the neckline and midriff, and Nati the Bible teacher said I looked like a junkyard.

Time resumed its previous conduct: unexpected and sudden. In the middle of class, it would suddenly break apart or tear into shreds. And a breeze from the sea would blow me out, to the road, where one of the cars would pick me up. Some of the anonymous drivers succumbed to my implorations and dropped me off inside the kibbutz. One of them told me, "Take care of yourself, huh?" I didn't fully understand what he meant, but I felt he was right. The drivers unloaded me in the parking lot, and from there I'd sweep into Ronnie's bungalow or burst in, depending on the direction of the wind. Ronnie would wait for me in a faded tracksuit, and our bodies usually preceded us, as if they had been waiting for us for a while, and now that we'd joined them, they were breathless, growling at us, huffing and puffing, minimizing some kind of gap. Ronnie's body was usually warm and moist, or else it was my body, and sometimes I needed to peel my skin off him carefully, as if separating two pieces of cling-wrap stuck together.

Time didn't exist. The hours would arrive one by one, or sometimes together, in pairs or trios, with no time separating them. Our embraces gripped us, our kisses gnawed and bit at the flesh, at lips, at nipples, at the neck, and when he entered me, my throat let out unfamiliar animal sounds. Occasionally we'd stop, staring at each other as if sharing testimony. Ronnie would caress my body, which really did resemble a junkyard, and I liked to look, observing the dereliction. Sometimes I cried. Sometimes I laughed. He did, too. At night we showered, or didn't, and in the morning I dragged myself to the school bus. I carried the backpack with its pencil case and notebooks that very soon were no longer up to date, deriving a strange pleasure from the misleading image of a schoolgirl. I wore yesterday's clothes, or those from the day before that, or Ronnie's clothes, or Ronnie's underwear, and Adam aftershave. Sometimes I made it to the end of the day, or else I fell asleep in the grass and Arbel woke me up to board the bus back to the kibbutz. And there was that week when we didn't leave the bungalow at all. Stayed inside for an entire week. Through the gaps in the blinds, we could see daylight replaced by the kibbutz streetlights, and vice versa; we didn't count how many cycles went by. We ate the two last cucumbers in Ronnie's fridge and a tin of cookies, as well as some anchovies from a can.

One evening, we heard my mother from the path, crying and yelling that she didn't know where Noga was. I buried my head in Ronnie's shirt and waited for the attack to pass, but she continued in a hysterical voice: *what am I going to do, I'm losing my mind, I don't know what to do, why does everything keep happening to me, somebody help me*, and Ronnie said, "You have to go to her."

"No way," I said, and he said, "Go, and then come back."

We decided I would wait a few minutes so that she would drift away and wouldn't see me leaving the bungalow, and in fact, her whimpering faded a bit and I got dressed and began making preparations. I was almost out the door when the phone rang, and when Ronnie answered, I heard the same voice I had heard from the path a few moments ago, now broadcasting from inside the receiver.

"Ronniiiieeeee," she sobbed. "Noga's disappeared."

"Are you sure?" he asked, and his voice sounded like the same voice in which he talked when we went to eat at the dining hall together on Friday evenings. I realized that I actually knew him, that it was the same guy.

"She's disappeared. I'm going crazy. Do you have any idea where she is?"

He looked at me and replied that he didn't know where Noga was. For a moment, it was possible to believe him. He went on to say that if she wanted, he could go look for me. Meanwhile, I went out and began to walk in the direction of the kibbutz's old people's neighborhood, toward the parents' house.

The paths were tainted with all kinds of fallen fruit, and leaves, and I knew I was now stepping on paths that all of the kibbutz's old people had already stepped on, and all the children of the kibbutz would step on, even the ones who hadn't been born yet, and that none of this was mine at all, and my mother hadn't even been born here, and my father was barely here, neither were my brother and sisters, and all the animals I'd loved here were already dead, buried in the yard of Palm Tree Preschool, where kids I didn't know were growing up, and I don't know where I found the obedience not to turn on my heels and be gathered back inside the bungalow, into Ronnie's warm sweat; he wasn't born here either, and probably wouldn't die here, but in the meantime, he was here, a guest in my junkyard, and there was the rotting old people's neighborhood, with Clara's cats, with the loquat peels spat out on the wall of Kalman's house. Ew. And here was the murky light in the kitchen of the parents' house, where Mom was on her own, waiting for me.

"What were you thinking?" she whimpered at me when I was standing on the threshold of the house. "What are you doing to me?"

I didn't even look at her as I tried to escape that voice that had been tracking me ever since the path by the bungalow, penetrating the receiver of Ronnie's phone, and now here, inside the house, whirling around me.

"I'm dying to get some sleep," I told her, and she asked, "Where were you? Where were you? Where did you disappear to?"

"I didn't disappear. I was here, in the kibbutz."

"I understand you haven't been at school for a week now. Carmel doesn't know where you are. Einav doesn't know where you are. Ram doesn't know where you are. No one knows where you are."

"Don't tell me you called their rooms."

"I didn't call, I went there. They have no idea where you are."

"Mom, are you nuts? Have you completely lost it? Do you want to ruin my life? How come you're looking for me at their places? I'm here, in the kibbutz. I'm always here in the kibbutz. Where could I possibly go? Don't you dare do that again, ever."

"Okay, enough, my Nogi, my pretty girl, sweetie, the important thing is that you're here. Everything's fine. Come in for a hug."

I resignedly succumbed to a short, second-long hug, and quickly extracted myself.

"Look how skinny you are. Are you hungry?"

I had to admit I was starving after a week of cucumber and cookies and anchovies from a can.

"Is there anything to eat here?"

"Come on, I'll make you something," she said, and instantly transitioned to an active state, and while she was dicing a tomato and making her *foo-foo-foo* sound, I knew that any minute, I would also hear "There you are," and "You deserve it," in the mother tongue.

"Call Ronnie, he's looking for you all over the kibbutz," she said before she began to sing the song about the sadly playing lyre, closing her eyes and surrendering to the words, "*Oh, why have you brought me into the world and dressed me in prisoner's garb.*"

***

I asked to go to the talk with Motti the principal without her. It wasn't surprising that she agreed. The surprising part was when she said: *Dad will come.*

He came. This time from Tel Aviv, not from abroad. He offered to drive me to school and said he would come by in the morning to pick me up from my room, and for an instant, the thought crept into my head that Ronnie might think I was a kid. Just a little girl with parents and a family and a kibbutz, and a father who picked her up from her room to go to school. But the thought dissipated quickly.

The room I shared with Carmel was empty of pictures or potted plants. In recent months, it was also empty of Carmel, who spent most of her time in Udi's room, and when I went in, I found packed, dense darkness. Sleeping without Ronnie felt like something I didn't know how to do. It had only been a month since I snuck under his blanket, and I couldn't remember how I would fall asleep before then. I climbed into bed with my clothes on and waited for sleep to descend on me like life in the bungalow had descended on me: all at once. I don't know how long Dad had been knocking on the door before I woke up the following morning, and it was a good thing I slept in my clothes. I brushed my teeth quickly and went out to meet him.

"Nogi, honey, look how much weight you've lost. Way to go."

On the way to school, he told me about a new academic foundation called the Israel-Germany Foundation and about a research proposal he intended to submit to the foundation, about evidence pointing to the existence of the Gamla Synagogue from the first century BCE. He was excited and said he thought the proposal had a chance. In any case, even if it wasn't accepted, it could also be submitted to the Israel Science Foundation, where it had an even better chance, as well as to the U.S.-Israel Binational Science Foundation, and "Let's keep our fingers crossed, Nogi. *Cross your fingers*," he said in English. If the proposal was approved by even one of the foundations, it could fund a research assistant or a doctoral student as well as an international conference. He also told me about another large conference for which he was a co-organizer, scheduled to take place in May that year at the University of Oxford, focusing on Jewish settlement in the Golan Heights.

He then asked what was going on with me and what the deal was with the mess I was making at school. "After all, you were always the smartest student in class."

I told him Mom had just lost it. "You know Mom and how she goes crazy sometimes," and both of us laughed at how easily she lost it, and he said we had to make allowances for her, she had not had an easy life. "Try to be kind to her, Nogi." He also asked after that neighbor of ours, Ronnie, the solitary soldier who had no family in Israel and whom Mom had adopted, and I answered that he was no longer our neighbor, that he had moved to a different neighborhood, and would soon go back to the army after apparently going through some issues, and Dad asked me to say 'hi' and wish him the best of luck.

We parked in the school parking lot next to the buses. While we were waiting to see Motti, Dad looked at the walls a bit and said the school looked very impressive, and who was this beauty, he asked, pointing at Hamutal from ninth grade, and I told him it was Hamutal from ninth grade, and when Motti opened the door for us and said, "Professor Glover, it's good to see you," they shook hands, talked a little, and decided that Noga would make up everything she missed during the last month, and she had special dispensation, as a one-time exception, to hand in papers instead of exams, and "let's join forces and help Noga get through the home stretch, it's too bad, up till now she's actually been a good student," and Motti ended with a saying by Janusz Korczak,[10] "Do not give a child a teacher who loves books but does not love people." On the

---

10   Janusz Korczak (1878–1942) was the pen name of Henryk Goldszmit, a Polish Jewish educator and children's author. After spending many years working as director of an orphanage in Warsaw, he repeatedly refused offers of sanctuary and stayed with his orphans when the entire population of the institution was sent by the Nazis from the Ghetto to the Treblinka extermination camp in 1942.

way back to the kibbutz, we stopped for falafel, and Dad said it was really fun spending time together, and that we should do it more often.

***

Ronnie opened the door for me in the same pair of faded sweat pants. I noticed it had been a while since he'd shaved and he resembled a primordial caveman. He, too, had lost weight like me during the last month, and for the first time, I saw that he was a solitary soldier here.

"Are you in trouble?" he asked, and I pulled down his sweat pants and dragged him to bed and told him there was no need to ask unnecessary questions. We picked up where we had left off when we heard my mother on the path, but this time without my mother's interruption. It was strange to think that of all the people in the world, it was actually my mother who had created some narrow crack in the loss of time. And that under different circumstances, that statement could have been true.

The next day, I got up in time for school. I walked among regular people my age, who talked about regular, normal things, and also caught up on what was going on in the world and in the kibbutz while I had been committed in the bungalow. It turned out the old Israeli shekel had been replaced by the New Israeli Shekel. People were interviewed on TV and said it was more convenient now because you no longer had to walk around with so many bills and coins. As for me, I didn't really care, because I didn't have any kind of shekels, or any change, in bills or in coins. Anatoly Sharansky[11] was received with cheers in Israel and changed his name to Nathan Sharon. The United States extradited John Demjanjuk to Israel and everyone had something to say about his defense attorney, whether it was actually okay to be his defense attorney, and whether he was really Ivan the Terrible, since, if it wasn't him, how could he just sit there, apathetic, while the witnesses recounted the horrors of the bayonet he would walk around with in the camp. Jonathan Pollard confessed

---

11   Anatoly (Nathan) Sharansky was a longtime 'refusenik' during the 1970s and 1980s, refused the right to immigrate to Israel by the Soviet Union, and spent nine years in Soviet prisons. In 1986, he was freed from Soviet incarceration as part of a prisoner exchange and received an Israeli passport with his new name. Currently, he is a human rights activist and political figure.

to spying for Israel, soldier Ron Arad was taken prisoner by Hezbollah, and the United States outlawed any kind of genocide. I told Arbel I hadn't known that genocide had ever been legal. She answered that it was nice talking to me, even about things like genocide, legal or illegal, since in the last month, it had been impossible to talk to me about anything. At the kibbutz general assembly, they started to talk about privatization,[12] and the subject evoked a highly volatile debate. Some said that the age of cooperative settlement was over, and as Martin Buber phrased it, "The kibbutz is not a product of the Torah but of the circumstances," and circumstances, as we all knew, had changed.

At recess, I went to the library and checked out materials for papers in biology, Bible studies, and grammar, and for my paper on the concept of hubris: everything I'd promised Motti to make up. When we got to the kibbutz, I headed for the parents' house first thing, before going to the bungalow. The house was dark, Mom was sleeping, and the primordial beast lurking in the living room was still there, but I felt it could touch me less. I thought that certainly at one time, when there had been kids in this house, they were a group, and the beast had a harder time against them. I, in contrast, had to walk around this house with insulation.

I placed all the books on the kitchen table in a pretty high stack, along with a little note with a heart drawn on it, containing detailed instructions about all the papers. I wrote to Mom that Dad and I had agreed with Motti that if I submitted the papers on time, I wouldn't get suspended from school, and that way I could get through the home stretch. I also wrote that I'd be happy if she started with the biology paper, which was the most urgent, and then continued on to the Bible paper, which was also a little urgent. "If you don't understand something, it's not critical. The main thing is to hand it in on time." I also added, "Thank you very much, from the bottom of my heart," and that in the afternoon, I had all kinds of errands, and she shouldn't worry. I also told her Dad said 'hi,' and that he said it had really been fun and we should do it more often.

---

12   The privatization of the kibbutzim consists of abandoning the traditional socialist, communal values and institutions and employing a more capitalist, mainstream economic model of operation.

***

Ronnie and I began to know each other's touch. Sometimes we had recurring rituals. Every day, we also tried new things, which made us sad and happy. We came up with nicknames for each other. He called me Rabbit and I called him Tortoise. We were skinny and wanton. We lived on snacks and canned food. We shared a few pairs of underwear we'd hand-wash, and occasionally, I remembered the driver who had dropped me off in the parking lot and told me to take care of myself. After a few weeks, we suddenly started talking.

"Tell me about your family."

"Now you ask?" he wondered, and I realized I had known him for eight years now and had never asked, other than knowing they lived in Canada.

He told me his mother was eighteen when she got pregnant as a result of a casual affair with a married Canadian guy.

"How did her parents react?"

"They didn't. She had no parents."

"Come on…"

"She was a little girl when the war ended and came from Poland on her own. No one else from her family survived. Let it go, Rabbit, it's a bummer of a story."

"So, you don't have any siblings? Or uncles? No grandparents either?"

"Nothing."

I remembered that when Ronnie had arrived at the kibbutz with Eli, he had been just a year older than I was today. My father was right when he referred to him as a solitary soldier, but it wasn't my mother who adopted him. It was me.

"As my mom says, you don't get to choose everything in life."

"How did your mom come up all of a sudden?"

We cracked up. I put my fingers on his face and began to draw animal shapes with them. "My poor Tortoise, my poor solitary Tortoise. I could make a really nice animal out of you." We clung to each other on the bed and our love was compassionate, and a little tired, too, like a nurse at the end of her shift. Ronnie opened the blinds and a screen of stars burst into the room, looking as if it had waited in the sky until the sky overflowed and shattered into our bungalow. We wrapped ourselves up in the blanket and looked at the stars.

"Why don't we go for a walk in the kibbutz?"

It was the first time we had left the bungalow together. We held hands and walked down the lane of Indian rosewood trees. Most windows in the kibbutz were dark or shuttered, and there were no crying babies in the neighborhood where we were strolling. The babies in this kibbutz cried in other areas. We went down the path toward the pool, along the blue jacaranda lane.

"This is where a bee stung me."

Ronnie laughed.

"And here, too. And here."

"Come here, I'll take all your stings out."

"When I was a girl, I was happy to discover that when a bee stings, it also dies."

"Don't worry, Rabbit. No one's dying tonight."

I asked Ronnie if he remembered Blackie, and Billie Goat, and Polynesia, and the ant farm. I couldn't remember at precisely what time he had entered my life, and it was unclear if he was my insulation or the other way around. He wanted to hear about Nadav too. Not about Nadav the rabbit. About Nadav.

"I barely remember. I was three when he died. I remember images, sort of, where he's lying in bed, and I come over to check through the crack in the door whether he's died yet." I remembered more things that I didn't tell Ronnie. Like when Mom brought Nadav postcards Dad had sent him from abroad. I remembered asking Amnon when Nadav would die, and Amnon said you didn't ask questions like that, and too bad it wasn't me who was sick, and instead, it was the only brother he had. I remembered running to Mom and saying I was very sick too, and Lily said one sick sibling in the family was quite enough, and that I should leave Mom alone. I also remembered the day when Nadav died. Mom didn't get out of bed. She sent Iris to bring me home from preschool, but I said I didn't want to come. Iris dragged me down the path all the way home, and at home, she spat out to Lily, "Next time, you go." And it was only Nadav himself whom I could barely remember. I remembered Mom said he had loved me best, and that he asked to see me before he died, but I was already asleep.

"I can barely remember," I told Ronnie the truth.

Ronnie wiped away my tears with the sleeve of his shirt and we began to walk toward the old people's neighborhood.

"Your shirt is dirty. At some point, we need to bring the clothes to the laundry."

"Right, we need to bring the clothes to the laundry, and get a little food, too."

The old people's neighborhood was dark. Clara's cats were asleep and so were Kalman's bats. Shmul and Hilda were asleep. Only a window in the parents' house was illuminated with a murky light, and through it, we could see my mom, hunched with straining eyes over the kitchen table, coffee and bread and jam next to her, writing school papers.

6.

First was the notice on the street. Black letters on a white page. The old, familiar format; the printing presses issue them every day. Only the order of the letters comprising the names appearing before the "RIP" changed from one notice to the next. And the notices, experienced, conveyed the short, pragmatic information to passersby before they were replaced by other, more timely notices. *Our beloved. Our dearest. Our dear father and grandfather.* Briefly striking the faces of passersby, weighing down their steps, slowing down traffic. And later, the notice on the house door, identical to the one on the street but scarier, as if the notice on the street was only a bleak prophecy about something that was taking place now. Soon the reinforced door would open, and the steel surface intended to protect the house would not be able to provide protection from the house itself.

I went in. Ever since I had met Adva, I often wondered what the Appel family's house looked like. I had imagined, in detail, the kitchen island at which Adva sat with both her parents during one of the louder arguments about the motorcycle. This must have been the chair she sat in when she tossed out that she had no desire to grow old like them, in a barren relationship, with a barren job, with a life that sucks ass. It must have been right under this contraption to hang pans and pots when she told them that just because they had already made that embarrassing mistake once and brought her into the world, probably just because they were bored, didn't give them the right to make another mistake and decide things on her behalf. It might have been this exact window with the minimalist frame that Israel Appel was leaning against when he yelled at her with a beseeching gaze to talk civilly, and before she asked for things, maybe to watch her mouth a bit, to pay attention to the way she was behaving, to her conduct at school, and it might have been exactly that door, the pantry door, that Ariella had leaned against, and from which she approached him, placed a soft hand on his shoulder, and told him there was no need to shout. A solution could be reached. "Why don't we try therapy? That might be a good idea. Regardless of the court order."

I fumbled my way to the living room, allowing the sights of the house to validate or disprove the way I had drawn it so many times in my mind's eye. The consolers were sitting on the couches and on plastic and wooden chairs creating various circles inside the house, as well as standing in the kitchen and in the foyer, making sure they had someone to talk to, looking around, smiling generously and compassionately to one another, occupying themselves with guessing games—who belonged to whom, who came from work, who was family, who came from school, who was truly sad now, who came because it was the proper thing to do. It was possible to discern who was more skilled under such circumstances, who didn't lose control, who knew what to say and who was sitting with shining eyes, leafing through a photo album—Adva on the day she was born, and on her first birthday, and then two and three and so on, in a bikini on the beach, and mostly with girlfriends, hugging and leaning against each other in staged poses, as if designed in advance to serve as a memory. What did they know about me, about the woman now standing idly in the living room? Could any of the visitors here to console identify me as her therapist? A therapist who made a U-turn in the middle of the road while her mother waited for her? Could anyone see through me to the mother, my mother, laid out at the unit? The one who didn't need people staying with her any longer?

"Want to see her room?" Ariella generously offered, and we went in. There were the curtains Adva bought at the flea market, seeming like an exact copy of the way she described them to me at the clinic. There was the collection of scented candles. I fluttered my fingers over them, trying to grasp something, to move the limbs of the body, to make the blood flow. There was the collection of seashells, the one from the poem she read me, not long ago:

The sea
looks different every hour.
Only the seashells in the room
are still.

And there was the motionless air. And Ariella, who didn't leave the room, standing next to me and breathing the breaths of a bereaved mother. So, this is what the room of a girl who wasn't there anymore looks like. The room of a girl who left her mother to stand in it without her. To stand in it with me, staring together into the empty space. "Who is missing in our little house?"

What have you done, Adva? Where did you find the nerve? Where did you find the courage to go all the way, to pose us this way, in our wretchedness, inside this adolescent bedroom, with its flea-market curtains and scented candles? And now is the time to admit: your poems aren't really good. You were right when you said I only said they were because I was your shrink. So, there you go, I'm no longer your shrink. You fired me yourself. And your poems are the poems of a confused adolescent girl who doesn't know the first thing about anything. They are the poems of a spoiled girl with a dirty mouth and plenty of pretension. And your mother, standing next to me now, probably thinks that when she suggested trying therapy, she didn't mean to send her daughter to a creative writing class.

I fled from the Appels' home. I closed the reinforced door after me and breathed in. Maybe that's what houses were for. To escape them. I walked toward my blue Opel. Light was streaming from the windows of the adjacent houses, and I imagined mothers busy preparing dinner for the kids who were encased, along with them, within "the routine." There was the smell of omelets, signaling seven p.m., emanating from every window in the street, right on time. Soon, the rattle of dishwashers would sound. Afterwards, window blinds would be closed, separating home time from street time. School bags would be organized in preparation for tomorrow, unloaded of the previous day, and charged with the one to come. From some of them, sandwiches, forgotten and now changing colors, would be retrieved. Obedient children would be tucked into bed to the sound of lullabies, fulfilling their part in the labor of family life before being gathered into a dream. Before waking into a new day, to exchange one garment for another, to wipe away the cobwebs of sleep and reinforce the circular motion of planet Earth along with the other household members. And I had "time off." I walked down the street during my time off as if I had fallen out of the schedule. Maybe the house in which my children were growing now smelled of omelets too. Maybe it was seven p.m. there as well. And in the swaying illumination of the streetlights, I couldn't remember what day it was today.

***

I don't know how I finished eleventh grade, or whether it was finished in any case, regardless of me. Summer came to the kibbutz, bringing the allergy attacks, and the night swimming in the pool, and the blossoming of the Syrian thistle and the milk thistle and the cotton thistle and the globe thistle. In kibbutz general assemblies, privatization matters were still passionately being discussed, and the members cast harsh insults at each other.

Ronnie returned to the army after sorting out his affairs and I kept sleeping in the bungalow, waiting for weekends in order to cling to his body and infuse oxygen into my pores, as if I was breathing through my skin with gills. His scent would hit my most internal organs, and his fingers managed to touch places that had long been covered with neglect. Before he returned to the army, I breathed in enough air to last me a whole week, sometimes two. Occasionally, I went to the high school dorms. Carmel broke up with Udi and Einav broke up with Amit. We'd sit outside, smoking and talking against the background of the buzzing and chirping and croaking of the dragonflies and crickets and toads. Carmel said that ever since I became friends with Arbel and Lior and Nitzan, they barely saw me. "Once, you used to be a lot more of a presence." They asked if I had heard the latest on Ram, and when I said I hadn't, they'd told me he'd lost it. That he'd been found running around naked in the kibbutz, telling everyone there was no such thing as an axiom. That everything we were taught in school was so that we wouldn't think and wouldn't ask questions, since if we did, we would find out we were being conned. But the truth was that parallel lines could meet and more than one line could be drawn between two points. They told me that, at the moment, he was hospitalized in the psychiatric unit and still wasn't allowed to receive visitors.

"Really, you didn't know?"

No. I didn't. I was suddenly sad and didn't know whether it was because of Ram, or because of me for not knowing, and I remembered that afternoon in third grade when he asked me to come with him to put rocks in his father's bed, but I went to the cabin, to operate Ronnie's drill.

One Thursday, when I returned from school, I found the bungalow clean, and a pleasant lemony scent of detergent spread through the air. It was so strange that I looked around to confirm that it really was Ronnie's bungalow.

There was food in the fridge, there were flowers in the vase, and next to them was a Bundt cake with a note in my mother's familiar handwriting: "*To Ronnie, a good Sabbath, from Ruthie.*" I felt I couldn't stay there. I ran to the parents' house, where I found my mother asleep. I sat down on the rug next to her bed and waited for her to wake up. I wanted to tell her something. I didn't know what I wanted to tell her, but I wanted to scream that something. To scream until she woke up from her terrible sleep. The entire house was breathing heavily, as if the house's breath were synchronized with the beast lurking in the living room. The peace pipe looked small and worn, and the bag with the postcards had grown grimy on the top shelf of the bookshelf, and even it let out a smell of mothballs and pajamas. I fled from there. I returned to the clean bungalow. I waited for Ronnie. Waited for him to come back.

At the end of the year, Motti summoned me to his office. "We're all very impressed, Noga. The entire staff at the principal's office and the teachers. We were happy to see you hand in the papers on time. Not only were they submitted in a timely manner, but the level of the papers was fine, all in all. Here and there, there's room for improvement, but I have to tell you we were already extremely concerned, and you've proven to us that when you're really determined, you can get the job done. Genius is one percent inspiration and ninety-nine percent perspiration! I've also personally called your father to thank him for his cooperation. Way to go!"

Motti said that during the Jewish holidays next year, a youth delegation from the kibbutz movement would be leaving for Poland, and the staff of the principal's office had chosen me to represent the school. "We think you can do us proud, because of the effort you've put in, because we know you, and also because of your familial connection to the Holocaust." Over Motti's desk hung portraits of Israel's president, Haim Hertzog, and Prime Minister Shimon Peres, and between them was the Israeli flag.

Arbel and Nitzan and Lior were waiting for me outside the office. "Don't ask," I blurted out to them when I came out.

***

In honor of the birth of Nadav, Lily and Ilan's new baby, Iris and Yossi arrived from Meyerland, and we all got ready for the long drive to the Golan Heights.

On Friday night, Dad slept over with Mom at the parents' house, and the plan was that the next day, Amnon would pick all of us up on the way from Tel Aviv. Iris and Yossi would arrive separately. I, too, decided to come over to the parents' house. I found Mom and Dad sitting in the kitchen, drinking coffee together. She was wearing a dress and had put the copper broach that was a family heirloom in her hair. Occasionally, she leaned into Dad and he hugged her.

She said, "How clever of me to have finished all the school papers on time. Now I can help with Nadav."

The house was spick and span. The pipes in the collection glistened in a straight row, and it was clear that in her preparations for Dad's arrival, Mom had once again won the race against time. We sat down in the little kitchen, the three of us: mother, father, and daughter. Mother, father, and daughter, preparing for a family get-together. Dad went to the living room and took the family albums down from the bookshelf. Nadav emerged from the photos with fair hair and childish smiles. At the bottom of one of the photos was a caption in Mom's rounded handwriting: "*Look what a cute son you have.*" In some of the photos, he was seen riding a bicycle. In one photo, baby Nadav was embraced in the arms of Lily, who was still a child herself, and in another, he had drifted over to Iris's arms, and you could imagine how neither of them wanted to be short-changed when their new brother was born.

Dad said, "Our son had a happy life."

I sat there silently. I felt that talking about him after so many years was like crossing an ocean. I tried to understand what language they were speaking when they carried on naturally with the type of conversation that was apparently discontinued some years ago. I tried to understand what kind of history I was witnessing now, and whose family was now sitting together in the kitchen reminiscing. Mom took a black-and-white photo out of the album, showing the five of us: Lily and Iris as smiling high-schoolers, with topknot hairdos. Lily was holding Nadav's hand, while Iris was holding me, a one-year-old baby, in her arms. Her cheek was right against mine and she was closing her eyes as if she was inhaling me in. Amnon, apparently in the midst of his bar mitzvah year, was standing with a soccer ball in hand. We were all looking up at the camera.

There had been such a time. The time before time. A time when people hung out at this house and little kids played on the rug, where the beast now dwelled. Another photo showed Dad, a young, tanned man, holding his twin daughters on either side of him, while Mom, next to him, held Amnon. In a different photo, Mom was sitting in a chair, with me in her arms, while around us were Lily and Iris, Amnon and Nadav. Perhaps we were a real family?

"Where are you going?" Mom asked when I rose from my chair.

"To visit Ronnie. He's been away from the kibbutz for two weeks."

"How nice that you two keep in close touch," Dad said, and when I was already at the door, Mom added, "Nogi, tell him that he's invited to join us tomorrow. After all, he's family."

***

The alarm rang too early for Saturday, and I couldn't remember how I had agreed to go with the entire family to see Nadav. The remains of the night's dream were still clinging to me as I tried to shake off the image of a hairless baby talking to me in adult language. "I don't understand," I yelled at him. "I don't understand. Talk clearly!" And Ronnie's elbow brushed against my ribs. I had a hard time getting out of bed. I got dressed and was brushing my teeth when I noticed that Ronnie had gotten up after me.

"It's great that you came," Mom and Dad said together when they saw him dragging his feet to the old people's neighborhood, heading for the parents' house. Amnon also clapped him on the shoulder and asked how things were going in the army. All of us got into Amnon's car, which began to wind its way out of the kibbutz, and for a moment, it seemed like we were on our way to somewhere new, to magical landscapes far from here. The road ran north, and east, and north again, to the land of basalt, the land of Bashan, the land of the eagle in the air and the serpent upon the rock, the land of red mountains and river crevices. Dad told us about the archeological excavations in Gamla, headed by Shmaria Guttman, for whom he had great respect. He told us about a unique bronze coin that was apparently forged in Gamla, with the words "For the salvation of Jerusalem the H," which was apparently 'Jerusalem the Holy.' "Do you understand what that means?" he asked us, excited, and Mom said it was wonderful when people worked at a job they were passionate about. It was mentally healthy.

Dad said, "Ruthie, honey, come on. It's got nothing to do with mental health. Think about what this means," and I gritted out through my lips that I didn't understand that whole deal with Gamla that Dad was so enthusiastic about, and I heard Amnon mutter back, asking why I was surprised. After all, there were more dead people in Gamla than in our family, and Dad, who was sitting in the front seat next to Amnon, who was driving, said that for now, we should keep it to ourselves, but he had received an indication that there had already been one supportive review regarding his research proposal about the synagogue built in Gamla during the first century BCE. "Everyone, keep your fingers crossed."

In the back seat, the three of us were crammed tight: Ronnie on my right, Mom on my left, me in the middle.

"Oh, Ari." Mom patted Dad's knee as he sat diagonally from her, rubbing against me on her way to him. "What a beautiful day, right? Didn't we get lucky?"

And Dad replied, "A fabulous day."

And Mom said, "Ah, Nogi, it's so great that we're all together," and I nodded and Mom went on to address Ronnie this time, "Your adopted family is expanding," and Amnon turned up the volume on the radio, looking for a station with good music.

Amnon's overloaded car, with the small hole in its exhaust pipe, passed through the changing landscape, leaving behind a slight mist of soot, and I tried to find the most viable pose between my adopted brother and my adopting mother, who was enjoying the way there and the beautiful day. Meanwhile, Amnon found a station playing Chava Alberstein singing "Kinneret,"[13] and all of us, including Dad and Amnon and Ronnie, joined in:

Though I grow penniless and stooped,
my heart a beacon for strangers,
how could I betray you, how can I forget,
how could I forget the grace of youth?

---

13   From "Kinneret (Perhaps)" by poet Rachel Bluwstein.

Lily was waiting for us in the doorway, her face tired. She was holding Nadav in her arms, like in the black-and-white photo in the album in the parents' house. Amnon's car unloaded its contents onto the parking spot and the entire cargo trapped inside it dispersed, finding a new spot on the rug of another house. Iris was already there, cleaning and organizing, chatting with Ilan while Yossi sat in front of the TV; she was obviously feeling at home, and it was clear that Ilan and Yossi, like Iris and Lily, also talked to each other besides the times when we all met. Lily passed Nadav to Iris in order to greet the guests.

"What a surprise." Lily hugged Ronnie with familial fraternity. "It's been years… Good job keeping in touch." And he smiled and said Nadav was really cute.

"He looks like you," he said, and it wasn't clear who he was looking at.

"So, does it make you want to have one of your own?" Mom asked him.

And Dad said, "What's the rush? Let him find a wife first," and Mom said, "No rush at all. These days, the young kids take their time, right, Amnon?" And Lily and Iris and Amnon all exchanged looks. Ilan and Yossi were already sitting in the living room when the entire family joined them, and it took less than five minutes for the mother tongue to take control of us.

"So, did Mom excel at the school papers?"

"Well, you know, you deserve it."

"I heard there was room for improvement here and there."

The four of us cracked up, and Amnon added, "Mom's become really industrious over the years. No way would she have written our papers."

Lily rushed to break the silence. "After all, Noga's going to Poland. There's an orchestra there that plays gas."

"And there's also *I scream* there."

The language emerged from my throat, demanding to be spoken, taking over, and for a few moments, I wasn't an only child. I was surrounded by a brother and sisters who occasionally appeared, speaking my cruel, incomprehensible language, casting it off themselves, forging a momentary alliance with me against a shared, anonymous enemy, and although I was not a part of their trio, we belonged to the same ceremonial tribe speaking the same dialect. Yossi and Ilan were already well-practiced at this scenario and waited for the fit to pass. Ronnie sat not far from me, and I couldn't remember how he had gotten here. We were a multi-membered family.

On the way back, we were all silent. Even Mom. It was dark outside and we were sad. As we approached the kibbutz, Mom said: *Nadav's so sweet. Such a cute, sweet boy. Isn't he, Ari?*

***

Ram was discharged from the psychiatric unit and I went to visit him at his mother's house. She said he was pharmaceutically well-balanced now. He told me he knew something was wrong with him, but he wanted me to know I'd always been his best friend. I told him something was wrong with me too, but I was too healthy for it to be official.

"It's tiring, isn't it? Being healthy, it's tiring," he commented, and asked if I remembered that weird day when we were in second grade and "your weird dad, with his weird mistress, came to tell us about Gamla during the Second Temple."

We both started laughing. It was the first time I had heard such a clear definition of what had happened there. I asked him if he remembered talking about slicing a cat in the bread machine, and he said he did, he just couldn't remember if it had actually happened. He asked if I remembered Storio the Elf, and I was shocked that he did.

"I knew right from the start that you weren't Tova Hershkovitz. She happens to be a relative of my parents. But your stories were better."

"Ram," I told him. "I love you. You're a good friend."

"And you, Noga, have to be a therapist after you finish your 'wrong' period. It'll go away, after all, that 'wrong' period, and you'll be a really good therapist. You know all about mental health and that kind of stuff."

I told him that he and I weren't the only ones who were nuts. Motti the principal had lost it too, and the teachers had chosen me to be a part of the delegation to Poland.

"So you're going to Poland?" he asked, and I nodded. "I bet you're going to miss that boyfriend of yours, that soldier you adopted in third grade."

"How do you know about that?" I asked him, and he replied, "Are you serious?"

I told him I'd been chosen not just because of the excellent papers I'd turned in, but because my mother was a Holocaust survivor, and now I had to interview her again.

Oh my God, he said in English. Weren't we done with all that yet?

***

Mom was waiting for me as usual with the coffee and the bread and jam.

And this was how it went down:

When Mom and Grandma were in jail in Rava-Ruska, a German officer saw them there. He liked the look of Grandma (why?) and asked her to come with him to a camp he was going to run in Belzec and be his housekeeper. That suited her very well. Not that anyone cared whether it suited her or not, but she wanted to be in Belzec. She told him she would take the girl with her. Or maybe she didn't tell him, and that's just what happened.

Belzec was a little town in southeast Lublin, next to the railroad tracks connecting Lublin and Lviv, where Mom was born along with many more Jews. In 1941, as part of Operation Reinhard,[14] a mass-extermination camp, the first of its kind, was founded in Belzec.

"There, I've collected some news clippings with reports from the archeological excavations and photocopies of testimony about Belzec in Polish. There are almost no Hebrew-speaking survivors from Belzec."

"Just you?"

"Just me and Grandma, who's no longer with us, as you know, and I heard there's someone else. I don't exactly know."

Oddly, when Mom talked about the events of the war, the mother tongue detached from her and a different, linear language clung to her, the kind I could follow. A language in which events emerged one after the other, and not all together, although occasionally they would collapse into each other once again, and I would turn my head, wary of them. Of her.

The master plan at Belzec included stationary gas chambers made of wood, into which carbon monoxide was streamed through pipes. These were efficient chambers, powered independently of an external gas supply by soviet tank

---

14   Operation Reinhard was the codename of the German plan in World War II to exterminate Polish Jews in the General Government district of German-occupied Poland, marking the introduction of extermination camps.

engines. In 1942, the three gas chambers began to work systematically, but as they could not deal with the volume of human deliveries flowing into the camp daily, they were replaced by six concrete chambers, an efficiency measure allowing the number of victims per day to rise to two thousand.

"Two thousand a day, imagine that. Two thousand a day." She stabbed me with that number: two thousand!!!

And I replied, "Mom, move on, please."

In any case, as you can imagine, Grandma didn't know all that when she decided to sew me a pretty dress and make me pretty shoes and ran away from the ghetto in Lviv to Belzec, of all places. She was just born there. She had that saying, "The people, where they were born, that's where they'll find help." What she didn't know was that what was happening in Belzec was intended to be a revolution in the extermination industry, and at the beginning of 1942, the first transports of Jews on whom the new method of efficient mass extermination with gas would be tried out had already been chosen.

Every time she said the word *gas* I felt I had reached my limit. I asked that we take a short break. "You want bread and jam?" she asked me.

And I answered, "No! How can you eat bread and jam all day?"

From the binder, Mom extracted a colorful map with a diagram of the camp, including its watchtowers, the gates, the barb-wire fences, the cabins where the Jewish forced laborers lived, the train station, the arrival platform, the gallows, the hall where clothes were removed, the hall where the women's hair was removed, the gas chambers, the mechanized gas manufacture system, the crematoriums, the mass graves, and a mess hall too. Horrific.

"How come, out of all the women there, the *Kommandant*[15] chose Grandma?"

Mom shifted a little in her chair, which made a noise as if saying that was enough. The chair had spoken and there was no need to elaborate.

Some things, Nogi, can't be explained.

In any case, Grandma came with the *Kommandant* to Belzec. No one knows how it happened, but she came to Belzec, like she planned, and not by train. Out of all the places, it had to be there. She thought that's where she had been born, and that there would be people there to help her. That's what was going through her head. *The people, where they were born, that's where they'll find help.*

---

15   German: Commander

"Okay, Mom. You've already said that sentence a couple of times."

Grandma was the *Kommandant*'s housekeeper. *What did she do for him?* Everything. She washed his clothes. *And what else?* She ironed his uniform. And shone his boots, too. And cooked for him. *And what else?* Tidied up his room and sewed for him. Grandma was an excellent seamstress, really. *And what else?* Anything he wanted. She did everything, everything.

"Come on, Mom, do you think I'm retarded? What else did she do for him?" Silence. *Foo-foo-foo.*

While Grandma was tidying up the *Kommandant*'s house, her little daughter was running around the camp. When Grandma ate something, she gave some to Mom, too. When Grandma went to sleep in the storehouse, Mom was sleeping there next to her, too (*On the rug? Just kiiiiding*), on the floor. And when Mom was bored, she had a rag doll she had brought from the ghetto with her, and a book in Polish that one of the Ukrainian laborers on the train had given her. But when Mom asked where all the people who arrived on the train had disappeared to, where were they? Where were the crowds of people who arrived on the train cars three times a day? Grandma slapped her on the mouth. It happened every day. A slap to the mouth. Mom didn't understand how such quantities of people could arrive, making so much noise, screams, shouts, dogs barking, the cracking of whips, and within a few hours, she couldn't see any of them. All was still. She and her mother went to sleep. And the people, where did they disappear to?

It was only from afar that she saw the bodies, later cleared in wheelbarrows and carts, piled up in stacks.

Are these the same people? Mom asked Grandma. *The ones who came on the trains? Is that what's inside the wheelbarrows now?* But Grandma warned her not to ask. She had a recurring response: *Go in to sleep. It's already dark. I'll join you soon.* And mainly: *Don't go there. Don't go there. You can't go there.*

Mom got up from her chair and put on the water. I never understood how water could be "put on," but Mom could put on the water. She could actually do that. She plugged the kettle into the outlet and when it buzzed, she said: *Oh, there, it's buzzing.* She asked if I wanted coffee, too, as if she still hadn't realized that I never drank coffee while she did, that it was impossible for both of us to drink together. "Should we keep going, Nogi?"

Belzec. A small camp with a pastoral landscape. One square kilometer surrounded by fences entwined with branches, with trees planted around them. No one knew what happened behind those fences. Even Grandma and Mom only roamed the external part of the camp where the administrative buildings, the residential buildings, and the depot all stood. Mom saw the overloaded trains enter through the northern gate and also saw the people led to the cabins, where they were forced to take off their clothes and store their possessions, which, they were promised, would soon be returned to them, after they showered and were disinfected. She saw how the men were separated from the women, how the babies were torn away from the mothers, and how the children suddenly vanished. As if someone had gone *abracadabra* and simply made them disappear. There one moment, gone the next.

She remembered one girl, about her age, a moment before she disappeared, standing alone in front of the cabin. Mom imagined that girl's name was Fania. She just decided, for no reason: Fania. She remembered Fania standing and looking around, and Mom tried to imagine to herself what Fania was thinking about at that moment. What she thought was going to happen. And then she saw everyone start to walk, a kind of strange mass walking. Everyone walked and walked, and slowly got smaller until they disappeared. Fania disappeared too. No one was left to play with Mom. She didn't see the path that was fenced off on both sides, the "tunnel," where the naked people were led, marching a few dozen meters to small shacks with double tin-coated walls with a layer of sand between them, their wooden doors covered in rubber, closable only from the outside. She also didn't see the pipes installed on the shacks and the opening for the removal of the bodies.

She did hear the shouting. The shouting reached all the way to where she was. At first, it seemed like strange sounds, some kind of moan, some of it in Polish or in Yiddish, which she understood, but some of it in all kinds of languages she didn't know. Cries of despair of some kind, as if someone should come and save all those people from something, but apparently, no one came. Then the cries turned into screeching, like a million owls or jackals. And there was crying, too, inside that screeching. Mom remembered she wasn't supposed to cover her ears. She remembered what they had told her and Grandma that day by the carousel in Lviv, and remembered that when the orchestra was playing, you had to listen. And the orchestra was playing. And sometimes singing as well: *Drei Lilien, Drei Lilien, kommt ein Reiter gefahren, bringt die*

Lilien. Three roses, three roses, the horseman came and brought roses. And Mom listened. But she didn't clap. There was no need. There was no one to clap, either. All the people had disappeared. The shouting stopped and instead came the smell. That part, Mom understood immediately: you shouldn't ask about the smell.

Damn. What an oppressive story. I asked Mom to skip the part about the smell when she described what had happened there to me. "It's unnecessary, I get what's going on there," I told her.

"What's going on with you?" She gave me that stare.

In any case, Grandma realized Mom couldn't stay there. Every day, the *Kommandant* told her it was just a matter of time, and that in the meantime, he was leaving her the child. And here, a new character joined our story (thank God!). It was actually not a new character and was even a truly old one: Grandma's brother. Mom's uncle. But in this story, he arrived abruptly. Someone had already hinted to Grandma earlier that her brother was spending time in Belzec, with Aryan papers (he was blond too, like Mom), working at the bakery and in charge of distributing bread in the camp. Every day, he would enter the camp with a horse and wagon, and loaded on the wagon were enormous straw baskets with loaves of bread inside them (no, not for the prisoners. There were almost no prisoners in Belzec. People came there for one night only). On one of his visits, the uncle told Mom quietly: *Next time I come here, you'll quickly hop into the basket. Don't talk to anyone, don't say anything. I take the bread out of the baskets, I give you a sign, you jump in and cover yourself with a sack.* Mom knew enough to listen to him. She always knew whom to listen to. It's a fact. She knew not to listen to the nice man in Lviv who told her to come to the Goldna Roisa Synagogue. But she knew she should listen to her uncle, and maybe that's the main point in life: to know who's on your side and who's against you.

The next day, the uncle arrived with his horse and wagon again. She heard the wagon arriving and was already waiting outside. He took one basket of bread and brought it into the Germans' living room. He then took out the empty basket, put it in the cart, and while he went in with a different basket, he signaled her with his eyes, a kind of wink, and she looked around, made sure no one could see, and leapt inside. She covered herself up with sacks, he climbed up to the wagon, and just like that, they were out. *Pony Boy, Pony*

Boy... Here we go across the plains. That was how Mom escaped from the camp. She left Belzec in a basket, like Moses in the Bible. She was the only Jewish girl in the world to leave the camp through the gate, although 600,000 Jews arrived at that camp.

Six-hundred thousand?

Six-hundred thousand!

Amazing.

Yes, amazing.

Unbelievable. And what happened to the uncle? Is he still alive?

So, it was like this: After Mom disappeared, the *Kommandant* gave Grandma a thorough beating. But he didn't kill her. He left her with him; he simply wanted to make it clear to her that he was the one who made the rules, and not her. And she understood. No one suspected the uncle. He died a few months later, when his mother, Mom's grandmother, arrived at the camp on the train, and he fainted when he saw her being led to the gas chambers. After he fainted, his Aryan papers didn't help him anymore. But maybe everyone has a role in life, and that was the uncle's role: he got Mom out of the camp. They couldn't get too far from the camp, and he brought her with the basket to Julia Pepiak's house.

Julia remembered Grandma's family from the old days and brought Mom into her kitchen. The kitchens in those places were big, long rooms, and inside the kitchen was a bed, too. Once, the kitchen used to be a proper room. There were plenty of duvets on the bed. On top was a tall eiderdown duvet, and over the duvets lay a giant board, on which they kneaded the dough and prepared the bread. Everything done in the kitchen was done on that board. There was always something on the board that was just being made: noodles or something to be chopped. Julia told Mom: *You go here under the duvets on which the board rests, and don't make a sound.* It was shortly after Mietek, Julia's son who had joined the Polish underground, was killed, and Julia, who couldn't recover, decided God had sent her a pretty little girl to ease the pain of loss. It turned out Grandma was right: The people, where they were born, that's where they'll find help. And even if this saying wasn't always true, it worked for Grandma.

"I just remembered I have to do something," I told Mom and ran to the bungalow. I threw up into Ronnie's toilet bowl and sprawled across the bed until the next day.

The evening before the delegation left for Poland, I had a fever of 104. I was burning up, and Mom suggested that I go to bed in the parents' house. I told her I'd rather die.

***

In twelfth grade, I looked like a normal student. I had a backpack, I was still friends with Arbel and Nitzan and Lior, and here and there I'd also do my homework, participate in class, and read out loud. My gills grew, and I managed to breathe without Ronnie for two weeks in a row, and even more if necessary. My hair was long, my skin was tan, and the boys at school would hit on me as if I was available. In lit class, we studied S.Y. Agnon's *A Simple Story*. In history class, we learned about the Holocaust and Revival, and in biology, we learned about "metamorphosis," a phenomenon that took place among certain species in the natural world, especially insects and amphibians, when the offspring did not resemble their parents in the slightest: not in shape, not in diet, and not even in the environment in which they lived.

I completed my matriculation exams successfully and Motti said he had always believed in me. "Both in you and in the system, as Janusz Korczak said: 'One who cares for days—sows wheat, one who cares for years—plants trees, one who cares for generations—educates people.' Oddly, I passed the screening process to serve as an army welfare NCO during my military service and thought to myself that maybe Ram was right when he said I understood about matters of mental health.

7.

My cell phone had all kinds of moods. When Julie called, it played "Call Me" by Blondie. Tomer, in contrast, fixed me up with a more original ringtone, and every time he called, my cell phone would be taken over by 'Funny Future Voiceover,' spouting out, 'Yo, what's up, hey there, hey there, no littering from your car,' and if I didn't answer quickly, I could hear more and more such inspired statements.

"Cool," I told him once about the choice, and he replied, "Come on, Mom, I know you have no idea what it is."

"I have no idea, but it's still cool," I insisted on not backing down, and he and Julie exchanged looks that said it was true, no doubt about it, "Mom's definitely one of the cool ones."

"If not the coolest…" I heard myself letting out another desperate attempt into the space of the house, refusing to be resignedly gathered into the previous generations of mothers preceding me, those with their copper broaches, while facing Julie and Tomer, who had already moved on to other matters.

But when most people called, my cell would play the same four-tone melody and I tried to infuse my "hello" with an empathetic, therapeutic intonation. This was also the case when it rang one afternoon, about two weeks after the wretched U-turn on the road, two weeks in which the last thing in the world I wanted was to be "one of the cool ones." The sun was right at the center of the sky. Its light entered my clinic through the window, parts of it filtering in through the gap under the door, and perhaps also through additional places I didn't notice, and the call caught me sitting idly in the armchair. Just like that, in the middle of the day, in the sunlight, I was sitting idly in the armchair.

"Hi, good afternoon, am I speaking to Noga Sarid?"

"You are."

"This is Stanza, Adva Appel's counselor."

"Stanza?"

"Yes, that's my name."

"Yes, of course that's your name. That's just fine. How can I help?" I asked Stanza, thinking about how I was already in trouble. The conversation had just begun and already I had to apologize. I sat up straighter in the armchair and imagined Stanza sitting in the counselor's office, the tumult of school around her, teachers running around in the corridors, a phone ringing in the principal's office, students filling up the classrooms and the schoolyard; perhaps they had already recovered from the absence of one of their own, who hadn't shown up for classes frequently anyway.

"My homeroom teacher has a face like Cookie Monster's," I remembered Adva's description. "And what's the deal with starting school in the morning? Why don't they let us sleep in and start around noon?" promptly followed by the usual question, "How much longer do we have to go?" and after I replied came the usual sigh, "Damn, life's long, what a fucking manufacturing defect," and I wondered who actually did design life that way, who took on the ministry of time, and how the idea of the fifty-minute therapy hour came about, and how come it was actually toward the end that Adva wanted to stay, wanted me not to pretend that I was sorry that we had to say goodbye, and perhaps wanted me not to pretend at all. Maybe that was what she'd wanted, to pull away the screen of pretense, the screen behind which I marketed the product called her life to her. If I had chosen to turn around on the road, to turn my back on my mother, it had nothing to do with her. And if you really want to save someone, there are ways to do it.

"Adva's counselor?" I asked Stanza, and she corrected me, "The school counselor."

"Okay, what do you want?" I couldn't hide my impatience.

A report. Stanza asked me to write a therapy summary report. The parents had signed a medical confidentiality waiver, and there I was, getting a call from the school and consigned to the computer to write about Adva. My body, which had already undergone a few experiences since the last time I was required to write a school paper, sat down in the chair to write a report for the counselor.

Adva, Adva. Now is no time for poems. Now is the time to report to the establishment on your despair. To report to the system on one girl who decided to retire, just like that, in mid-battle. To report on the therapy I administered to you, which was unsuccessful. You were the one I turned to when I turned my back on my mother, to the girl in you who I thought was waiting for me. I didn't believe you'd do what you did. I thought we'd traverse these years, tinted with the darkness of five p.m., and beyond, together.

At the end of every session, I silently recounted to you the tale of another girl, and after all, I've gone through that age, that age resembling an electric short circuit. Here I am, right here. Where are you, then?

∗∗

I was assigned to basic training camp in the Jordan Rift Valley just as the Intifada[16] began, which didn't stop me from hitchhiking at any hour of the day, every time I felt my gills had reached their capacity. Ronnie, who had left the standing army, was an organ in my body. An organ whose location was unclear—under the skin or over it, but an organ nonetheless. I gained weight, my hair became a dust trap, the uniform clung to my flesh like a type of skin disease, the corps badge perched on my shoulder like a bothersome twitch. I was a foreign body moving through space in one direction—toward Ronnie.

When I occasionally showed up at the parents' house, I noticed that the mother tongue had gotten worse, and even the most inanimate objects were spasming. The kettle stopped buzzing and started dancing ("Nogilee, unplug the kettle, it's dancing."), the K300 bug spray "walloped" ("It really walloped those big black cockroaches today.") and the coffee just "went crazy" and turned bitter. That's what happened: the coffee just went crazy. I visited infrequently, but on Saturdays, I'd send Mom to bring the laundry, since the soldiers' laundry facility closed before I even woke up. The clean clothes waited

---

16   The Intifada or First Intifada was a sustained series of Palestinian protests, including violent riots, against the Israeli occupation of the West Bank and Gaza, taking place between December 1987 and September 1993.

for me, folded up, at the entrance to Carmel's and my room, and I took them from there to the bungalow. On Sunday mornings, Ronnie would drop me off at the bus station, and when my body disengaged from him, I imagined I heard a kind of sudden *pok* sound.

I learned the work at the military base quite quickly. I grew skilled at telling people what needed to be said. The soldiers' complaints tended to repeat themselves, and my meetings with them tended to have a recurring chronology, other than that frightening moment, during a home visit with Dan's parents, when I was appalled to hear myself telling them that it was a good thing that Dan felt he could come to me with anything. It was mentally healthy.

Time became heavy and awkward. The bulletin board in the dining hall filled with notices about emergency assemblies, and about weddings, and about funerals, and one Thursday afternoon, Clara suddenly died.

"Did you hear? Such a tragedy," Mom told me.

Other than that, nothing notable happened in the army. The Intifada bubbled up, Molotov cocktails flew through the air, we were hated all over the world, and soldiers underwent training on how to look less bad for the TV cameras, but my foreign body still moved in only one direction and knew only two modes: with Ronnie or without him. And during the summer at the end of the army, when the nausea began, I realized that a period that was a month late was not only the result of faulty nutrition and mental stress.

***

I thought Ronnie would be happy about the pregnancy. I was already past the age of twenty, two years older than his mother had been when he was born. But he just said, "Okay." It seemed as if our foreign bodies had preceded us again. Once again, they made their plans before we did, making room for something, while we just needed to fit in inside them, in the appropriate spaces.

"Okay," he said, and I, too, said: *Okay*. I concluded my military service and was assigned a room of my own in the young people's neighborhood in the kibbutz. Out of everyone, Ram was the only one who asked why Ronnie and I didn't move in together. Meaning, not officially. In actuality, my room stood abandoned, and now that I wasn't sharing it with Carmel, the darkness in it became denser, and when I occasionally turned on the light, the bulb was startled. One time, it suddenly shattered, and it took me a month to change it. The dust stopped being granular, and perhaps for that reason, became invisible. I noticed it only when I reached out one day for a hairbrush that had been left behind, and when I shifted it, I recognized various shades of grayish-brown that covered the shelf.

My body turned mysterious and scheming. I would encounter it randomly in front of the mirror, or across from window panes, as if it were emerging from the outside, and inside the room, my shadow climbed the walls and sometimes seeped palely to the floor. My chest filled out in a day. I went to sleep, and when I got up in the morning, I found it waiting for me in full bloom. My face assumed a grayish hue and I was nauseous all day, but I couldn't throw up. I was assigned to work at Palm Tree Preschool, and every day, I walked, pale, between the preschool walls, waiting for four o'clock, for someone to declare they were all going to the parents, and I could go to Ronnie. I'd reach the bungalow before he did, lie down on the bed, and turn on the radio-tape with the Mati Kaspi cassette.

Soon, almost, as one we band,
Forever, you've placed your hand in my hand,
I'm afraid, and you understand,
why my whole body trembles tonight.[17]

---

17   From the song "Eternal Covenant" (*Brit Olam*) by Mati Kaspi and Ehud Manor.

8.

Saturday morning at the Glover-Sarid home. As I wake up to the heaviness of the body, it always takes me a moment to remember what day it is and how old I am, as if my body still carries the remains of the previous ages that need to be removed. Eli is still asleep, and in the living room, electricity in all its forms awaits me. The hum of air conditioning, the rattle of the refrigerator, and the exhalations of the computer. Soon, the noises from all the other machines will begin—the dishwasher, the washer. Mild electrical charges will shake the house in brief pulses, nearly indiscernible. Cell phone charger cables dangle in all corners of the house, reflecting the household members' anxiety about dead batteries. Tomer and Julie are still asleep as well.

Usually, I fear the moment when everyone wakes up. The "good morning" someone has to say first since it feels wrong to skip it completely. We still maintain everyday civility. Friday night dinners with steaming soup, and washed-out chicken, and mashed potatoes, and salad. Cleaning and tidying, more or less. *Good morning* and *good night* and *bon voyage*, and *how was your day*, reinforcing the beams of the house with a scaffolding of kind words and role division and a daily schedule. But today, there's a plan. Tomer is getting ready for a school expedition to Poland and driving to interview Grandma at the kibbutz is already a bit too complicated. She doesn't really remember anymore, and it's gotten hard for her to talk about it. Besides, "She goes way too deep." He prefers me to Grandma. That's what he said: "I'd rather have you tell me."

Have me tell him. It might be easier, to tell the story of Tomer's grandma. Grandma, who in some way already belongs to history, and actually, all this happened long ago, and I too am no longer the girl I once was, the one who would run off to throw up at the end of each Holocaust story. So here, Tomer. Here's how it went down:

When Grandma arrived at Julia Pepiak's house, Julia initially hid her under the duvets in the kitchen. No one from Julia's family knew she was there. Not Jan, Julia's husband, not her daughter Adela, who had already left home and was a teacher in Janów Lubelski, not her son Zygmunt, who was a novitiate priest in Krakow. And certainly not Mietek, who was already dead ("Mom, I don't think it's necessary to mention that."). Julia didn't tell anyone. When Grandma heard the voices of Polish children playing outside the house, she asked to join in, but Julia explained that she couldn't, and told her not to talk; it was dangerous to talk. *Why?* Grandma asked, and Julia always told her the truth: *Because it's dangerous to be Jewish right now. Then why did my mother give birth to me as Jewish?* Grandma asked, and Julia told her that that's how it was; you didn't choose how and to whom you were born. But Grandma had already made up her mind: Julia would be her mother. She didn't know Julia thought God had sent her from heaven after Mietek died, but she did feel how much Julia loved her. She felt it; love is something you feel (*Right, Tomer? Obvs*).

But it gradually became too dangerous. Julia's house was only half a kilometer away from the camp, and German officers would arrive there several times a day. They came to stay over, to rest, to drink some coffee, to smoke a cigarette, and Julia was hospitable. She couldn't continue hiding a Jewish girl there. Especially since a few of the neighbors were already suspicious. Someone said he had seen Julia washing a girl's clothing, although everyone knew Julia's children were already adults and had left home. Someone else said he had seen Julia making more food than usual. Another said she had heard Julia humming a children's song to herself, after months of not singing and barely talking. You know how it is; people started talking. (*Not just on the kibbutz, huh?*)

Everyone knew that if Julia was caught, not only she but all of the neighbors could be sent to the camp. Everyone was well familiar with the sight of Jews jumping off the train. Everyone was familiar with their frenzied expressions as they burst into yards, with their terrified eyes, begging for shelter in Polish homes, in the barn, in the cowshed, in the stable: *Please, I beg you, at least just take the boy, just take the girl, only for tonight, until we can find somewhere else.* Everyone knew that when they heard the sound of the train coming, they had to take care to lock all the doors, and slide the deadlocks carefully into place, and keep a really good eye on the yard, and make sure to thoroughly check that no Jew who decided to jump off the train here, of all place, had invaded the cowsheds, and the stables, and the barns. And everyone knew what had happened to the Japoshnik family when they found a mother and child in their cowshed, under one of the cows. It didn't help when Branislava Japoshnik swore they had no idea that Jews had broken into their cowshed, and even asked them to let her murder them herself. It didn't help their neighbors, either. And the most dangerous part was that when they discovered that Grandma had disappeared from the camp, they organized a manhunt to find her, going from door to door and searching. "Is there a girl here?"

But Julia was a believer, a devout Christian. A picture of the Virgin Mary, holding the baby Jesus in her arms, was hanging in her home, and she thought that if God had seen fit to send her a girl like that from heaven after Mietek had died, it was her duty to protect her. It was all a matter of signs. She told Grandma: *Summer is coming now, and you'll go hide in the wheat fields.* The wheat in Poland was high and dense, and Grandma was small and skinny (great combo!). *At night,* Julia said, *you'll go sleep in the crypt, under the floor of the church, where the dead are buried. The Nazis don't go in there at night, and in the winter I'll come get you. I'll find you, don't worry.* And that's what Grandma did. She knew to listen to Julia. She ran into the wheat fields, which were next to Julia's home, and disappeared inside them.

"She's the coolest," Tomer said. "We should submit her to the Weekly Children's Drawing, like Where's Waldo: Where's Grandma?"

And I played along: "Please, kids, color in the whole drawing in pretty colors, and leave only Grandma in white."

In any case, while she was in the wheat field, she didn't really have anything to eat. Occasionally, when she could, Julia went out to the fields as if calling her dog. She shouted out to her dog, and if it wasn't dangerous, she'd sneak Grandma a little bag with a bit of bread that would last for a few days. And when it wasn't enough, she ate raw stalks of wheat (*lethal!*). Occasionally, it rained (*In the summer? Yes, that was Poland*), and then she had something to drink, too. Grandma opened her mouth wide and gulped the rain. Sometimes, she managed to cup a little in her hands. And when it didn't rain, she waited patiently. Grandma had infinite patience. After the rain, the sun would come out, drying her clothes. Grandma knew she couldn't get sick. If she got sick, there was no doctor to cure her. And at night, she would go sleep in the crypt.

There was a flat surface there, on which the bodies were prepared for burial, where Grandma would sleep. It wasn't the most comfortable place, but it was a flat surface. Grandma lay there as if she were a corpse. Julia told her that the people in the neighborhood didn't go into the cemetery at night. They were scared, which was fortunate: one person's fear was another's salvation. Julia pretended to come to the cemetery in order to visit her parents' graves, and when possible, would smuggle in a little food for Grandma.

There was one more spot in the cemetery: the grave of a soldier who died in the war against the Russians, before World War I. It was a cement grave, with a cement cover. It wasn't flat, but rather a kind of container from which the soldier's bones had been taken out in order to bury them in a military cemetery. It was an empty grave. And the empty grave became Grandma's home. In the morning, she was a field girl, and at night she slept in the cemetery. She did that for a few months, waiting for Julia to come get her.

"And for her mother?"

"What about her mother?"

"Wasn't she waiting for her mother?"

Good question, I thought to myself. "Good question, Tomer." How come I never asked that?

During this time, her mother was working for the *Kommandant*. Cooking for him and cleaning for him and doing his laundry and tidying up his house. And getting beaten, too. He didn't believe her when she said she didn't know where her daughter had vanished. How could a girl escape from the camp like that? Someone had to have helped her. He didn't believe her daughter wouldn't tell people outside what was really going on in there, inside the camp with the pastoral landscape, with the branches decorating the fences. And mostly: it was unbearable to think that one little girl would make a mockery of the supreme order reigning there. That was the ultimate impudence since, other than that little mishap, everything there was going precisely according to plan.

"So, I don't get it. How come the *Kommandant* kept Grandma's mother alive?"

"Where were we?" I found myself evading the question, just like she had.

9.

The tadpole sprouting in my belly was not discernible, but my entire body swirled and took part in the happening as if it was something much bigger than thirteen millimeters. In all the commotion, I had a hard time recognizing the tadpole itself without all the surrounding noise. When Ronnie would come back from work, he seemed sadder than ever. When I asked, "Are you happy? Are you pleased?" I was appalled to find my mother's voice emerging from inside me as if it were her inside my belly, and parts of her were already starting to seep out. Most of the time, I was exhausted, and one morning, I fainted at Palm Tree Preschool, in front of all the kids, and Adi the preschool teacher took me to the clinic.

My mother wasn't in Israel at the time. It was her first trip outside the borders of the State of Israel since I first knew her. The Jewish Agency for Israel had invited her to testify at an event taking place with American teenagers in Washington, DC, and in preparation for her journey, she briefly resembled a worldly sophisticate. Dad brought her a suitcase from Tel Aviv, and when I came to say goodbye as well, I found her packing and humming *foo-foo-foo*, singing the song about *s'brent, briderlekh, s'brent*.[18] Occasionally, she said she had plenty of work in preparation for the trip, and that she was in a race against time. Dad and I sat and watched her pack, sharing our wonder in response to this woman packing a suitcase and humming, when suddenly, with no warning, she looked up, gazed at me, and said: *What happened to your breasts? Did they swell up?*

A brief moment of silence froze between the three of us, until Dad said, "Ruthie, hon, you better leave the girl alone and focus on the work you need

---

18   "Fire, my brothers, fire!" is the first line of the Yiddish song "It is Burning" (or "Our Town Is Burning,"), written in 1936 by Mordechai Gebirtig in response to the pogrom of Przytyk, which occurred on March 9, 1936.

to do," and I joined in, "Yeah, Mom, vork sets you free, ja?" and Dad and I started laughing.

"*Meshigene*."[19] But she was not distracted, telling him, "Ari, can't you see? Are you blind? The girl's awfully pale," and I hurried to intervene and suggested that she not take the tight turquoise pants and matching blouse on the trip. That's how the three of us spent the evening before her journey, and Dad said, "We'll miss you, Ruthie," and I added that she could send a postcard.

On the kitchen table was a cardboard file containing all the documents and newspaper clippings and the story of Mom's testimony was printed, laminated, and ready to be presented. And this was how it went down:

All through the summer months, Mom hid in the wheat fields, and when night fell, she went to the crypt under the church and lay down to sleep on the surface where the dead were prepared for burial. She knew not to sleep too deeply, and even before the first ray of light infiltrated the room, she ran back to the fields. That way, for several months, she waited for Julia to come get her like she had promised. Julia had promised, and Mom knew Julia didn't lie. But one morning, loud pounding was heard on the door of Julia's house. *Mach die tür auf: Open the door! Open immediately!* Two Gestapo men, in their uniforms and boots, were standing in the doorway and informed Julia that the staff housing at the camp was overcrowded, and they were now moving into her house. She told them: *Welcome!* They smiled back and said there was a rumor she was hiding a girl in her house. She replied: *You know what Jews are like. A Jew is not a pin. He has a certain size. If you want to, you can search.* They searched. And searched. Turned the house upside-down. Beat at the furniture with the barrels of their guns, took the pigs out of the barn, checked the cellar. Made so much noise that the neighbors were looking out their windows. No one dared leave their homes, but everyone was peering through the windows. Everyone knew what it meant if they found a girl there. And they didn't. They found nothing!

"I told you, a Jew isn't a pin. If he's there, you'll see him. Can I offer you something to drink?"

And from that day on, Julia lived with the Gestapo in the house. They began to feel more and more at home, and every time they had a break in their day of hard work at the camp, they would come to Julia. Eat, shower, rest, chatter,

---

19   Yiddish: "Crazy."

smoke, smoke endlessly, inquire about the pretty picture hanging in the living room, a picture of the Virgin Mary holding the baby Jesus in her arms, her gaze full of tenderness and grace.

There was not a day that Julia didn't think about what was happening to the girl that God had sent her from heaven, who was waiting for her in the fields in the morning, and at night in the casket in the crypt; the girl who was thinking, *when and where will Julia come? Will she come in the morning to the fields? Or maybe at night to the crypt?* And what would she tell Julia when she came? Maybe about the birds who had saved her from death one day, when she fell asleep at the edge of the wheat field, just as the Wehrmacht's Stormtrooper jeep passed nearby. The birds noticed that a girl had fallen asleep there. They recognized the danger after they themselves had escaped the camp and flown through the skies of Belzec. They were almost the only ones who knew what was really going on at the camp. They knew where people were disappearing to. They knew what Mom only sensed: that the many people arriving by train and the many bodies in the wheelbarrows were the same people. When they noticed that Mom had fallen asleep suddenly, at the edge of the field, they gathered together in a flock and chirped as loudly as they could. Each individual bird was barely audible, but together, they formed a choir and woke Mom up. And so, one day, inside the camp, while people were walking in the tunnel a moment before disappearing, while the engines of the Soviet tanks were thundering and the carbon monoxide was already flowing in the pipes, while, against the background din of the people screaming and the commotion of the orchestra, Grandma took care of the *Kommandant*, while he watched over her and also endlessly beat her, Grandma heard the chirping of birds. Birds in the skies of Belzec. The *Kommandant* was annoyed to see her smiling, and he beat her harder, but she didn't care. And during this time, as the birds were chirping and Grandma was taking a beating and smiling, Mom woke up. She heard the jeep and burrowed deep inside the wheat. Mom disappeared. And the birds flew away.

Winter had already come to Poland and people began to prepare for the cold season. Julia was worried. She knew that a seven-year-old girl would not make it in such conditions. She also believed that if God had sent her a girl like that after her son died, He had to watch over her. He couldn't take a child from her twice. And she began to plan what to do while the Gestapo was in her house every day.

When all the neighbors in the street began to stack up firewood to keep the house warm, Julia did the same. It was an opportunity to make some noise and reorganize the barn, where the pigs were kept along with the firewood, and dig a little pit there, not too big, so that no one would ask what was going on. Every time the Gestapo went to the camp to work, she installed the little pit under the firewood. She dug with her hands, placed the soil in the pockets of her robe, and went out to the fields to toss the soil, so it wouldn't pile up too close to the house. Julia knew very well that with every step she took from the house toward the field, eyes were watching her from the neighboring houses. But she walked with the soil in her pockets and sang.

And when one of the neighbors ambushed her behind one of the fences, grabbed her, and threatened that if she was hiding a girl, the neighbors would put an end to her long before the Germans did, to her and to her entire family, and that her dead son was just the preface to everything that was going to happen to her, she told him: *Jews aren't a pin. They can't disappear. If there's a girl here, why can't anyone see her?*

The Gestapo were a bit drunk when they came to Julia's house on their lunch break in the middle of the week, which was a bit odd, since usually, they would get drunk only on the weekends and only at night. They brought salami and said that that night, there would be a celebration. *Standartenführer*[20] Walter Griffen was coming for a visit to the camp, and the preparations were in progress. Therefore, they had only come for a brief rest and had brought a small gift to thank Julia for being a devoted host. Julia thanked them warmly: it was good to know that even in such times of deprivation, there were still generous souls. And when they left, she knew: tonight was the night. Tonight, when darkness covered the street, she would go to the crypt to fetch the girl that God had sent her as a gift. She would march to the church, take the stairs down to the crypt, and bring her pretty girl up from the deep. And if it had been her fate to send one child into the ground, now she would bring the girl up from there. And that's exactly what she did.

Mom knew Julia would come. The entire time, she held on for her. She drank the drops of rain and ate the wheat grains. She obediently visited the crypt at night, taking care to sneak away in the morning. And Julia came. Julia

---

20   "Standard leader," a Nazi rank.

really came. While the *Kommandant* proudly presented his camp to *Standartenführer* Walter Griffen and his entourage, and while her mother, meaning her real mother, meaning Grandma, cleaned and tidied up and cooked and prepared everything for the visit, Julia went down to the crypt.

She found her: lying like a corpse on the flat surface, pale and skinny, all ready to be buried.

"You're here?"

"I'm here. Like I promised."

She swept her up and took her home, hiding her in the barn, where the pigs were.

"I want to sleep with you," Mom told her. "I thought you were coming to take me to you, to your bed."

But Julia told her, "We can't. Only where the pigs are. The Germans don't go in here, to where the pigs are. They're scared. But you have no reason to be afraid. You'll see, the pigs will like you and keep you warm at night. You won't be cold anymore like you were in the fields. I'll put a hard-boiled egg for you inside the pigs' slop, and sometimes I'll put in an apple, too, which you can wash in the water bucket the pigs drink from."

And that's what happened. Julia would bring the pigs their food inside a wooden tub, pour the food in the trough, and use a stick to show Mom where she could find a hard-boiled egg or an apple, and sometimes a potato, too. She couldn't hide too much food, since every once in a while, the Germans would use a stick to search the pigs' food, to see if there was anything suspicious. They were familiar with this technique and had frequently shot women and children who hid where the pigs were in neighboring houses. Until that was no longer safe, either.

And one day, when the Germans weren't home, Julia took action, and very quickly, before anyone could come, arranged the pit next to the pile of firewood and padded it to hide Mom inside. She told her: *Quick, there's no time, get in and I'll cover you with the rest of the wood. I'll cover you like with a blanket. A wooden blanket.* And there was lots of wood there, enough to last till the end of the long, cold Polish winter. No one would think of starting to move all that wood. However, there was no time, and the pit Julia had dug was too small. Even smaller than Mom. Maybe Julia thought it was only for a month, or for half a year. A year at most. A year and a half at the very most.

How long could this horror last? Julia didn't know how long it would be before Mom could come out of the pit.

I wished Mom bon voyage and a moment before I left, we stood looking at each other. She told me: *You're awfully pale. And your breasts have swelled up.*

***

My tadpole grew a little every day, but with an indiscernible, invisible motion. It swam alone in its little pool while I did all kinds of other things, mostly sat and stared at the objects around me through the nausea. Every day, I waited for the end of work at Palm Tree Preschool, where most of the smells were impossible. Mostly the smell of coffee that Adi the preschool teacher would drink in the morning, the smell of the cream she put in her hair (*ew*) and when Dafna, who worked with us, arrived one morning wearing a new perfume, and Adi said, "Wow, what a great scent," that was the first time I finally managed to throw up. I ran to the preschool bathroom and felt my body turning inside out, dragging me after it into an uncontrollable whirlwind, and allowed myself to surrender to the drift, to let the fluids that burst out from me mingle with those in the toilet bowl.

When all the kids finally went to their parents at four, and I went to the bungalow, I discovered that smells were still assaulting me. That there were no breaks from this pregnancy. It went on all the time. Any woman who crossed my path with any sort of cosmetic product was hostile. Any house emitting evidence of cooking evoked new levels of rage within me. And once, when Ronnie returned from work smelling sweaty and stood in the doorway, I pushed him out of the bungalow. "Get out of here!!!" I screamed at him and he kept standing there with his mouth gaping open. I lay down on the bed and cried. I waited for him to come back to me, but with a different smell. After a few minutes, he knocked on the door and asked if he could come in. I asked him to go shower, with soap, and not to put on his Adam aftershave, or any other scent, afterwards. He did what I asked, but it took him a little too long to get out of the shower. When he came out, he found me crying in bed.

"What am I going to do with you, Noga? Are you sure you want this pregnancy?"

I looked at him in disbelief. "Don't you ever, do you hear me? Don't ever talk to me like that."

Over the next few days, I noticed the difference between my affection for the bungalow and my affection for Ronnie. While I always hurried to the bungalow at four, having a hard time bearing the distance, with Ronnie, things were more complicated. I couldn't stand his presence, and I couldn't stand the hours when he wasn't there. He had already gotten used to me pushing him out the moment he arrived, then getting mad at him if it took him too long to come back in. Sometimes, he would ask from outside the door whether he could come in, to avoid the pushing. Once, he reminded me, "You know, this is my bungalow," and I burst into tears and said I was sorry. That I was a terrible person. That I didn't understand how he could stand me. How anyone in this world could stand me at all. He hugged me and kissed me and we made love.

"What do you say, Rabbit, should we give our tadpole some food for thought?"

"My solitary Tortoise," I told him. "My poor solitary Tortoise, how did you get stuck with such a crazy Rabbit?"

He hugged me tighter and told me I was his most Rabbit in the world.

***

For a whole month, Mom was away from the kibbutz. When she returned, she said she had to talk to me. "I heard," she said.

"Heard what?"

"I heard. Everything. You can't go on with this."

"Excuse me? Since when do you know what I can or can't do?"

But she wouldn't be distracted. She said, "You can't go on with this. Pe-ri-od." As far as she was concerned, the conversation was over.

"So I understand you're back from your trip to Washington, with your Holocaust stories, and now you suddenly have an opinion?"

"Noga." She gave me the stare. "Noga," she said, not Nogi, or Nogilee, or any other pet name. "Noga, listen carefully. Washington isn't the only place I went."

"Well, what are you trying to tell me?"

"I went to Canada, too."

"Well, that's hunky-dory, you went to Canada."

"I went to see his mother." Then she added, "End of discussion."

Usually, I would willingly flee the parents' house. Now, too, I wanted to flee willingly, but right by the door, I got dizzy and sat down on the rug. She looked at me from the corner of her eye and said nothing. A river of blood began to flow out of me and flood the house. Within the stream of blood, for the first time, I could see my little tadpole. I saw him. He had a head and legs and arms and he lay curled up. She called Dad's apartment in Tel Aviv and ordered him to come right that moment, that very moment, to take me to the hospital. I bled in his car the entire way.

***

Bei dems yingls kranke betl
Veint dos mame shtil
un dos yingl redt fun hits
mame ikh shtarb ikh fil.

Mame mame beig tsu dein kepele
beig es tsu tsu mir vel ikh dir nor tseyln
oi mein kholem dir.

By the child's sickbed, the mother weeps quietly,
and the boy speaks from his fever: Mother, I'm dead, I'm dying.
Mother, Mother, bow your head, bow it toward me,
and I'll tell you, oh, my dream.[21]

For an entire month, I lay in the hospital, and when I was discharged, I lay for another seven months in my room. Mother sent Carmel and Einav, by turn, to bring me food from the dining hall, to open the blinds on the windows once a day, and to try and talk to me. That was how I found out that Ronnie had left the kibbutz. They didn't know where he'd gone. I barely talked to them, but to my mother, I swore, I would never speak again.

---

21   From a Yiddish folk song called "The Sick Child."

10.

"So what have you got to offer me?" Adva asked, laying her feet, clad in shoes, on the couch.

"You can rest your feet there, but take off your shoes."

"That's what you've got to offer me? Man, killer!"

"The truth is, you're right. Think about it. It can't be the worst offer you've gotten in your life."

"What do you know about bad offers?"

"You'd be surprised."

"You'd be surprised?"

"You'd be surprised? Isn't it supposed to be the other way around?"

"What's the other way around?"

"That I'm supposed to be the one repeating your words, instead of you repeating mine, right? Isn't that what they always say about shrinks?"

"Damn, sis, you're witty. Can I smoke?"

"You know you can't."

"Right, right. No chewing tobacco or littering either."

Silence.

"So, hey, do you like that Sudanese guy?"

"You mean Ibastam? You're cracking me up. I actually have a boyfriend. His name is Amar."

"Arab?"

"Why, do you know any Jewish Amars?"

"And do your parents know?"

"He eats Friday night dinner with us every week. He's really become part of the family. But they think his name's Omer and that he's from Jaffa. They don't know it's Amar, and that he's from Ramallah."

"Huh."

"Huh."

"Are you echoing me again?"

"Okay, can I go?"

"Sure, in forty minutes."

"You're boring the crap out of me."

"So, how do we pass the time? You want us to talk? Want to tell me about Amar, or about Omer, whoever you want?"

Weary minutes crawled on the clock. I had already learned to know time in all manners of variations, but during sessions with Adva, something new occasionally happened to it. I started to fear it. It was impossible to know how it would behave and what to expect from it. Sometimes, it seemed to exit the room and leave the two of us alone, with no adult in charge. One time, I discovered the clock was turned the wrong way, and during the entire session, I didn't dare turn it back toward me. I kept trying to guess the time based on all kinds of signs: calculating the number of words, assessing the pressure on my bladder, but it was hopeless. At some point, I said, "Hey, the clock's turned around," and turned it back.

"I think you're actually the one who's turned around today," she said, and I answered that she allowed herself to say all kinds of things to me. "Damn it," she said, "you're such a shrink," and I said I was guilty as charged. At the end of the session, I let her go quickly, before Ariella had time to come into the room.

And there was also that day when time went by without me. Adva arrived for our session and I wasn't there. It's true that there wasn't supposed to be a session. She was the one who had gotten mixed up. But that didn't change the fact that she was there. And I wasn't.

***

The kibbutz health committee decided to send me for psychiatric assessment. Dr. Mirando suggested a short hospitalization, to allow monitoring and selecting appropriate treatment. I maintained the same position, on my back, with my eyes on the ceiling; only the scenery changed a bit and my musty room at the kibbutz was replaced by a fairly clean, whitewashed room on Unit B, which I shared with a woman with crooked bangs who lay on her back with her eyes on the ceiling, like me, but who would occasionally giggle and say that Hani, the unit's psychologist, was actually a street hooker and that she gave all the money she earned at our expense to Dr. Mirando, her pimp. At eight a.m. there was breakfast, with salad, scrambled eggs, quark cheese, and sliced bread, served on blue plastic plates. Then, they distributed medication at the nurses' station. There were two kinds of nurses in the unit: pregnant and not pregnant. I received one pink pill from a non-pregnant nurse. Lunch was at twelve-thirty. They gave us a serving of something resembling schnitzel, with mashed potatoes and peas, but a different nurse, also not pregnant, gave me permission to stay in bed. Even when everyone went to occupational therapy, she allowed me to stay in bed. I lay in my bed for hours, looking at the ceiling and thinking about my little tadpole, who, for a few minutes, I got to see swimming on the rug at the parents' home. I also thought about Ronnie, who had disappeared suddenly, without me knowing where he'd gone and whether he knew about our tadpole.

After a few days, they called me in for a conversation with Dr. Mirando and Hani the psychologist. They asked how I was doing and I didn't answer. Hani said she knew I was going through a rough period, that I had gone through some things that weren't easy, and that sometimes it made sense to react the way I was to situations like that. She said sometimes an extreme reaction was the most reasonable way to react to extreme events, and that paradoxically, my reaction could be viewed as a form of communication. That maybe I had no other way to tell them what I was feeling. I sat there and felt the tears rolling down my cheeks. They were warm and wet, and their touch on my skin was something I could feel. Hani rose from her chair, sat down next to me and hugged me. She said there was no point in me staying in the unit, but that I was welcome to come talk to her.

In the afternoon, Lily came down specially from the Golan Heights. She went into the unit to take me home. "Nogi," she said. "I didn't know. I didn't know any of it."

We went to her car in the parking lot, and it was only when we were sitting that I saw she was pregnant again.

"Look at you," she told me, "you look like a *muselman*,"[22] and we both cracked up.

I knew that after she dropped me off at the kibbutz, I wouldn't see her again for a few months, and it was important to me to ask, "Say, do you have any idea what happened to Mom in Canada? What was so horrible about her meeting with Ronnie's mother?"

***

I returned to the kibbutz and was assigned to work at the laundry. I ironed and folded and distributed the clean clothes to the members' cubbies. Twice a day, I went to the dining hall to check if I'd gotten anything in the mail, but the only thing that came was the kibbutz newsletter on Fridays, with updates from the secretariat desk, congratulations on new babies born, and death notices. Three or four times a day, I circled the bungalow to see if anything new was happening there, and nothing was. The bungalow stood abandoned. I slipped the key I had kept into the keyhole, but the bungalow replied with a locked door, as if it didn't recognize me anymore. As if everything between us was over. In one day. This repeated itself every time I tried to open the door, checking whether anything had changed or softened after all, but the sound of a harsh squeak of refusal cut through the air every time anew, like a broken record. "Enough already!!!" I yelled at it one day. "How much of this can a person take?" There was no trace of the box of cookies and two cucumbers that Ronnie and I had devoured over an entire week. No trace of the Tortoise and Rabbit who had once shared a rumpled bed there, with one tiny tadpole.

After a few months, I saw a light on in the bungalow and ran to the window. Through the pane, I saw the figure of Dana Walensky, who had moved in there. I saw her opening the fridge and taking out a carton of milk. I remained standing by the window until it seemed like she saw me, and then ran off. And after a few months, I dropped that habit.

Twice a week, I went for sessions with Hani. Carmel and Einav took turns driving me, and every time, they swore to me anew that they had no idea what

---

22   A *muselman* is a living skeleton, a slang term for the malnourished, exhausted victims of Nazi concentration camps.

had happened to Ronnie. "You swear?" I'd ask Carmel, or Einav, in turn.

"I swear, Noga, I'd tell you."

Occasionally, Dad would drive me, too. He was at his most productive after his new research proposal was approved by the Israel Science Foundation. He claimed that very soon, he could publish his article on the destruction of the Jewish settlement in Gamla, in which he intended to bust a few myths. It turned out that the Jews in Gamla were not exactly the heroes they were usually portrayed as being, but in the meantime, he was being very cautious about publishing his findings, since they were not yet final. "It's a very sensitive topic, as you can probably imagine, and it's a matter of life and death. With these sorts of matters, I'd rather be extra careful."

When we approached the parking lot, he said he would wait for me here, and that he hoped that before I knew it, I would be okay, with a little help and support, of course, and that I would start talking to Mom again, since after all, even if she made the occasional mistake, and was a bit strange and hysterical, as we all knew, she only wanted the best for me.

"And what about Ronnie?" I asked him.

"You mean that boyfriend of yours? You'll get over him."

For two years, I went to see Hani twice a week. She continued to insist that my strange behaviors were normal reactions to events that the mind was having a hard time dealing with. Everything was potentially normal to her. Adopting Ronnie in third grade seemed normal to her, "under the circumstances." Screaming at him seemed normal to her too, under the circumstances, and so did barely getting out of bed for a year after he disappeared. "It's called mourning." I asked her whether it was mentally healthy, and she said sometimes it was the only solution for mental health. I asked whether, according to that logic, my mother was also normal under the circumstances, and when Hani said you could see it like that, I thought, what was the point of being normal, if under the circumstances even what was normal took on all kinds of strange forms. And yet there was something a bit soothing about it.

At some point, I got a driver's license and drove to Hani on my own. I'd park the kibbutz car in the unit's parking lot, and on the way to Hani's room, would think which of the people around me were completely normal, who was normal under the circumstances, and who wasn't normal in any way, shape or form, and whether Ram was right when he said it was tiring being healthy.

The image of my little tadpole swimming on the rug in the parents' house was still like a stain within my thoughts, but gradually, the stain soaked in a little and was diluted inside all kinds of other thoughts. Ronnie was the only thing I couldn't stop thinking about. Some days, my body missed him so desperately that I was overcome with weakness and had to stop any activity and rest my body on a chair or bench or on the floor, whatever was closest, and wait for the attack to pass. That was how I discovered that when you cut a limb off the body, it didn't stop hurting. On the contrary. It grew and spread, and there was no way of knowing where it began and where it ended. I told Hani that sometimes I couldn't bear it anymore. She said that made sense, and she was glad I could tell her about it. She also said she hoped it would pass, and that in the meantime, we had to figure out how to do things despite the pain.

In the hours after work at the laundry, I studied for my psychometric university application exam and resumed hanging out with Carmel and Einav. While I was doing things despite the pain, all kinds of things were happening in the world. Two important treaties were signed: Israel's peace treaty with King Hussein of Jordan, and the treaty between Israel and the PLO, granting the Palestinians the right to govern themselves. Yitzhak Rabin, Shimon Peres, and Yasser Arafat received the Nobel Peace Prize, and Dad said it was a vision of the End of Days. Who would ever have believed they would stand side by side with Arafat. Alongside this vision were constant terrorist attacks, and in the Cave of the Patriarchs, Baruch Goldstein butchered dozens of Muslim worshippers. Israel abducted terrorist Mustafa Dirani, while terrorists dressed up as Jewish settlers kidnapped Israeli soldier Nachshon Waxman. Some people said this country would never be peaceful, that those seeking a peaceful life should go elsewhere. Others said we couldn't lose hope. That pessimism was a privilege, and that we needed to continue procreating. And, indeed, lots of new children were born in the kibbutz, with unusual names like "Hod," meaning 'splendor,' and "Shunit," meaning 'reef,' and two more new neighborhoods were built. Also, there was an earthquake in California, while Rwanda stood on the verge of genocide.

***

I started studying psychology at the university. In a lesson on Maslow's hierarchy of needs, we learned that the hierarchy was arranged so that no need could be entirely satisfied without first satisfying the need that preceded it. Thus, for example, those deprived of food, drink, comfort, and elimination would have a very hard time attaining self-actualization. When I raised my hand and asked how come some Holocaust survivors who had been raised under sub-standard conditions had come a very long way in life, Prof. Barak said there were always exceptions.

In Developmental Psychology class, we studied Freud's psychosexual stages, constructive drives, destructive drives, and fixation, which took place when a person got stuck in a certain developmental stage. Harel raised his hand and asked what the point of these stages was if you always got stuck in them, and Prof. Klein said that was actually one of the problems with Freud's theories.

We also studied Statistics, Physiological Elements of Behavior, Theories of Personality, Research Methodology, and Psychopathology. Unlike Hani's theory, which claimed that almost everything was normal, potentially and under the circumstances, the books we studied stated the opposite, and every day, we discovered only abnormal things in each other and in ourselves.

I met Tal and Ophir, both kibbutz girls like me, and shared an apartment with a male and female roommate—Noa, who was majoring in computers, and Gil, a law student who was older than us by a few years. Tal and Ophir tried to introduce me to all kinds of cute guys, but all of them reminded me of Ronnie by being so unlike him, and I became increasingly full of despair after each date.

"What is it about him?" Tal asked me. I'd walk down the university corridors, dragging my deficient body after me. When the lectures began, I remembered I had to do things despite the pain, and learned to use that small part of my thoughts that was relatively free to take in the material. That was how I learned about various kinds of disorders, about regression toward the mean, about the question of duality of body and soul, about psychological testing, about neural pathways in the brain and about attachment styles between babies and mothers. I finished the first semester cum laude, and Ophir said there was definitely something misleading about me.

***

Spring is when things happen. We were sitting in the evening at the Iguana Pub: Gil, Noa, Ophir, Tal, Ohad, a friend of Gil's, Orna, a friend of Noa's, and some other people I didn't know. We were drinking beer and listening to Oasis's "(What's the Story) Morning Glory?" The first semester of freshman year was behind us and near the end of the exam period, we took a break from time. My head was crammed with theories and formulas, and the answer to the question of what was mentally healthy and what wasn't became less and less clear.

I was wearing leftover clothes from high school: a checkered Sabi sweatshirt and Levi's 501 jeans, and it was odd to notice that despite all the upheavals, the clothes remained the same. We sat and argued about Ernst Kretschmer's theory, whether he was correct or not in his typology based on different physiques. Everyone other than me thought it was utter bullshit, and there was a reason the theory ultimately wasn't covered in the exam. Nevertheless, Orna declared that if there was something to it, she preferred the mesomorphic type, and Tal, who had already embarked on a relationship with Ofer, the Research Methodology TA, said she didn't actually buy into that theory, but if she did, she would definitely prefer the ectomorphic type. I tried to think what my type was, and realized I was having a hard time imagining Ronnie. His body was something my body remembered from the inside, with no clear outline, and I had a hard time finding an image I could retrieve from my memory. Actually, throughout the entire time we were together, we had no shared photos. We never thought about documenting. We were us in such a dense manner that no electronic sensor separated us from life. And that was also why I had no memory that could simply be erased, deleted in order to go forward. Tal, Ophir, Orna, and Noa appeared liberated to me, available for something, while I didn't even have a name for a place where I knew Ronnie was, a place in which I might be able to store him. Ronnie had just disappeared. He had evaporated. Vanished. The only one who probably knew where he was was my mother, whom I also hadn't seen since I stopped seeing him. I did run into her here and there on the paths of the kibbutz, but I would immediately change direction. I imagined her standing and watching me walk away down the path, becoming smaller and smaller until I disappeared into the horizon, but I didn't turn back toward her even once. Dad had talked to me about her only that one time, when he drove me to the session with Hani, and the strangest part was receiving a letter from Iris, of all people, one day, via airmail, in which she wrote that I was taking it too far, with all due respect.

In the heat of our argument about the connection between physique and personality, I saw Gil waving hello to someone, and a figure with a familiar face, hair that was a pretty brown and a little curly, darting eyes, and a tiny beard approached the table.

"No way," he said. "I can't believe it."

"No way," I heard myself repeating.

"Do you want to share with the rest of us?" Gil suggested when he saw that our gazes were stuck, and Eli said it was a long story.

"Very long."

We didn't know how to start catching up. He had broken up with Hila a long time ago, but in any case, she hadn't been the reason why he left the kibbutz. "You probably heard about the whole mess with Ronnie."

"What mess?"

"You know, his mental breakdown in the army. And the whole deal with his mother."

"What?"

"You didn't know? I actually heard you two were very close before he left the kibbutz. I meet people from the kibbutz here and there. I saw Noam from the secretariat not that long ago, and Itamar Nave."

We sat in the garden under the building where I lived with Gil and Noa. The spring was the same spring as the one when I met Ronnie on the paths of the kibbutz seven years ago. The same spring in which a few years earlier I ran to Ronnie and Eli's window to invite them to my ninth birthday party. The same spring like all those springs in which the Judas-tree and the tipu tree and the blue jacaranda and the flame tree and the coral tree all bloomed, and the silkworms hatched from their cocoons. And we, too, were the same us suddenly, only Eli's beard had grown a little, and when he laughed, his face creased up, and my body, encased in my high school clothes, always gained five pounds during the exam period. Other than that, you could think that nothing crucial had actually happened.

"You've grown, Noga," he noted as if to challenge my thoughts.

"It happens, you know."

"Right, that's what happens naturally, isn't it?"

"I think so. What are you doing here?"

"I'm a doctoral student in law. Researching the provisional courts for Jews suspected of collaborating with the Nazis."

"No shit."

"Yup. And you? You're a student too?"

"I am. Majoring in psychology."

"Well, that's not too surprising."

"How come?"

"You know, your mom, with her thing about mentally healthy and all that. How is she, actually? Still a bit weird?"

"A bit?"

"Okay, maybe a major bit. But you had your issues too."

"Eli," I called him by his name, like back then. "What's the deal with Ronnie?"

I noticed that this was the first time I had addressed that question to someone who also might be able to answer it. That we were really conversing.

"I was sure you knew. His mother was in and out of psychiatric hospitals. She was never entirely sane. Ronnie was always on the edge too. I'm sure you're familiar with her story, how she came to Canada on her own, with no family, everyone was murdered, and that she got pregnant with him when she was eighteen, from a married man. Unrequited love, you know, can be really cruel sometimes."

"Yeah, tell me about it. It can be awful. It's like mental illness only without the medication."

"I always had a hard time with Ronnie, but I really loved the guy," he said sadly. "He'd isolate himself for days at a time, and you could never really talk to him."

"I really loved him too," I said, wondering. *Did I really love him? Did I know him at all?* I thought, and noticed that we were talking about him in the past tense as if he didn't exist, or, on the contrary, as if he finally did exist, and we could talk about him.

"Do you have any idea where he is?"

"No, none. You?"

"I don't either."

"How did that happen?"

Eli and I decided to stay in touch. Now that both of us were here in the city, near the university, it seemed natural. The truth was, he didn't understand how it had taken us so long to meet up. After all, he was a really good friend of Gil's

***

After the last exam in Personality Theory, there was one week left before the next semester started, and we decided to all go out to the Iguana. The air outside smelled like citrus, and we played a game: each of us told the others something about ourselves that they didn't know yet. Tal told us she was once the Israeli high-jump champion.

"Really?"

We were happy for her as if she had just been informed of her win.

"Your turn," she told Ofer. It was clear they were still in the process of getting to know each other. He said his father was the Israeli ambassador to Columbia.

"Really?" we all asked, mainly Tal, and he looked at Ophir and said, "Your turn."

She told us that when she was in elementary school, she was an actress in Orna Porat's children's theater, and was cast as the Little Prince in a play. Before we could say "Really?" she looked at me and said, "Your turn."

"My brother died when I was three," I found myself saying, and everything went quiet. I looked at Eli and said, "Your turn."

"Hold on a minute, Nogi, let people recover," he said.

"What was his name?" Tal asked, and I asked them to switch topic, that I'd just blurted it out and hadn't really meant to talk about him at that point, but Eli said, "Nadav."

I apologized for ruining the evening and said I had to go. I left money on the table and went out to the street. The air was full of all kinds of flying bugs and I started to walk toward the apartment when I noticed that Eli had followed me out.

"Noga." His breathing was labored. "Let's keep playing on the way."

"My mother is almost the only survivor from Belzec."

"I know. Try a little harder."

"Okay, when she says, 'you deserve it,' she means something good."

"Getting better, but you're only talking about her. The game is about you."

"You're right. Your turn."

"I have a twin brother."

"I know," I replied and remembered I actually didn't know. That, in fact, I knew nothing. That almost anything he said would be new and that I really didn't know him. That the familiar scent drifting from him was not actually related specifically to him. Or to his twin.

"Your turn," he said. We kept going until the middle of the night. He told me about a rare stamp collection he'd had since he was a boy, and I told him I had four nephews and one niece, that sometimes it seemed like new ones were constantly being born, maybe even right now, at this moment. He told me he liked playing the guitar, and I told him that when I was a little girl, I had dreamed of founding an animal hospital. He told me about his doctoral thesis, and I told him Ronnie had gotten me pregnant, and that I'd had a miscarriage, and that I'd seen my fetus swimming on my parents' rug like a tadpole, and that afterward, Ronnie disappeared and it had taken me nearly a year to get out of bed. And I told him about Hani, and about things that could only be normal under the circumstances. He was silent for a while, then said, "My turn?"

By the time the semester started, we had made quite a bit of progress in the game. We had learned all kinds of things about each other, but those were just facts. Just pieces of information, and during the day I tried to think what it said about him, that his father was an ophthalmologist, that his twin brother was married to a gentile, that he had a scar behind his ear because of a bike accident. I tried to revive early memories from the era when Ronnie and Eli would go to the dining hall with us on Fridays, an era when I didn't care which one was Eli and which one was Ronnie. A time in which, when I wrote to one of them, I also wrote the other more or less the same things. I tried to revive the shared memories, the things we had already discovered once, long ago, through the window of an old cabin, the daring trio we had been when we strode to Mom's garden for my ninth birthday, in the age when things were still being discovered. In those springs, the old ones, whose blossoming was more than just yearning for a bygone spring.

***

The second semester began leisurely and Eli would come to our apartment often. Classes didn't stress me out. What did was actually routine. In the evenings, we would sit in the living room in front of the TV and watch "Seinfeld" or the European World Cup games. Noa would bring loquats from the tree growing in the garden under the apartment, Gil brought sunflower seeds, and I sat in sweatpants on the couch and tried to find some interest in the shows. There was something ordinary about those evenings, ordinary in a way I didn't know. I was constantly thinking about what I still had to do and hadn't yet done. There must be something else to do. Just hanging out in front of the TV scared me. I felt that time was going by without me, and when Gil and Eli cracked up in front of "Seinfeld," I realized there were situations like that: where people just cracked up. Not a desperate laughter, like we laughed in our family at the mother tongue. A different laughter. A funny laughter. I realized that within the general mass of time, there were hours when people just had fun. Without doing anything. Without it taking them out of time. It bored me to death.

Eli became part of the milieu of the apartment, and we were all okay with the fact that it wasn't clear whom he was coming for—for Gil or for me or for the apartment. Once, he went out with Noa to buy coffee and sugar at the grocery store, and we all felt relieved, for some reason. When they came back, we couldn't tell Eli to leave, since no one had invited him in the first place. It was as if he had always been there, and was just waiting to reveal himself. Sometimes, he sat down on the couch next to me, and occasionally I found his arm around my shoulder and tried to continue breathing naturally. It was actually one evening when he didn't come that I realized something was missing. That I was waiting for something. It was strange and oppressive, since I had gotten used to things happening first before I had time to wait for them or call them by name. The next day, at school, I felt a weakness in my legs, and told Ophir I thought this whole university thing wasn't right for me, that there was too much psychology. But when I came to the apartment in the evening, I found him and Gil playing FIFA on the console.

"Don't you ever do that again!" I told him.

"Do what?" he asked.

"That."

But deep inside, I knew "that" wasn't really it. It was only reminiscent of it. Very faintly.

As the semester progressed, Eli synched in with the apartment's scenery in such a stealthy, imperceptible manner that I had no way of knowing if I was happy or not. I once asked Ophir if she thought I was happy, and she said it was something only I could answer. I asked her if I looked good and her answer soothed me. "You look regular, as usual." It was calming to think there was something regular about me, something that could look "as usual." That I was part of the scenery. Normal under the circumstances. And when I found myself hurrying home from the university when classes ended, I hoped the irresponsible cancellation of my library study time and the last-minute ditching would remind me how a reckless girl in love felt. When I found him in the apartment, I tried to initiate fights, to get angry or offended, but it never took off. He asked how school had been while all kinds of daily programs like newscasts or sports shows were on TV.

The city air bothered me less than it had in the first semester. My hair became more tolerant and learned how to get into fewer tussles with its environment, and one evening, when I encountered a regular young woman in the mirror, with a pleasant, bored expression and not terribly allergic skin, I realized it was me.

Eli stood behind me and hugged me in front of the mirror. "Look what a good fit we are," he said, and in a moment of distraction, I sighed, "Oh, solitary Tortoise."

I was preoccupied with troubling thoughts: what would have happened if it had been him, rather than Ronnie, whom I'd met then, in the spring of my junior year of high school, on the path leading to the dining hall? Would things have unfolded in the same way? Would any figure walking on the path have arrived at the same place? Are people different from one another, or are we all variations on the same thing? And what would have become of me? Or of my little tadpole, left to swim on my parents' rug?

But Eli was not troubled by all this. He was busy with his doctoral thesis and liked to hang out with us, and when I fell asleep on the couch in front of the TV, he would cover me with a blanket and carry me to the bed in the bedroom. Sometimes he would also sleep over. And one evening, when he told me he had read my paper on the biblical Exodus through the prism of Bowlby's attachment theory, and that he thought I brought my creativity to new heights there, I realized that even if this was a new version of Ronnie, or of something else, it didn't matter anymore. Eli had already been absorbed into the everyday.

A few weeks went by that way, until, one evening, as we were standing in the kitchen and making coffee, he asked me how I would feel if he came to the kibbutz with me for Passover. For a moment, I got scared. He leaned against the fridge and his shadow was split right down the middle, the shadow of a solitary soldier. But it was only a shadow, just a small area obscured from the main source of light.

"You can if you want to. It's your kibbutz too, right?" I asked, and thought that Eli didn't even know that I wasn't speaking to my mother. He didn't know how much blood, sweat, and tears had flowed on the rug in my parents' house since he left the kibbutz. He didn't know she had made his ex-roommate disappear. Maybe he wasn't even familiar with her magical powers. And for a moment, I actually enjoyed the idea that I, too, had some tricks up my sleeve. I could show up to Passover dinner at the dining hall with Ronnie's roommate and sit down at the table like it was nothing at all. Like it was no big deal. My adopted brother disappeared? Well, look, I brought a new one instead.

***

In each and every generation, a person is obligated to regard himself as if he had come out of Egypt, and in every generation, they rise up to destroy us; and the Holy One, blessed be He, delivers us from their hands.[23] The choir sang, "*Whither is thy beloved gone, O thou fairest among women? Whither is thy beloved turned aside? That we may seek him with thee,*" and the low voices replied, "*My beloved is gone down into his garden, to the beds of spices.*"[24] The dining hall was filled with round tables covered with white tablecloths, kibbutz members were reading from the Haggadah in accordance with instructions from Dina from the Culture Committee, and the third graders staged a skit of the song *Chad Gadya*[25].

Everyone was happy to see Eli, who hadn't been there for seven years. They asked what he was doing, and how it was going, and how great, and this

---

23   These are quotes from the Haggadah, the text read at every Jewish Passover Seder to commemorate the exodus of the Jews from Egypt.

24   Song of Solomon 6: 2

25   *Chad Gadya*, meaning "One Little Goat" or "One Kid," is a playful cumulative song in Aramaic and Hebrew sung at the end of the Passover Seder.

matter of the provisional courts was disturbing, and how could you even judge collaborators, what criteria did you use, after all, everything that took place during that era was incomparable to anything else. Some people also asked what was going on with Ronnie, whether Eli knew where he was, and that was the moment when they looked at me, too: how was I doing, what was up with me; but no one dared ask what they really wanted to know, and we didn't get into it, either. Meaning, not out loud.

Eli sat down at the table with my entire family, other than Iris and Yossi, who didn't fly to Israel this time: Dad, and Mom, and Amnon, and Lily and Ilan with Nadav, Roy, and baby Gilly. Just like that: we all sat down around the same table like it was nothing. As if all a family needed in order to sit down together was a table and chairs and a white tablecloth. And together, we picked up the family exactly where it had been interrupted the last time we met: we chatted, and made noise, and laughed too loudly and tugged together at lines of resemblance. Gilly resembled Lily and Iris when they had been babies, she was a dead ringer, and maybe she also looked a little like Ilan's sister. Roy resembled Amnon (after all, blood wasn't just ketchup), Nadav resembled Nadav, and it was obvious to everyone that the game began and ended in the grandchildren's generation, that the rules were very clear, and that if we wanted to get through the Haggadah safely, then nothing else resembled anything else.

We followed the instructions of the ceremony obediently—a time to raise your glass, and a time to eat the matzah. A time to sing together, and a time to applaud. And a time to pass things to each other: *Who can pass me the water? There you are. And the salt? There you are. Tasty, right? Are you enjoying it? You deserve it.* Eli and I snuck looks at one another. *The "You deserve it" from the game, it's real, see? There. It's happening now, I didn't make it up.*

I didn't address Mom directly, and when it seemed like she was saying something, I pretended not to hear her. And maybe it really was true; maybe I didn't hear her. Maybe the words flew over my head, or behind my ears in all kinds of indirect, invisible routes. Lily and Ilan looked tired; parenthood pursued them like the eleventh plague and they operated it like two well-coordinated parts in a well-oiled machine, passing each other the bottle, and the pacifier, searching for the rattle in the depths of the bag, changing a diaper, picking up the toy car that fell under the table, suppressing a yawn. Amnon sat Nadav in his lap and talked only to him all evening, and Mom and Dad sang all the songs from beginning to end, as if they had boarded a couple's highway together, which would finally lead them safely to the end of the road, and if they only stuck to it, all of us could get to the end of the occasion safe and sound, and the People of Israel shall attain their liberty. It was just that every once in a while, Mom paused and said, "Great holiday, isn't it?"

When the ceremony ended, the kibbutz members went down for folk dancing in the plaza under the dining hall, and I went to talk to Carmel, leaving Eli to manage on his own. It had been a while since we'd seen each other, and she was happy to see me.

"Any chance you'll dance for once in your life?" she asked, trying to drag me to the plaza.

"No way. But you dance and I'll watch." I assigned our roles.

The members danced in circles, "Bonfire Hora," "The Little Shepherdess," "A Stalk of Wheat," "With You Once More," "To the Walnut Grove." I didn't recognize most of the young people who were in high school now, and found myself, like the old people, standing there and asking: *Who's that? And this girl? Wow, they've really grown.*

From the corner of my eye, I saw Eli talking to my mother. I almost ran there, perhaps to prevent some catastrophe that was evident in advance, but the sudden touch of a hand laid on my shoulder stopped me: "What are you worrying about, Noga? After all, what could happen that hasn't already happened?"

"Ram, so cool you're here."

"It's weird to see me out of the hospital, right? Some of the kibbutz members don't recognize me in that state."

"I actually always recognize you, you know."

"So, did you trade in your old boyfriend for a new old boyfriend?"

"Are you saying that's an option?"

"I have no idea; I've never tried. Does he happen to know where Ronnie is?"

"No, Ram. How do you always know what to ask?"

"I ask what I don't know. So no one knows where Ronnie's disappeared to?"

"I, for one, don't know. I assume my mother actually does."

"She definitely knows, and there's no chance she'll tell anyone. Including Eli. Definitely not now. Sometimes your mother acts like a woman who knows exactly what she wants. But never mind all that, how's university? How's studying mental health professionally?"

"Sometimes it's interesting. Did you know that one out of every hundred people will come down with schizophrenia?"

"I don't know about the hundred people, but I definitely know about that one guy."

"I love you."

And although he had asked what I had to worry about, and what could happen that hadn't already happened, I hurried toward my mother and Eli. Oddly, she wasn't talking, but actually listening, or at least that was what it looked like. He was telling her about his doctoral thesis, and she seemed to be truly interested in those provisional courts that had formed in the displaced persons' camps, in order to "purify the Jewish camp of collaborators with the Nazis." Eli talked about the American occupied zone in Germany, and she listened, and then they switched places: she talked, and he listened, and I noticed she was in her linear state, the one where things followed a certain sequence. They agreed that the next day, she would tell him more about what she had gone through during the war.

**

And this was how it went down: Mom went into the pit that Julia had prepared for her. Both of them knew the pit was too small, and both of them had worried expressions on their faces, but Julia said: *Go in, quick, and I'll watch over you. You just need to know: two Germans live in this house. They shower here, and eat here, and sleep here, and have other Germans over. They drink and get drunk and talk lots of nonsense. You can't make a sound. Not a peep. You can't sneeze. You can't cry. You can't move too much. The logs can't make any noise. It's as if you're not here. I'll know the entire time that you're here. And you'll know you're here. It'll be our secret, the two of us. And all the others won't know that there's a girl here.*

"Tough," Eli said, and she went on: Julia gave Mom a few rags with which to cover herself, as well as the New Testament. She did take care to put that in the pit. She created a little gap between the pieces of wood, through which she could insert food and a small container for waste, and placed a small stool for herself, on which she could sit daily and talk to Mom when no one else was around. She told Mom: *Once a day, when no one else is here, I'll come take care of you. I won't always be able to talk. Based on the color of my shoes, you'll know what day it is. On Sundays, before going to Mass in church, I'll put on the white shoes. Every time I put them on, you'll know a week has gone by. On all the other days, I'll wear black shoes.*

"I'll be here more than a week?" Mom asked, and Julia answered that they couldn't know that. It was impossible to know anything during that time. The world had gone mad.

"Want some *matzah* with jam!" Mom offered Eli, and he said he wasn't hungry. That he was interested in hearing more.

"The *matzahs* are great," she said as if she had made them herself.

And I interfered, "Mom! What part of this aren't you getting? He told you he wasn't hungry."

She spread some jam on a *matzah* for herself, and when the *foo-foo-foo* began, I walked to the other end of the rug. I sat down on a big pillow that Dad had once brought from the flea market and looked at the squares and rhombuses on the rug, the lair of the primordial beast. Lily and her family were sleeping in the room allocated to them by the kibbutz, and I knew they would be arriving in the afternoon. Nadav, Roy, and Gilly would probably play on the rug, imbuing it with life after even I had abandoned it, and no one would know whether the beast would hurt them or not. And whether the blood left behind from my little tadpole had already been absorbed, or maybe there was a stain left inside the rhombuses I was staring at now, while Eli was patiently waiting for the story to continue, and Mom was eating *matzah* and jam in a house reeking of mothballs and pajamas.

She continued:

Julia told Mom she would come whenever she could, she would talk to her, but Mom wasn't allowed to answer her. Julia would sit on the stool next to the woodpile and read from the New Testament. When no one was around, she would tell Mom what day it was today, and what was happening outside her hiding spot. She would also read her books. She would stand holding the hymnal in her hand. If the house was empty, she would tell her made-up stories, about children, about animals, and about faraway lands. About a world where all the people strolled the streets, mothers promenading with their children in the park, and fathers taking their sons for bicycle rides on Sundays. And if someone suddenly entered the house, Julia would simply pray. She would read out verses from the prayer. Everyone would know that there, where Julia was sitting, was her favorite prayer spot. "Do you understand where I'm hiding you? I'm hiding you in a place of prayer," was what Julia said. And prayer was necessary. There was a God in heaven. This was the God who had sent Mom to Julia, the God who would watch over Mom for Julia. And when the German officers were home, it would be the God who would make sure Germany won the war.

"But the moment they're out, you hear? The moment their feet are no longer inside the house, God resumes behaving in a sensible way. And it doesn't matter how tight it gets for you inside the hiding spot, you can't get mixed up."

After this manner therefore pray ye: Our Father which art in heaven, Hallowed be thy name. Thy kingdom come, Thy will be done in earth, as it is in heaven. Give us this day our daily bread. And forgive us our debts, as we forgive our debtors. And lead us not into temptation, but deliver us from evil: For thine is the kingdom, and the power, and the glory, forever. Amen. But thou, when thou prayest, enter into thy closet, and when thou hast shut thy door, pray to thy Father which is in secret.[26]

***

Eli and I moved in together. Gil and Noa helped Eli transport his things, while for my things, no help was required. I had nothing. Not even a photo album. I shoved some clothes and toiletries into a plastic bag, put my textbooks in a separate bag, and walked to the new apartment. Eli opened the door for me and said, "Welcome to our life," and I slammed the door and remained standing in the outside staircase. Then I opened the door and said, "Welcome." The furniture hadn't arrived yet, and we were standing in the empty living room under the light bulb and staring at each other in the swaying light. I was a vagrant in the city streets and Eli, with the apartment he had rented, was an innkeeper.

"Your hair is goldening," he told me.

"Your eyes are greening," I told him.

---

26   Matthew 6: 6-13

"Your stomach is rumbling."

We cracked up and ordered a pizza.

That was how life in the new apartment began. There were already several trends in Israel that made life convenient: sushi takeout (a hit!), cable TV, and a few of Eli's friends also had mobile phones, a new way to "reach out and touch someone." Also, the phone company had introduced call waiting, which became truly annoying if you ignored it, and when I was talking to Tal or Ophir and hearing the insistent tone in the background, I knew that on the other end of the line, a primordial woman was sure to be waiting, with infinite patience, hoping I would eventually answer her.

The living room window let the remains of summer into the apartment, bringing with them the scent of honeysuckle and the buzzing of bees. One day, around five p.m., when I was sitting on the balcony with coffee and a cigarette, time fell apart into tiny particles, which felt as if they were passing along my skin and caressing it. Without interrupting.

11.

"And don't you dare tell my parents about it. Every time you talk to them about my cutting, I can't leave the house afterward. As if when you don't talk to them about my cutting, it doesn't exist."

"I won't tell them," I promised Adva. "But not because I don't dare."

"Oh, right, I forgot, you're a superhero."

"The truth is that every time you step out of here, I'm scared. I don't need your parents to be scared."

"Well, at least we've got that much in common."

"We might have more things in common."

"Oh no, don't you start all that. The last thing I need now is for you to be like me."

"I'm sure you can imagine that I was once seventeen too."

"The thing is, I don't want to imagine you being seventeen. I've got myself, which is already way, way more than I can deal with."

"So, what do you like about Amar?"

"I see you like to talk about forbidden love. I've got no problem telling you about him. I like to sit with him in my parents' living room and think that my racist father is sure he's talking to a Jew."

"That's what you like about him?"

"How much time do we have before the session ends?"

"Too long to start counting."

"Bummer."

There really was something frightening about it. I was attracted to her age like a wound that needed to be prodded. I was also wary of it, as if it had never happened, as if you could truly protect yourself. And every evening, on the way back to Eli's and my house, I donned the mantle of age, my advanced age, the one that made my hair go gray and dropped glasses over my eyes. The one that made me ask, "What?" every time Eli or the kids addressed me. The one that saved money for me, piled on the degrees, and kept me a safe distance away from myself. And, most of all, it misled. Misled me, misled all of us. Misled us to believe that time really was going by, and that the mother tongue was fading, and that the primordial beast had gone extinct or aged. It wasn't the beast, it was merely its memory that was not mentally healthy. The beast itself wasn't dangerous at all; it was merely its shadow cast on the rug. It was merely its growl sounding in the background. Suddenly, or all the time. It wasn't the beast that couldn't touch me.

"Mommy," Julie opened the door for me. "How was work?"

"It was fine. And how are you?"

"I'm cool. Grandma called. She wants us to come on Saturday. It's been a while since we saw her."

***

My second year of university was mentally healthy. We studied the development of empathy in babies, altruism, processes of perception and cognition, and taste aversion, which was classical conditioning that took place when an individual associated the taste of food with symptoms characterizing poisoning, such as nausea and stomachache. The ability to develop taste aversion was considered to be a survivalist trait training the body to avoid toxic materials before they could cause harm. Prof. Greenberg showed us a movie where wolves were allowed to feed on sheep after having been injected with toxins that caused nausea. The next time they encountered sheep, the wolves were wary of them. The sheep, which realized the situation had changed in some highly unexpected way, taunted the wolves, taunted them more, and more, and the wolves did not retaliate in any way. Harel said it was too bad that the Jewish underground, which had poisoned the Germans' water, didn't do it while they were killing Jews, but later. Ophir said those studies were important, but she thought there was still an ethical issue there. That it wasn't okay to inject wolves with toxins and then put them in such an unpleasant situation with the sheep. That it was true that wolves fed on sheep, but it wasn't out of evil, and that made them different than the Nazis. Harel claimed in response that the

Nazis, too, didn't commit their crimes out of evil. The discussion developed, and all of us provided examples of natural circumstances in life that brought on taste aversion. For example, nausea after drinking too much alcohol. For example, morning sickness. For example, bread and jam.

In Israel, Operation Grapes of Wrath broke out, aiming to return peace to northern Israel.[27] When four mortar shells accidentally hit a UN base, killing and injuring hundreds of civilians, Prime Minister Shimon Peres stated, "We are sorry, but we do not apologize." And when Eli was summoned to reserve duty, I began a hunger strike so that no food, of any kind, would mingle with those terrible days, which smelled like fish that had gone bad. And standing water. And mold. Eli returned a few days later, tired and filthy, and found me sitting by the door, waiting for him.

"I'm starving," I told him. "And I haven't slept for four days. Did you at least bring something to eat?"

We went back to the routine of school. The grapes of wrath that had arrived with no advance notice evaporated just as suddenly along with all the things that came and went and came again, and if I allowed myself to be focused, I would certainly have recognized that once routine was re-established, I missed the painful thrill of not knowing where Eli was. I missed the expectation of finding something that might have disappeared.

The load of assignments for submission was peaking, exam period was approaching, and in the race against time, it was possible to ignore the fact that my fists were clenched during most of the day, my shoulder blades drawn tight, my breath gripping my ribs from the inside, and my mouth uttering things that were regrettable.

"I'm sorry," I told Eli after accusing him of racism when he attacked the government's tolerant approach. "I'm really sorry," I said after not talking to him for two days. "I'm really, really sorry," I said after weeping because of a sink full of dishes.

"You don't have to be sorry. Just wash them."

---

27   Operation Grapes of Wrath was a sixteen-day campaign against Lebanon in 1996 during which Israel Defense Force (IDF) attempted to end rocket attacks on northern Israel by Hezbollah.

***

While in my second year, my breath held my ribs from the inside, in my third year, the pressure to get into the clinical track in graduate school also grabbed hold of the belly, the kidneys, and some areas in the windpipe. Only limited areas remained relatively free, and I grounded myself in them to try and deal with the assignments and application interviews. We tried to assume a therapeutic appearance and make our speech sound relaxed. "If we get in, we get in, and if we don't, it's a systemic issue." "We could always go study abroad," "Or else there's Birzeit University in the West Bank."

We compared grades and calculated GPAs. We asked for recommendations and bet on who would be admitted and who wouldn't. We consulted each other, and stopped talking to each other, and consulted again. But most frightening of all was the thought that they might actually reveal something about us. They might discover something. The despair piling in front of a sink full of dishes. The great deception. And what was this desire to treat other people, when the mind had not yet learned to distinguish itself from dust. Rumor claimed that anyone not in therapy themselves would not get in, and people started to go find themselves a therapist. Within this turmoil, I experienced a sudden satisfaction. After all, I actually was in real therapy. Not in order to get admitted to graduate school. I was in therapy since I had stayed in bed for an entire year. I was in therapy and was decreed normal under the circumstances. I felt real and convincing and authentically suffering.

In preparation for my interview with Dr. Nathaniel Hazon and Ms. Meital Shovinski, I needed to fill out a questionnaire. In the questionnaire, I was asked to describe low and high points in my life, as well as positive and negative traits. I was asked to describe, in detail, my mother, father, brothers, sisters, a good friend, and another significant figure. A pet, a hobby, my external appearance, and my credo as a psychologist. I sat down in the living room in the apartment with coffee and a cigarette and dialed.

"Raaaaammm!" I yelled at him over the phone. "Heeeelp!"

"Nogi, you're worrying again. I told you, what could happen that hasn't already happened?"

"But this time it's different, Ram. This time I'm not worried about what might happen. I'm worried about what might not happen. I want to get in."

"You will. Why wouldn't you?"

"Because everyone wants it. And besides, you know I'm nuts."

"True, but wasn't it decided that it was under the circumstances?"

"Well, the circumstances haven't really changed."

"That really is a problem. You'll have to do something about that. But I'm telling you, Nogi, you'll be a good shrink. I don't know what they're teaching you over there at the university, but we both know that no one really knows what's mentally healthy, and you have a good grasp of it, relatively speaking. You're the only one who didn't argue with me when I said there was no such thing as an axiom. And if you really want to know, I still believe that parallel lines can meet, and that more than a single line can pass through two points. But don't mention that during the interview."

"Don't worry."

"By the way, I gather your mom's gone to Canada again."

"What?"

"You didn't know?"

"Are you sure? She didn't say anything about it to me."

"Well, Nogi, you don't really talk to her."

"But no one else said anything about it to me, either."

"Maybe they'd rather you didn't know."

"Why would they want that?"

"I don't know. There must be some reason."

***

I came to the interview without having filled out the questionnaire. I explained that I couldn't find a page on which I could write about my life. There was no page where I could put down my mother. Two months later, I called the department to ask whether I had gotten in.

"What's your name?" the secretary asked.

"Noga Glover."

"Noga Glover? Yes, yes, you're on the list. Congratulations. Way to go."

The next day, I called the department again, just to make sure. I thought maybe there had been a mistake, and it was Noa Plover who had gotten in. The woman who answered me told me she wasn't from the clinical track; she just happened to have passed by and picked up the phone. It was Saturday, and everyone was gone. She suggested I call again on Monday, but if I still hadn't received a response, it was probably negative.

***

There were ten students in the clinical track, five girls and five boys. We felt chosen, but the reason wasn't clear. No one knew, as if we were a secret cult. The relief over getting in was replaced by embarrassment. We sought clues in each other to the special quality we shared. We felt like cheaters without knowing we felt that way. We spoke in a hyper-elevated manner and practiced telling each other what we really felt, but we weren't certain what that was. We read constantly. Endlessly. Freud, Winnicott, Melanie Klein, Heinz Kohut, and Kernberg. We tried to quote them in the appropriate context. To agree with them but also to oppose them. To recognize whether the burger, the pizza, or the salad we ate during our break was a product of the wishes of the "true self" or the "false self." Whether we were subjects or objects or both, and which predisposition controlled each of our relationships. Behind everything we did lay a hidden motivation stemming from our early childhood, and everything we said had an obvert meaning, a covert meaning known only to us, and a covert meaning that was not known to us, and which was the most meaningful.

Our relationship was a lab to study relationships in general, and we spent lots of time together, deepening the investigation. At the end of the day, when I walked with Joy and Aviram to the train, I thought the human mind had never been more out of reach. And when Joy said the train car was crowded and smelled like ass, there was a momentary relief.

Eli would wait for me in the apartment. He was in the final stages of his doctoral thesis and shared his findings about the provisional courts with me. I told him about the psychological determinism principle, which stated that every act originated in the infantile life of the mind, and the manner in which we behaved was determined long ago. Determinism clashed with the principle of free choice and essentially described our behavior in a causal manner. Everything had a cause. But the causes were so early and repressed that it was very difficult to know what they were.

He replied that he was familiar with the idea, but that he had to note that when examining the behavior of the Jews both during the war and in the displaced-person camps after the war, you could form the impression that in certain situations, free choice did exist. He said that was precisely the question at the root of the research being conducted by Prof. Rubin, his advisor. Several months ago, he had submitted a research proposal under Prof. Rubin's name to the U.S.-Israel Binational Science Foundation, and they were waiting for an answer. If the proposal was accepted, he could find funding for his post-doctorate. "That's great," I told him. "Are you happy?" and immediately grew silent.

Outside, winter was quite stormy, and every morning, when I got up into the wind, it was unclear whether it was the early causes driving me to go to school, or the practical goals motivating me. My body had ideas of its own at the time. A rash in the shape of half an apple appeared on my palms, of all places. Around my armpits, a kind of reddish swarm of ants crawled, progressing in a circle and returning to its point of origin. Thoughts of Ronnie began to visit me again, like something that had come with the storm. I remembered how, in the period when I was with him, death, aggression, and sex drives controlled me, and things were clear. At the time, I knew exactly where my mind was: wherever Ronnie was.

In the class on the clinical interview, we were split up into pairs and I was with Aviram. We were asked to interview each other and then share with the circle what we had identified during the interview. Aviram was born in Be'er Sheva to an accountant father and a teacher mother. He was the second of three siblings but had never felt like a typical "middle child." His parents had always given everyone the feeling that each of them was a person in his or her own right, regardless of the order in which they had been born. He was a tantrum-prone kid, who had grown up into an old-before-his-time teenager. In the army, he had served in the Artillery Corp, where he met Miri, his first love, who was a regiment clerk. In retrospect, he wasn't sure if it really had been love, but he thought the same could be said of almost any relationship, even the connection between parents and children. "Don't you think so?" He got his bachelor's degree from Tel Aviv University, double major, Psychology and Israeli Studies, which, by the way, was a great combo.

"So you studied with Prof. Aaron Glover?"

"Aaron Glover who would hit on his female students? Yeah, sure. He's actually a good lecturer. Very passionate."

After the interview, we switched, and Aviram interviewed me. I was born on a kibbutz, the youngest of five siblings. Twins Iris and Lily, Amnon, and Nadav, who died of an autoimmune disease when I was three.

"I'm sorry."

"Me too. My mother, Ruthie Glover, a social worker, is one of the only survivors from the Belzec extermination camp. It would be too much to talk about her now. My father, Prof. Aaron Glover, studies the Jewish settlement in Gamla."

"Shit, Noga. I'm sorry. I'm really sorry."

"Me too."

In the evening, Eli told me excitedly that Prof. Rubin's research proposal had been accepted, and that he intended to continue on to do a post-doctorate. He talked about his research with such enthusiasm that I thought he wouldn't even notice if one day I got up and left. If he got up in the morning and I wasn't there. If I just took off.

"I can't," I told him.

"Can't what?"

"Can't be with you."

***

The apartment Aviram and I rented together was within walking distance from campus. Each of us had our own room, but both of us ended up sleeping in the living room since the rooms smelled funny, as if the tenants living there before us were still sticking to them. One day, the phone rang in the living room. Aviram answered and passed the receiver to me: "One of the only survivors from Belzec is on the line. She wants to talk to you."

"Don't ever talk like that," I gritted at him and answered her.

"Nogi, my pretty girl, is that you?"

"No."

"So who's speaking?"

"My grandmother."

"What?"

"Come on, Mom, what do you want?"

"I'm just freshening up the house and I thought you might need a few things for the apartment."

"You're freshening up?"

"Right. Maybe you want the rug?"

Silence.

"Nogi, sweetie, are you there?"

"Mom, I understand this time you've decided to officially lose it?"

"You don't have to if you don't want to. I can offer it to Amnon or to Lil, but I wanted to offer it to you first."

"How do you even have my number at the apartment?"

"Eli gave it to me," she said, and I said I had to hang up.

"She called Eli," I told Aviram. "Can you believe it? She called Eli."

Aviram walked around the apartment looking as if his hair had been electrocuted. Outside, the wind was whistling and I thought that if a utility pole collapsed now, the darkness would know no end.

***

There once, on the rug, lived a primordial beast.
Perhaps it was brought here from the forests of the east.
Was it comfortable there, where it had been flung?
No one knows, since the beast doesn't speak our tongue.
Reticent and heavy, full of growls and sighs,
it had one sharp tooth and two red eyes.
With a long tongue and sharp perky ears on its head,
on the rug it awoke, and there it went to bed.

***

We began to choose topics for our research seminar. Joy joined the Facial Recognition lab, studying an area in the temporal lobe about the size of a raspberry, where single neurons had been recorded in macaque monkeys. The basic premise was that there was no essential difference between us and the macaques. The same basic premise was also at the core of the studies Shiri and Shirin were conducting in the cognitive lab and of the studies conducted by

Dan and Yossi, who had joined a project at the pain lab. I was having a hard time deciding, and when Dr. Nathaniel Hazon invited me to join him for a study in the Holocaust Research lab, I replied that it would be over my dead body.

"That's what I told him, staring him right in the eye: 'over my dead body,'" I told Aviram while we watered the two poor plants wilting in our apartment.

"You might be making a mistake," he said casually, once again looking as if his hair had been electrocuted.

"Why do you think so?" I asked and he said he didn't, but hypothetically, there was always a chance that I might be making a mistake.

"Come ooooon."

"What do you mean, 'come on'? If you're saying 'come on,' there must be something there. It might even be determinism. Maybe you don't have free choice here," he said, adding, "I think we need more water," and I replied that it was unnecessary. *Take a look; that plant wilted a long time ago.*

Nathaniel Hazon suggested I focus on Holocaust survivors' autobiographies and examine them with literary devices, using a narrative approach.

"The part that interests us here is not only what actually happened, but also how the survivors conceptualize the events to themselves. Do you understand? We'll take terms and concepts developed in literary research and use them to examine the autobiographies of holocaust survivors."

"What terms, for example?"

"You'll decide on that. You can focus on imagery, metaphors, the concept of chronotope, questions of genre, anything you choose."

"Come on," I said, then remembered that if I said 'come on,' then apparently there was something there. And that it might actually be determinism and there was no free choice there.

"You can start with your mother's life story. I was very impressed during the application interview when you said you couldn't put down your mother on any page. But she did write down her story, right?"

Definitely right. And this was how it went down:

Mom went into the pit and didn't leave it for two years. The pit was too small and you couldn't even sit up in it. Only lie in a fetal position and reach for the narrow opening that Julia created in order to pass the food, which would arrive sometimes, and the container for waste, of which there was not much. That is not a metaphor or an image. That was simply what happened. If you wanted to, you could say that Mom had returned to being an embryo in the pit dug by Julia, who was already fifty-something years old ("No need"). But if you wanted to, you could say Julia's hand, extending into the pit and withdrawn again, once with a hard-boiled egg, once with a slice of bread, once with a small container full of water, resembled the umbilical cord. It's said that embryos hear the voices outside the pit and sense the atmosphere outside. Apparently, this is also true when dealing with seven-year-old embryos. And it's said that fifty-something-year-old women can no longer have an embryo, and apparently, that's true as well. It's also not a metaphor. Even if they really, really want to. More than anything. Even if they've lost a son. Even if they look for every possible way to grasp at life again. Still, the body has its limitations, after all. It can't get pregnant at age fifty-something. The body doesn't know about imagery and metaphors.

"Damn it, Nathaniel."

"Keep going."

"But it might not be true. All this research. There might be stories that you can't explore using literary tools. There might be stories that are outside of literature, like there are people who are outside of psychology."

"Keep going."

"Why did you let me into the clinical track?"

"I didn't let you in. You got in. Keep going."

When it was raining, or snowing, Julia couldn't come out to the woodshed and sit on the stool. She also needed to justify every step she took. Why was she going there, of all places? There were a hundred eyes on every step in Belzec; that was how they walked in Belzec, with the eyes. It was a period when everything had eyes. The trees, the walls, everything was observed. And so, when Mom heard the rain, she knew Julia might not come to sit by the pit. And since she couldn't hear the snow, she didn't know why Julia didn't come, and waited to see her shoes. Sometimes, mice would enter Mom's pit. Once, a whole family of mice got in there. A mother mouse with a few baby mice. Mom whispered to them: *You'll be my friends*. One time, ants came. But when they bit Mom and she couldn't make a sound, she squashed them with the hand she could move.

And once, the opening letting in air and light grew suddenly dark. Out of the darkness, Mom recognized the Nazis' polished boots. She heard the Germans talking to Julia. They told her that the day before yesterday, they had killed the entire adjacent street after they found a girl there, and no one had snitched. There was no need to waste a bullet or raise a bayonet at them. It was very simple, they told her. *The camp is a mere 500 meters away, if you know what we mean. Five-hundred meters. You can start counting. But we know you're a smart, loyal woman,* they told her. *We know that if you happen to find out there's some girl in the area, you won't endanger yourself or your family, right?* they said, and stroked her hair, her face, and took off her clothes, and she tried not to make a sound. She knew embryos could hear sounds from outside, and she tried to be quiet. But Mom heard everything. The heavy breathing and the moans in German, and the sighs in Polish. And the quiet weeping after the pounding of the polished boots faded away, walking off. And it was only after Julia whispered, "That's it. They're gone," that Mom asked if Julia wanted her to read to her from the New Testament.

Nathaniel said that a delegation of students was leaving for Poland in the summer. He wanted me to come along. I agreed, but once it was summer, I came down with dysentery, and Aviram said that in some situations, determinism and free choice could go hand in hand.

12.

"I've found a way how to be happy," Adva said, breaking into an Amy Winehouse song: "*Well, sometimes I go out by myself and I look across the water...*"

"That's a cool way to go about it," I said. "Too bad it didn't really work for Amy Winehouse."

"It's okay, don't worry. It's not really working for me, either."

"Sometimes nothing helps, huh?"

"Maybe I'll stay and sleep over on your couch?"

"What's so great about my couch?"

"Please don't answer my questions with a question. Just tell me: can I or can't I?"

"During our session, you can sleep on the couch. Afterward, you can't."

"Okay, obviously. Let's not say anything new. Just don't say that sometimes nothing helps, because there are things that can help."

She crossed her long legs on the couch and straightened up. "But you have to want it, right? In order to help someone, you have to want it."

She got up and left the clinic, leaving a small dip in the couch, while I sat and stared at the fabric that had emptied of her body, straightening itself in preparation for the next guest. Once again, the clinic was all mine. A small island within life that I reserved for myself. An island to which my patients came and stayed for fifty minutes, while between patients, I was there alone. In the quiet filling the space, I could hear my breath. I felt my pulse thudding between the walls, updating me on my condition. "How am I doing?" I could ask myself there.   Between the clinic walls, my thoughts were free. The woman who sat in the armchair was me. Every day, I returned to the island from the exile in which I lived with Eli, from our well-organized house that Eli liked to tend to, where I was a guest. A very welcome guest. A guest scattering various objects around her, which cast their shadows over each other, hodge-podge, creating a shadow city dwelling at the bottom of the house, existing beside it, and from there, I returned to my clinic, day after day, to be myself within it.

**

For two weeks, I was laid out with dysentery and Aviram took care of me although the doctor said I constituted an epidemiological hazard. My body was wracked with spasms and twitches and I spewed fluids from every possible orifice until it felt like if there was some toxic nucleus inside me. Perhaps the dysentery would manage to locate it and destroy it, or else it might manage to destroy the dysentery first.

During that period, Aviram made his living by sleeping at the sleep lab, and during the day, he worked on his thesis on the effect of social construction on homosexuals and took care of me and of our two plants, which persisted in their wilting. He wasn't afraid of catching what I had and said it was one of his problems in life: that nothing stuck to him. We kept sleeping in the living room together, drinking from the same glasses and using the same bathroom, and when I felt a little better, we hugged and kissed.

"See? Nothing sticks to me."

By the time the delegation returned from Poland, I was already out of bed and Nathaniel called to ask how I was doing. "It's too bad you couldn't come." He said it was important to get back to working on the thesis quickly and suggested looking into correlations between an autobiography's literary quality and parameters of well-being, examined through questionnaires that had already been validated. The hypothesis was that the more a person's autobiography was told in a literary manner, the higher their mental well-being score would be.

"Very interesting," I told him.

Outside, summer came to a sudden standstill, as if it had had enough. As if it had exhausted itself mid-season. When I opened my apartment window, I found static air. The news announced that ten villages had been destroyed in Papua New Guinea due to an earthquake, and that Jean-Paul Akayesu had been convicted of genocide. The late newscast included Bill Clinton's recorded admission that he had indeed had an inappropriate physical relationship with Monica Lewinsky. I asked Aviram if he felt like being in an inappropriate physical relationship with me, and he suggested slotting it in before he left for the sleep lab. It helped him fall asleep more easily. That was how summer and then fall went by. In the morning, we worked on our theses. Aviram made progress in examining the effect of social construction on homosexuals, and I continued to explore literary aspects of Holocaust survivors' autobiographies. During the evening hours, we did inappropriate things on the living room couch and then fell asleep: me in the living room and him in the sleep lab. And when I realized he was right when he said nothing stuck to him, I invited him to come to the kibbutz for Jewish New Year with me. Iris and Yossi were planning to fly in from Houston, and he would have a chance to meet the well-regarded Prof. Glover and, of course, my mother.

***

By virtue of being Prof. Glover's daughter, I had a tuition waiver. Mom made sure my required work days at the kibbutz, already partially privatized, would be calculated accordingly, and I rarely visited. Other than Saturday shifts, the kibbutz existed from one holiday to the next. I found it blossoming in Passover, the spring holiday, and shedding its leaves during the fall holidays. My family, too, blossomed and shed accordingly. When I arrived with Aviram at the parents' house before the gathering in the dining hall, Iris and Yossi were already there, and their kids were playing on the rug.

"Aren't you freshening up?" I asked Mom when I saw that the rug was still the same rug, and Iris suffered an attack of hysterical giggles that I caught as well.

"Mom's freshening up?" she asked, and I replied, "Turns out she isn't, she's not freshening up," and we kept on adding more and more statements that included the words 'freshening up,' which reloaded the giggles every time.

"And what about you, you're not freshening up?"

"No, but I heard that Lily might be freshening up."

Iris's kids asked, *What's so funny about freshening up?*

And Iris and Yossi said it was simply surreal, what was going on with the roads in Israel. Every time they came for a visit, they were newly appalled by

Israeli driving culture. In Houston, no one dared behave like that. Dad said we were already familiar with that scenario of Jews who didn't live in Israel, but when they visited, had plenty of criticism, and Mom said it wasn't the time to moralize, now, during the holiday, and if anyone was hungry before the holiday meal at the dining hall, they had cake here, and *kreplach* (dumpling) soup. Lily, Ilan, and the kids entered the house along with Amnon, and all at once everyone embarked on an industry of noise, and taking care of the kids, and catching up, as if we were all bolsters helping each other hold on, watching out for hidden sinkholes, filling the house with words whose utterance forced us all to maintain a certain kind of focus.

Aviram introduced himself to my dad: "I was a student of yours," and Dad was happy to tell him that in the meantime, some startling developments had occurred in researching the Jewish settlement in Gamla, and what had once been perceived as an act of heroism was not necessarily interpreted that way nowadays, from a historic perspective. Everything must be viewed from a historic perspective, while watching out, of course, for anachronism, the enemy of science.

They sat in the kitchen, conversing with interest, and I went to the parents' bedroom to find some small expanse of quiet, but the quiet there was infected by the noise in the living room, or actually, it was the other way around: it was the noise that was infected, and in any case, I didn't know where to place myself. When I returned to the living room, I saw that Aviram was no longer talking to my father. He was deep in conversation with Amnon, who was inquiring about his thesis on the effect of social construction on homosexuals, and I felt the isolating material I had brought with me into the family this time was proving so effective that Amnon hadn't even noticed that Aviram and I might be connected. I didn't remember it either. On TV, they had footage from the riots that had broken out on the Temple Mount, and Dad commented that it would never be quiet around here.

I called Ram to let him know I was in the kibbutz. When he didn't answer, I called his mother, who said she was sorry to inform me that he was hospitalized again. His condition had worsened considerably, and he was back to his theories about nonexistent axioms and parallel lines that actually would meet one day.

"How's it going to end, Noga?" she sighed. "You're almost a clinical psychologist. Are there some things that can't be cured?"

The house stayed noisy, and I returned to the parents' bedroom. I took the bag with Dad's postcard collection down from the shelf. His handwriting was friendly, in clear print letters, and I found myself missing the father I'd had as I was learning to read. I missed the father I had missed when I was in first and second grade, the one who sent me postcards from all over the world. The one who had sent me the Eiffel Tower from France when I was sick and Mom slept next to me on the rug, and a long-necked woman from Thailand, and the Forbidden City from China, and koala bears from Australia, just for me. I missed missing, and expectation, and his pretty, misleading handwriting. I missed the Japanese woman from the photo, who didn't look the way I remembered her. She had stopped winking and the entire picture had faded more than the last time I had looked at it. I missed so many things that had never really existed. How could you miss something that had never existed?

The door opened and he came in. "What's going on, Nogi? Looking for a little bit of quiet?"

"Is there quiet to be found?" I asked, and he laughed.

"How's school going?"

I didn't answer. He saw the postcard collection spread out next to me and both of us looked at the colorful photos and the warm regards sent from all over the world, packed within clear print letters, postmarked by the Tel Aviv branch of the post office.

"Let's go, okay?" Mom called to us from the other room. "The holiday ceremony's about to begin."

***

When the semester began, Aviram said he had to talk to me about something.

"Shai from our course wants to move in with us."

At first, it took me some time to get it. "So the three of us will sleep in the living room?"

"No, of course not. Shai's joining me in the sleep lab, and you can keep sleeping in the living room. Or in one of the bedrooms if you decide to get used to the smell, whatever you feel like."

Shai joined the study on the effect of social construction on homosexuals. At night, the two of them went to sleep in the sleep lab, and I was left alone in the apartment to wilt along with the potted plants. I had a hard time falling asleep, but I was also scared to stay awake, and the nights would grab at me and hold me in an uncomfortable position. I would twist and turn, sometimes passing through the empty rooms to check whether they might be fit for sleeping in after all, since I was having a hard time finding the right posture for my body.

For two days a week, we were assigned a practicum, and that was how I found myself working at the same unit where I had been hospitalized a few years earlier. Some of the nurses didn't recognize me, but I quickly explained to the staff that I was here on my practicum.

"You're going to be a clinical psychologist?" some of them asked me in concern.

I arrived tired after restless nights, and I didn't know how to dress. Almost everything I wore was inappropriate, or just ugly. In jeans or corduroys, I looked too young to be a therapist; my good tailored pants weren't right for the unit; shorts, Bermuda pants, and sweat pants were out of the question, of course, and I didn't have any dresses. My blouses were too tight or casual or short or see-through, and there was also one that was right but was just ugly; I couldn't wear it every day and needed to mix it up.

I found myself dealing with problems I hadn't known when I was hospitalized, when I had nothing to hide. When my mind was exposed and naked, and I was wearing some rag or pajamas. When my mind lived in Ronnie's body, and my body was strangely abandoned and available. In a counseling meeting at the university, we talked about the quandary of what to wear in the units, and when I discovered that Joy, Shiri, and Shirin had a similar problem, we went out to shop for clothes one day. It was awful.

"Have you noticed that there are no good outfits for female therapists? I swear to God, the easiest thing is being a doctor or a nurse," Shiri said.

"Or a patient," I noted, and the three of them laughed.

"Word."

And yet I got the sense they were dealing with it a little better than I was. Despairing, I entered the dressing room with a pile of items. I took off the clothes I was wearing and found my body sulking at me.

"Well?" the three of them asked from the other side of the curtain.

"Hold on, let me breathe," I blurted out into the mirror, which was too close, confronting me with my body, which was repelled by it and by me, having a hard time deciding which of us was the scariest of them all. The sales associate was frightening and unpredictable, and at any moment, there was a risk she would suddenly pull back the curtain, and in the fluorescent light, my body and I would be exposed in our endless nakedness. I ended up buying two pairs of high-waist pants, two button-down shirts, and a bluish dress it was obvious I would never wear, but this ordeal needed to come to an end.

We went out for pizza, and I sat there exhausted and lost.

"Nogloom has undergone a traumatic experience," Joy said, and we all laughed at the new name and enjoyed the precision of the definition and the idea that sometimes, this was what was called for—precision.

"Joy, did you notice we have opposite names?"

As night approached, it was clear I had no chance of falling asleep. I watered the plants, left the apartment empty, locked it against any unwanted passersby who might display interest in it, and informed Aviram and Shai that I was sleeping at the sleep lab that night. I fell asleep so quickly and easily that none of the employees had the heart to tell me to stop sleeping there, even after several months had gone by.

***

The unit smelled strongly of medication and disinfectant and urine, and the detergents were clearly not managing to overcome the bad smells, but rather living alongside them in a delicate balance of power. The hospitalized patients would shuffle down the halls, crowding the nurses' station after breakfast to obediently take their pills, sitting at the tables during occupational therapy, and staring blankly at the TV at ten a.m. and five p.m. The schedule reminded me of the one we'd had at Palm Tree Preschool, but without the games, and without the pets, and without the songs. There were several people claiming they were God, and one who was Hitler, and a Jesus, too, and they fought among themselves, but it wasn't a game. It was real. Everything in the unit was real; nothing was make-believe.

Hani had been promoted to the position of head psychologist at the hospital and once a week, we met for a counseling session. It wasn't strange that she had become my counselor after she had been my therapist for two years. Nothing was strange with Hani. With her, I could be a direct continuation of the girl I had been. I realized one day that sometimes, I could be a continuation of myself. We talked a bit about the patients and a lot about me.

"We use our own personality as a therapeutic instrument," she explained her credo as a psychologist.

"Some instrument," I sighed.

She was wearing a long skirt and a purple knit, and there was nothing embarrassing about her.

I asked her what I could possibly do with the people in the unit. None of the theories I had learned at school were relevant when Hitler woke up in the morning crying because he missed his mother, and no one could calm him down; not Jesus, and not God. Not Freud, and not Melanie Klein, not Winnicott or Kohut or Kernberg.

She said it was important to listen to people in the unit. That I actually knew how to listen to them. That sometimes, you needed somewhere to place your mind.

"Oh, come on," I told her. "It's not like you can really put your mind somewhere."

And she smiled and said I was right. That sometimes, ridiculous statements came out of her mouth. But she still thought they should be listened to.

She inquired about my thesis regarding literary aspects of Holocaust survivors' autobiographies and suggested that maybe literature actually was somewhere you could place your mind. I said that was an interesting idea. That in order for the mind to exist, it needed a kind of make-believe. Exactly the kind that the unit was missing.

"So, is there make-believe in your mother's autobiography?" Hani asked, and I felt a sharp point touching some part of my body.

"Hani," I told her. "I feel my body."

"Cool," she said.

"Right, but I don't understand where my mom made Ronnie disappear to."

"You'll find out," she told me. "When the time is right. How are you living in the meantime?"

I told her I was living in an empty apartment with two wilted potted plants and two roommates and that for the time being, the three of us were sleeping at the sleep lab and two of us were also getting paid for it. I told her about my new friends from school, and about the new binary opposition in our academic track: Joy and Nogloom, and we both laughed at the idea that "they who sow in nogloom shall reap in joy."

***

The article about literary aspects in autobiographies of Holocaust survivors that I co-authored with Nathaniel Hazon was published in *Holocaust Studies* and was quoted and referenced several times. A review published in the journal of the German Psychoanalytical Association called the article "a turning point in the documentation of traumatic events," and the clinical track held an event to celebrate the achievement. I was invited to talk about our research in various forums, and when I was offered a chance to accompany a delegation of young researchers traveling to Poland, I had already acquired enough experience of sorts and thought there was no need for an attack of dysentery or a fever of 104 degrees in order to say no. I cut my hair short and made myself look boyish. I wore men's shirts, but "just because it was cool." And one day, I got a phone call from Dad, who said he was coming to "my university," as he called it, and that he would be happy to have lunch.

We met during my break. I told him about my research enthusiastically, and he praised the publication and "the prestigious journal."

"Do you realize the implication? Do you realize what it means? Do you realize that people deal best with traumatic events when they tell themselves about it in a literary manner?"

He looked at me and seemed to be listening. Suddenly, he said, "Noga, I see you're really interested in this."

"I am, it's mentally healthy," I answered and we both cracked up.

I noticed I had missed the mother tongue a little, that it had been a while since I had spoken it. That it was fun to speak it with him. And when he made some comment about my short hairdo ("A little masculine, isn't it?"), I suddenly felt like conducting an experiment and told him, "Maybe I'll submit a research proposal. Maybe I can hire a research assistant," but he didn't find it funny. He said the quiche was disgusting. "Ew." But that time, I was the one who didn't laugh.

When school ended and our residency began, I noticed my hair was having a hard time growing. It had developed a kind of weird stubble with curling ends and I had to cut it short again every time. Cutting my hair had been a mistake. What had I been thinking? Along with the puny salary from the residency, I was working in a boarding school for at-risk youth, which allowed me to leave the kibbutz and stay in the apartment with Aviram and Shai, who were now sleeping there at night after their gig at the sleep lab ended. I left the lab too and resumed sleeping at the apartment. Shai and Aviram had jobs advocating for gay teens, and they occasionally met Amnon, who worked for the same nonprofit. I came to kibbutz holidays with both of them, as a trio, and no one in the family asked anything, other than Amnon, who called sometimes to make sure they were really coming. However, while I occasionally found myself missing the mother tongue, this feeling ceased immediately when I got to the kibbutz and the *foo-foo-foo* would invade my cells, cutting the visits shorter and shorter.

Once I no longer had a room of my own at the kibbutz, the parents' house was the only place to be, and one time Dad blurted out, perhaps distractedly, that this was the reason he didn't come to the parents' house much, either.

I was sitting with Shai and Aviram on the parents' bed, watching TV as they covered the wave of terrorist attacks, including the murder of a baby by a Palestinian sniper in Hebron.

"It'll never be quiet here," I heard myself say, and Mom said a little noise in the house wouldn't harm anyone; when I was a girl, I had complained it was too quiet there.

The volume on Greek mythology in English was propped up on the bookshelf, next to the pipe collection. When Shai heard I had already read the book in third grade, he said that at least it was easier than reading about English mythology in Greek.

The rug smelled musty, like a beast grown old, along with something else, unidentified, and the postcard collection perched above us.

"Forget it," I replied when they expressed interest. "Those are postcards from nowhere."

"There's no such place as nowhere," they answered. "Every place is somewhere."

And Amnon said, "You know you're the only one that he sent postcards from nowhere."

"Did he send you guys postcards from real countries?"

"No, he didn't send us anything at all."

Mom and Dad were in the kitchen, moving things from one place to another, drinking coffee, chatting, restarting some unknown couplehood. Aviram, who already felt right at home, stood up and reached out for the bag of postcards. He poked around in the bags that were crammed in among the spider webs when suddenly, a white envelope dropped down from the depths of the shelf. The address on it was crossed out with a black marker, and a lined page like the kind we used in school was peeking out. My face was flooded with cold sweat when I saw the opening words at the top of the page: "To my most Rabbit in the world," and the date. January 1990.

13.

Some people can manage not to notice what's right in front of their eyes. Miss obvious signals, clear-cut facts, red cuts in the living flesh. There are theories that talk about the healing value of literary devices. Theories that posit that the darkness of five p.m., the one that gathers the earth as if it had never been illuminated, was nothing but a metaphor. That there was no other, actual darkness behind that darkness. Theories being published in prestigious journals, theories being quoted and reviewed.

"A cat, I wouldn't even entrust a cat to you," Clara yelled at her husband once, before she died.

"I wouldn't even entrust a husband to you," he yelled back at her, before he died.

They would fight like that every evening, before both of them died. Kalman didn't leave the house after Sarah died. What reason did he have to leave? Or to stay home?

The mothers of the youths from the at-risk youth center stopped being mothers one day. Their kids were removed from the home. Any woman who couldn't take responsibility shouldn't be raising a child. She should leave it to other people. There are boarding schools and kibbutzim. There are women like Julia, who are willing to hide a child at their place, who don't tell her: *You can't sleep here, we're out of time. See you next week.*

"Here, take all my patients, I'm giving you all of them." That's what I could tell the man with the suit and the badge who would come to check what was going on at my clinic. "Just leave me the kids, Tomer and Julie. Leave me those two," I could ask the authorities. "I've already miscarried one tadpole, I mean, he dropped, I didn't do it on purpose," I'd explain. "Please don't take these guys." And Eli would look at me, he would want to help me, but it wasn't certain that he could. And someone else would pass by, maybe a neighbor, or an acquaintance.

"You know," that person might say, "it's not about you now." That's what he would think. "Everything doesn't revolve around you. It was a different girl who suffered, who needed help. Different parents who are beside themselves right now."

The media reported air pollution due to a dust storm, recommending that the population stay home due to particles and high levels of sulfur dioxide found in the air. Depressive, liberated girls were walking around in the streets, girls with nothing to lose, and no responsibility to anyone, including themselves. Across from them strode groups of bored girls who didn't follow media announcements and didn't know what sulfur dioxide was. They wore hip clothing and conducted idle conversations over the phone with other bored girls. On a bench sat old ladies whom pollution could not hurt anymore, staring into space. But most of the people chose to stay home on a day like this. Close the windows, put on pajamas, and hide under the covers.

And in the home of the Glover-Sarid family, two teenage boys were sitting in front of the TV and playing on the Playstation. In the living room, one mother was walking around in an unfashionable sweatsuit. A mother who was once a girl who had made up being Tova Hershkovitz, the author who wrote about Storio the Elf, a girl whose father told her that if she looked around, she would see there was a story in everything. A girl who was later a graduate student who published an article about literary aspects of Holocaust survivors. After searching for metaphors and imagery in electrical barbed-wire fences and gas chambers. The important thing, after all, is not what really happens, but the way it's told. And now her mother, their grandmother, the grandmother who managed to hide from the Nazis for so long, had slipped in the shower while her daughter drove off to be with her patient in the ICU. Her patient, who wrote poems between one cut and the next. *Who knows*, their mother probably thought to herself as she chose to make that U-turn on the road, on the way from the kibbutz to the ICU, *who knows*, she probably told herself some kind of story, *maybe she can still be saved?*

***

To my most Rabbit in the world,

I don't know why you don't answer my letters, but I've decided in the meantime to keep writing anyway. You must know it wasn't my choice to leave the kibbutz. Your mother said there was no choice, and I can understand her, the way she must have felt after meeting my mother in Canada. I'm sure you noticed I'm not that good at letters, but I wanted to write you today in particular, because if our little tadpole had been born, it should have been today. I think about him, even though he wasn't born, what kind of tadpole he could have been. I think about you endlessly and miss you more than anything in the world.

Your Tortoise.

***

In the anatomy books, the heart sometimes looks like a fist, or a butterfly, red and shriveled. I don't know what my heart looked like when I felt it flutter, making its way outside the body. And if a stomach can really flip over, the way it felt like it did. And if something could really take your breath away, as the saying goes.

"Can I ask what exactly is going on here?" I waved the letter in front of my parents, who were drinking coffee.

"Where did you find that?" My mother leaped in a kind of involuntary spasm.

"I didn't find it, it fell on me." And she was silent. And he was silent. They had never been that coordinated before.

"Can I get an explanation?" I screamed at them.

"Shush, Nogi, sweetie, it's unhealthy to scream like that. We'll talk about it when your guests aren't here."

"We'll talk about it? We'll talk about it? Since when do we talk about anything? Can I just get an explanation? Now? Where are all the letters? Where are the rest of the letters? Where are they? How many of them are there?"

"We kept the letters since we planned to show them to you, but not now. We thought it was still too early. That you're not ready yet."

"Yeah? And who exactly is 'we'? Since when exactly are you a couple? Since when do you think, and plan and debate, and why do you think you know when I'm ready and when I'm not? And what the hell is wrong with this house? What's messed up here? What here is so mentally unhealthy? Huh, Professor Glover, tell me. You live here, don't you?"

I decided not to slam the door when I got out of there, but to let it slam of its own free will. Aviram and Shai went out after me.

"That's quite a scene you put on there."

Amnon came out too and all of us were standing between the parents' house and the cabin where old Katya had been living for a few years now. Her raincoat hung on the peg that Ronnie had once installed with the drill a long time ago, and when I looked at the aging peg, I imagined that echoes of that noise I made when I held the drill for a few moments might still be trapped between the walls of the neighborhood houses. Amnon and I stood and looked at each other without saying a thing, without knowing who had caused him to get out of the parents' house. Me, or "my guests." But he stood there silently.

"Come on, Amnon, say something for once."

But he was silent. For the first time, I noticed that around the top of his head, a small bald spot was emerging with a smidge of obsequiousness, and I thought about the fact that it wasn't just him who hadn't seen me all those years. I hadn't seen him either. Hadn't even looked. So that, by the time I remembered to look, Amnon's hair had already started losing interest and retiring, and I only noticed that after Shai commented, "Your brother's kind of cool." Who was my brother? What did he like? What interested him in life? What was left of my living brother, after my dead brother died? I thought about what Amnon had said, about the postcards from nowhere that Dad hadn't sent them, but only to me. And I thought about the sight of Dad and Mom having coffee together, and being silent together, like activities they knew how to do together, as a couple. Through the window, I could see their silhouettes, sitting at the table inside the house that had emptied out all at once. It seemed like I understood something, but I wasn't sure what it was.

"Come on, Amnon, say something. Say something already."

"What do I have to say to you, Noga?" he asked, staring fixedly at the neighborhood lawn. "Why would Dad send us postcards? He was home all the time before Nadav got sick. There wasn't any need for any postcard, from any country, real or not." He looked at Shai and Aviram, who seemed to resemble each other, like they were brothers. *Great, Amnon,* I wanted to tell him. *Great, Amnon,* I didn't tell him. *Great, Amnon, keep not answering my real questions. Did you know about Ronnie's letter? And about the other letters? Or did they come from imaginary countries too?*

We left the old people's rotting neighborhood and began to walk toward the parking lot. But halfway there, I told Shai and Aviram we were taking a little detour. Another spin we had to take before we could get the hell out of there. "It'll only take a minute," I told them before I walked into the living room of Rachel's house; Rachel, who had replaced Aviva at the post office.

"It's over," I told her. "From now on, the letters coming from Ronnie don't go to my parents' mailbox anymore," and I gave her my new address.

Aviram drove, Shai sat next to him, and I sprawled out in the back seat.

"Would you turn the radio down?" I asked them as we left the kibbutz, and they turned down the volume immediately. No one dared argue with me over anything that evening. At night, Shai and Aviram snored together, and I stood in the living room in front of the window, until morning came, and looked out at the street, trying to examine precisely how the light reached the road, which point it emerged from and how it spread, sending out long arms as it wrestled all of the objects out of the darkness. One by one. In the morning, I took our two wilted plants and threw them out in the garbage can under the building.

"How are you doing?" I asked Eli over the phone, as if we talked every day.

***

The provisional courts for Jews suspected of collaborating with the Nazis were established immediately after the war, when the Jews were still spending time in the displaced-persons camps, and before it was clear that one day, the State of Israel would pass the Nazis and Nazi Collaborators Punishment Law.

"Imagine the chaos over there. Jews living together, remnants of that appalling war, creating a community life of sorts and a culture after the horrors, when the local press began to publish stories and demands to fully bring to justice those accused of collaborating with the Nazi monster. They were sitting together, say at a soccer game, when suddenly someone pointed and said,

'Look! It's so-and-so who was a *kapo*,'[28] or 'Here's Mrs. So-and-so, who was in charge of Block 34B.' A doctor who had been a prisoner in Auschwitz and, under Mengele's orders, was forced to perform terrible surgeries, heaved a sigh of relief when the camp was liberated, but then she found herself accused by the Jews. What would you say about that?"

"What a wacky period. The world can be so insane sometimes."

"You have no idea. There was so much stuff going on. They had to be certain they could identify those people, and also decide whether they had had a choice or not, and what kind of punishment they deserved."

"That war never ended."

Eli looked at me and I could see he was choosing not to say anything about the fact that one day I had left the apartment. Or about the fact that one day I came back. As if you could just come in the same door I had left through with one bag of clothes and toiletries. As if the time that had passed between closing the door and opening it had indeed passed, but only in other places. He chose not to say that I didn't have to behave like that. That the wind didn't have to blow me from one place to another. That I was a clinical psychologist now. And it was a good thing he made that choice. He knew he had no better option. His doctoral thesis, already in its final stages, was keeping him busy, and he was dedicating his time to publishing the article he had co-authored with Prof. Rubin.

"If you publish it in *Holocaust Studies*, we can be neighbors," I told him, and he hugged me and kissed me.

Then he said, "We don't have to be neighbors. We can go back to living together."

***

In the first few months after getting back together, we didn't talk about Ronnie. We were busy with our professional development and felt that we were growing, each of us separately, witnessing each other's lives. I felt that Eli was creating an air bubble around me in which I could live in relative quiet. And

---

28   A *kapo* was a prisoner in a Nazi camp assigned by the SS guards to supervise forced labor or carry out administrative tasks.

while I had breathed in Ronnie through my gills, with Eli, I had plenty of air and the two of us could go to all kinds of places, and return to our apartment, and have friends over who saw us as a couple. We were Eli and Noga and our friends came in pairs. Gil and Yael. Noa and Yuval. Shai and Aviram. My hair overcame its stubble phase, and although it was still stuck in mid-growth, it could create the impression of having a destination. Like it knew where it was going. I bought some clothes and tried to develop a "style" of my own. We bought things for the apartment, too, some of them even expensive and okay looking, but I had no special regard for any of the items. They were spread out around me and matched each other well: the couch matched the lamp, and the chest of drawers matched the table, until it seemed like the apartment was actually theirs. That when I came home in the evening, I was interrupting them in the middle of something, and they would grow silent all at once. The mind had a kind of mobility then: sometimes I would encounter it and sometimes I wouldn't, and there was a general feeling that it was somewhere in the neighborhood.

From within the air bubble, I met my patients, who presented all kinds of variations on the mind. Sammy, who had broken up with his wife without knowing why. Dafna, who had gotten married without knowing why. Anna, who got pregnant every time she felt stuck, and then regretted it, although she couldn't actually say she regretted it, but she regretted it anyway.

Eli and I usually met in the evening, when we brought the experiences we had collected during the day to the apartment in order to fill our conversations and, quite quickly, we came to talk about the subject that connected us: the Holocaust, toying with the possibility that our articles would dwell together in the same journal. That through them, we could conduct conversations about that wacky period in history, which, other than Ronnie, was the only wacky thing in life I shared with Eli. No other wackiness touched him.

We bought a computer and set it up in the bedroom. The Internet had arrived in Israel several years ago, and we were excited to use it in all kinds of ways. But every time I looked up Ronnie Wertheim, nothing came up. Not a thing. I always found search results for Ronnie Wertheimer, the sportswear designer, who was too real, and too athletic to remind me of the solitary Tortoise I'd once had.

Ronnie's name gradually expanded between Eli and me the longer we avoided talking about him. It expanded as I walked to the mailbox expectantly, only to be met with bills to be paid and flyers advertising various businesses. And when I called Aviram to ask whether a letter happened to have arrived at my previous address,

"Nothing?"

"Nothing."

"Okay," I said, adding, "no news is good news. Right?"

I hid the one letter, the one written on an old lined page, in my underwear and bra drawer, which I took care to open only when Eli wasn't around. If he was in the room just as I came out of the shower, I would get dressed quickly, as if hiding some guilt, concealing evidence. Other than the letter, I had nothing through which I could experience Ronnie. We didn't have any shared photos. We had never bought each other gifts. We didn't leave notes. We didn't have any friends in common. Other than Eli, who was the closest thing to Ronnie I knew. Sometimes, I would be seized with resentment over the fact that he wasn't fulfilling his mission. At such moments, Eli seemed like a terrible waste. I recalled those Fridays on the kibbutz in fourth grade, when they would return from the army together, and I'd divide my speech equally between them, so that neither of them would be jealous, remembering that both of them were solitary soldiers and that both of them had no family in Israel. I liked to remember that Eli was a solitary soldier and weave various conversations around his solitary status, trying to blur the fact that he had not been a solitary soldier for a while now, and was actually not solitary at all. For a while now.

"So, were you all alone at the library today?" I tried to extend compassion, and he replied that it was fascinating, that this research was sucking him in. And so Ronnie's name gradually grew between us, until one day, with precise casualness, when we were talking about the traumas of Holocaust survivors, as was our habit, Eli said he had to mention that it was very strange of my mother to behave the way she had. That the fact she had told me she'd also gone to Canada and met Ronnie's mother there was no reason to behave the way she had.

"Even if Ronnie's mother is a highly unstable woman." Eli's words were decisive, which was typical of him. Both together and separately: "Not a reason to behave the way she had." "Highly unstable."

I should have stayed with Ronnie even if his mother was a highly unstable woman. But Eli went on to say what I, too, apparently knew. The fact that she was a highly unstable woman, who had gotten pregnant with Ronnie at the age of eighteen by a married man after arriving from Poland on her own, was not a reason. There had to be a deeper reason.

"But which one?"

Eli sat and thought. He was obviously making an effort. For some reason, it was not strange that the same man who had replaced Ronnie, that same faded, lukewarm alternative, was also the one now cooperating with me in an attempt to figure something out. I loved him for it. And I felt sorry for him. And I was angry at him. And I forgave him. And sometimes myself as well. Ronnie expanded between the two of us like a longing that was adjacent to life, intensifying it and growing distant from it. Ronnie expanded like a memory, and holding on to it was the only thing we did together. Almost.

***

Shortly before I finished my residency, Eli finished his doctorate. My parents came to the graduation ceremony, as if we were family.

"Who invited them?" I asked him, and he replied, "Why, didn't you want to?" and for a moment, I savored knowing Eli had invited my parents because he had no family in Israel. Because he was solitary, and once, long ago, in the old days of the cabin, Mom said he could come to her with anything. So he had. Dad was formally dressed, as if the event was in his honor, and Mom walked arm in arm with him, proud of the achievements of her adopted son.

The university president's speech praised perseverance and determination, striving for excellence and expanding one's knowledge. "As King Solomon said on this matter, '*Happy is the man that findeth wisdom, and the man that getteth understanding. For the merchandise of it is better than the merchandise of silver, and the gain thereof than fine gold.*'" [29]

After the ceremony, my parents suggested that the four of us go out for coffee together, and when Eli said we could have it in our apartment, "It's more simple," was what he said: "more simple," I let some force inside me surrender

---

29   Proverbs 3: 13-14

and go with Dr. Sarid and Prof. Glover and his wife to the couple's apartment, thinking that Eli was right that it was "more simple," although he hadn't said more simple than what. "More simple than what?" I might ask him one day, although we both knew the answer, and therefore there was no need to ask, and therefore I never would.

"Did you put on water?" Mom asked me, and Eli said he already had. He had already plugged in the kettle, and in a few minutes, it would toggle, and Mom could say, in my apartment, "Oh, there, it toggled."

Everyone sat down in the living room, me too, in the apartment where all the items of furniture matched each other, and Dad said, "It's nice here," and Mom said, "It's wonderful here, Nogilee, what a lovely apartment, did you insure against earthquakes and fire?" and Eli put things on the table and chatted cheerfully, and gradually, we all joined the chatter when Eli talked about the trials held for those suspected of collaborating with the Nazis, "the traitors," for whom the most severe possible punishment was "banishing them from the Jewish camp," and every time he said the words "betrayal," or "traitors," I felt I was having a hard time sitting there, that I wished I could go, leave the three of them to chat with each other in the apartment, and disappear to the place where I belonged—I didn't know what it was, but there had to be such a place. Eli seemed enthusiastic, glad that Prof. Rubin had brought his wife to the ceremony as well, that meant it really was significant to him, the ceremony, and the research as well, and Mom said, *Sure, I went to Ari's ceremony, too, and so did Lil and Iri and Amnoni, only Nadavi and Nogilee hadn't been born yet,* and Eli said right, "Right," he said, after Mom had finished unloading her five children, the living and the dead, including the ones who hadn't been born yet, in the apartment's living room. "Right, Ruthie, but Prof. Rubin's wife came to my ceremony, not her husband's," and Mom said, "True, that really is nice, isn't it nice, Ari, that Prof. Rubin invited his wife to Eli's ceremony? Are you happy, Eli? Are you pleased?" She switched from Dad to Eli in the span of one breath, and I thought there must be such a place, somewhere in the world, a place where, when the door closed after they left, a sort of click would echo, a sound indicating everything was in its place, and I could finally breathe.

Eli and I cleared the dishes from the living room. I handed him dish after dish and he arranged them nicely in the dishwasher. His broad back was turned to the kitchen and his busy hands were instilling order into our dirty dishes, as if there was nothing disturbing about them. No waste that could not be cleaned. He was satisfied. His movements were measured, and every time he moved, his shadow moved with him, exposing another shadow, which emerged suddenly. A similar shadow, but different. Eli was standing with his face to the dishwasher and humming the song "When the Saints Go Marching In," singing to himself, "*Lord, how I want to be in that number, when the saints go marching in.*" He had no idea what was going on behind his back, on the floor, and between the walls.

***

When Little Red Riding Hood finally entered Grandmother's house, she found her in bed, wearing a nightgown with a white nightcap on her head. But Grandmother looked different. Like her usual self, and yet different. *What big eyes you have!* Little Red Riding Hood said to Grandma.

The better to see you, my beloved granddaughter.
And what big ears you have!
The better to hear you.
And what big teeth you have!

I inserted a detergent pod, pressed Run, and remained standing there for a few more seconds to hear the rattle of soap and water removing the coffee remains from our four cups. I sat down on the floor with my head between my knees.

"Have you ever had sex with a doctor?" he asked, and I said I had a killer headache.

***

The months that went by smelled like apartment. I tried to find an animal name for Eli, but no animal was right. "Spotted Leopard" was too pretentious. "Monkey" was silly. So was "Pied Kingfisher." Occasionally, the embarrassing slip of the tongue recurred, and I called him "Tortoise." Sometimes it happened in the middle of sex. When it did, I trembled under the covers and he said I was cute and that he loved me. He really loved me and wanted to live with me his entire life.

"Why?"

"Because I'm happy with you. Because I like it that you still haven't decided what to do with your hair. Because I feel like family with you."

"Okay," I said.

"Okay what?"

"Okay, I'll marry you." I was trying to recreate Ronnie's 'okay' when I told him about the pregnancy, although it was clear that this 'okay' was a different 'okay,' and that the feeling of missing Ronnie would never let go of me, and that if I married Eli, I could be close to it, to missing him.

Eli got out of bed and stood across from me with disheveled hair and in boxer shorts. "Noga Glover, psychologist with funny hair, will you marry me?" He got down on one knee.

"I just told you I would."

"We should raise a glass," he smiled.

"Then raise it." I felt how I had no way to take part in this ceremony, and once again I felt sorry for him. Now, within my pity, he reminded me of something sweet. I almost loved him. Here I was, about to marry Ronnie's roommate. My mother's other adopted son. But Eli didn't know I felt sorry for him. As far as he was concerned, there was nothing pitiable about him. It was entirely my thing. He was pleased with his new academic degree and the new wife he would soon have and the nice apartment with the clean dishes. My problems didn't touch him. Eli was happy. I would soon be the wife of a happy man.

"Here's to our life." He poured wine for both of us, sipped from his glass, and fell asleep.

***

Our life together was suffused with daily tasks, especially after Julie and Tomer were born. A mountain of daily tasks covering life itself, although Eli said that was life. That's what he said—*That's life*—and I tried to cruise between the tasks, pretending to find meaning in notes from school, in sandwiches in the morning, in doctor visits and grocery shopping and appointments with the accountant and paying taxes and bills and fees and the mortgage. I discovered a practical side within me that amused me and felt that my marriage to Eli, with the two kids that accompanied it, had switched me to Run mode, which, oddly, was more relaxed than my previous mode. Time was measured out, calculated, well organized within calendars and weekly planners, made of a packable material so that you could think it was the one working for us, and not the other way around.

When I paged through my weekly planner, I could see the beginning of next year and how the days separating me from it were passing with the rustle of paper. Passover, Holocaust Remembrance Day, Memorial Day, it all passed with a rustle, including occasions that had yet to arrive. "Time will do the trick," we'd say. Like a one-trick pony. It would heal all wounds. Eli and I were a "good team," as he liked to say, and I was part of the good team. Sometimes we laughed about the fact that I was the less-good part of the good team, and Eli said that that was the good thing about a good team. That it could deal with the less-good parts too.

I straightened my hair and gained six pounds, which allowed me to maintain a gap between me and my body, to keep a safe distance from it, so it wouldn't burst into my life suddenly and mess up the prevailing order. Practical functioning kept me in constant motion that did not allow me to fall anywhere or sink or fly or evaporate. The centrifugal force of life kept me far from the center, and it was only at the clinic that I felt I could connect to something else as well. My friends were the mothers of Julie and Tomer's friends and I discovered I could talk to them about nothing for hours. Perhaps even for days or months. Once a week, Eli and I would have sex, usually sticking to a fixed format, and I managed to find all kinds of nooks in my body that released a certain pleasure from me, emerging like a distant echo, as if appearing out of some other woman's body. "So much pleasure!" Eli would say before he fell asleep.

The Saturdays were like traps that we managed to avoid most of the time using day trips and social get-togethers. Sometimes we stayed home and during the free time, I tried to imbue everyday materials with a literary spirit. That was what happened when Mitski, our kitten whom Julie had gathered up from the trash, got stranded in the top branches of a tree in the yard and couldn't get down. Tomer started to climb up in order to fetch her, but she panicked even more and climbed higher, and kept going higher, and higher, until she got stuck on a branch that was so high it couldn't even be reached by climbing.

"Mitski," we called her together, in a family cheer. "Mits-ki, come-on," we sang to her in a four-voice choir, and I thought we must look nice together, all peering up, our gazes fixed upon the top of the tree in a family prayer to our cat. But Mitski couldn't come down; no prayer helped. Julie began to cry at the sight of the frightened cat, stuck between the heavens and her new, helpless family, whose members were holding out their hands and urging her to have faith and jump into their arms.

"Someone do something," she begged. "She'll never come down from there," and then added that Mitski would have been better off just staying in the garbage can.

Eli brought a ladder, but it didn't help. The ladder was too short and Eli looked ridiculous in that heroic venture, with his limp hoodie and his goodwill. Time passed slowly, like it always did on Saturdays, stretching the hours to their limit, but when it started getting dark and Sunday's tasks were already knocking on the door, I felt I was over that family event and waited for Mitski to do us all a favor and come down from the tree so all of us could return to Run mode. But she didn't come down, and Tomer was helpless, and Julie was crying.

"Someone do something."

And then I thought of the poem about the athlete cat, Dahlia Ravikovitch's poem from the book *Family Party*, with its orange-and-white cover, which stood on the shelf in the parents' house in the kibbutz. "*Oh no, oh no, the kids are worried so,*" I proudly recited to Tomer and Julie, to show them that there, I had found a solution to the problem. "*The cat's in the tree, they said with a frown. And how will he ever come back down?*" But they didn't know what I wanted from them. "Listen to the words," I said with a maternal smile, therapeutically. "What's happening here is just like the poem," and I continued: "*The cat kept on climbing till he got to the top. He might fall, the kids yelled, if he doesn't stop!*" And I was just about to move on to the next verse, the one about safety nets and the fire department, when they both stared at me angrily and said, almost simultaneously, "Enough with the poems right now. How's a poem going to help Mitski come down from the tree?"

I went back into the kitchen from the yard and started to clean up the leftovers from lunch. Smears of ketchup on the plates, schnitzel crumbs, juice spilled on the table. I was defeated. I had been defeated in front of my own children's eyes. Soon Saturday would be over and I would resume doing what I knew: treating other people, letting the time packed up in the weekly planner "do the trick." From the perspective of the weekly planner, it was already possible to draw a checkmark over next week, and next month, and the costume that needed to be prepared for Purim, and the goodie bags, and the parent-teacher meetings. Everything was going by. From the perspective of the weekly planner, this Saturday was already over; it was only me still stalling here, although, after this Saturday, another Saturday would arrive, and then another, and I would observe my kids' life in a literary manner and clean the schnitzel crumbs and the smears of ketchup and the dribbles of juice. The mother figure clinging to my body would bend down to the floor to gather the scraps that had fallen off the table by gravitational force. The body trapped inside me, the one hidden behind the gap, would signal me occasionally with brief pulses, with rashes, with the molting of the face, with drooping eyelids, while I continued sweeping the floors and mopping them, and under every layer of dust, another layer would be exposed, and another; how far I had drifted from the bedrock of my life.

Eli stood behind me and hugged me. His large hands rested on my shoulders and I could feel the surplus of his goodwill.

"What are you worrying about, Nogi girl, none of it is serious. Soon she'll come down from the tree, see? There, she's already coming down," he said, and through the window, I saw Mitski making her way down as if she had only been waiting for me to go into the house and leave her alone. My optimistic husband returned to his own affairs.

"See? I promised you. No cat ever born has died on a tree."

***

I liked being a therapist, even if, for much of the time, I didn't really understand what it meant. Sometimes, the insights would come from the most unexpected patients, such as Tom, whose dream was to be a taxi driver: "You sit there in your taxi. If you're hot, you turn on the a/c. If you're cold, you turn on the heater. If it's stuffy, you open a window. If you're bored, you turn on the radio. Whatever's making you uncomfortable, you can take care of it in a taxi."

That's true, I thought while enjoying sitting in the clinic I had designed for myself, nearly the only place in my life that was mine alone, excluding the dusty apartment I once had in the kibbutz, which tended to me after Ronnie disappeared. The apartment I saw only from one angle, as I lay on my back for seven months, looking at the ceiling. But at the clinic, I didn't miss anyone, other than myself. If I was hot, I could turn on the a/c. If I was cold, I could turn on the heater, or wrap myself up in a sweater. And when Tel Aviv became too noisy for me, I closed the windows. And when I was too noisy for myself, I opened them, allowing the people on the street to see my silhouette revealed through the curtain. That was how I liked being a therapist, reflecting in the window occasionally, casting my shadow on the couch and the windows, lending myself by the hour to people who came to me. It was easy for me, lending myself to others, easier than returning to myself at the end of the day, opening the door of the Sarid family home, walking into the mess and the bustle, and declaring: *I'm here! Mom's home!* Maybe it really was easier dealing with the dust of the mind than with the dust on the kitchen floor.

I would lay out my clothes the evening before so that daylight wouldn't catch me unprepared. Eli's and my generous wages allowed me to have the wardrobe of a real woman, the kind I imagined myself being, and every morning, I'd insert myself into the clothes, start the car, and through the mirror, watch the woman now driving from her home to Tel Aviv, the light breeze blowing her tousled hair as she moved toward the rented apartment, her clinic, in which she could heat the room if she was cold, and cool it if she was hot, and rest from her own home.

The patients brought a variety of stories with them. Every time, when it seemed like I had already heard everything about the mind, a new variation showed up. The mind was like a dragon with a thousand heads. At least. There was Yitzhak, who had survived Auschwitz.

"How do you survive Auschwitz?"

"What you need, other than lots of luck, is initiative, and mostly to be good with your hands. As soon as we arrived at the camp, they asked: 'Is there a doctor here? Is there a tailor here? Is there a plumber here?' And I raised my hand and said I was a plumber."

"And were you really a plumber?"

"No, but I had initiative, and I was good with my hands. They took me to work at one of the officers' houses outside the camp. Every day, I was driven outside the camp, and I'd fix things."

That's how you survived Auschwitz. No imagery. No metaphors. Being good with your hands. In Auschwitz, no one would ask whether someone happened to be a psychologist. Or a poet.

Sometimes, at the end of the day, the therapeutic persona stuck to me. I believed in my patience and would call Mom, at the parents' house.

"Nogilee, my pretty girl, are you done with chemotherapy?" She flung me back out of myself. And sometimes, it took her a while to recognize my voice.

"Who is this? Iri? Not Iri? Lil? Not Lil? Who, then?"

And sometimes, she beat me to it and called me. "Who is this?" she would still ask.

14.

The ICU at Sheba Tel HaShomer Medical Center. It was only yesterday that I had been here, after making a U-turn on the road on the way to the kibbutz. It was only yesterday that I replied "no" to all the questions. No, I wasn't Adva's mother. Not her sister, either. Not family at all. A therapist. A therapist to whom no information could be conveyed. At three p.m., I would go to the funeral, and in the meantime, I was here, by my mother's bed, meaning the hospital bed, the one holding my mother close in a white sheet and a blanket with the logo "Sheba Medical Center" gently enveloping her, as if she were just anyone.

The receptionist recognized me. After all, it hadn't been that long since my patient bled to death here.

"Yes, I'm family," I would yell at her if she asked. "Yes, that's my mother. Damn right she is. I'm her daughter. I didn't get to her in time yesterday. I was here, you saw yourself that I was here. I mean, I was on my way to my mother, but I made a U-turn to come here. You understand, my patient cut herself, I had to come. I thought maybe she could still be saved."

But the receptionist didn't ask who I was. There was no need. Jenny was already sitting by the bed and gazing at my mother in devotion. Lily and Amnon were there too. They had handled all the forms. Now, Mom was already conscious and would soon be transferred to Orthopedics. "A hip fracture," Lily updated me, and Mom confirmed the statement with a nod.

"It's too bad you came, Nogilee," she said. "There's no point. Lil is already here and it's a shame if you have to miss chemotherapy. There are really nice doctors here and all of us are already friends. See, there's a nice Arab doctor here named Sasha Dimitri, and a very sweet nurse, what's her name, Lil? Rotem? Lotem? Rotem or Lotem, in any case, we're already best friends, and they're taking great care of me here. Everyone knows I fell headlong when you didn't show up yesterday, a very serious fracture, a really bad break for a woman my age. But Lil is here, and Rotem."

"Headlong?" I asked. "You fell headlong?" as my eyes sought out partners who understood the mother tongue. But now everyone was talking in a language reserved for other matters, a language that Rotem or Lotem and Dr. Sasha Dimitri, who could not have been an Arab doctor anywhere but in the mother tongue, could understand as well. The mother tongue had instantly turned into one of those languages forgotten a long time ago; even Mom, Lily, and Amnon knew when it couldn't be spoken, and here I was, the only one to still mistakenly assume its accent. My eyes tried to seek out Mom's eyes, she who fell headlong, and she actually looked at me directly, without blinking, and said, in a linear language: "Yes, headlong, I fell headlong. I just felt myself flying all at once as if someone came along and whoosh, pushed me to the floor." She mimed a pushing gesture with her hands and added sounds of exhalation and immediately sighed "oh" in pain. "I did an actual summersault in the air when you didn't show up," she pressed on, and the patients lying in other beds raised their heads curiously to see where these ongoing reports were coming from, and she made a gesture miming collapse, summing up the event: "Wham bam, and that was it. After that I passed out."

No one else said a word. You could only miss those days when Lil and Iri and Amnoni and I, Nogilee, would start laughing immediately after such an outbreak of the mother tongue, accompanying it with impressions of our own, *whooosh* and *oh* and *wham bam* and *that was it*. But Mom had recognized the potential inherent in this moment. And she was unstoppable. It was her moment.

"Don't you have to go to the funeral?" Lily asked, adding, "Go. We're here, there's no point in us all sitting here. Your patient committed suicide yesterday, didn't she? Go. If you want to help, come spend the night here. We'll let Jenny rest a little."

I looked to see whether Mom had anything to say about it. Some mention of her pretty girl. But Mom asked them to call Rotem or Lotem quick; she needed some painkillers. "The strongest they have." Inside the white linens, she resembled a giant baby who had finally found a fleet of babysitters. On her forehead was a giant purple splotch, and there were more on the two arms that had just taken part in recreating the incident, and there was no need to say another word. The body had had its say.

"So, should I go?" I asked, but no one seemed to hear. "Should I go to chemotherapy?" I hoped to light a spark of solidarity within a tribe speaking the same dialect, but no one heard, since two orderlies were just passing by with a bed bearing a woman in a cast.

"I'm going," I added. "I might still make it to the funeral," and when one of the orderlies asked, "Are you okay?" and I said I was, Lily smiled at him and said, *She thought you were talking to her,* and then quietly explained to me, "He meant the woman in the cast."

I dragged my feet toward the parking lot, or else they dragged me. The lot was full of all kinds of vehicles. Old and new cars, small and large ones, belonging to people. To families. Silent tin cans waiting under a winter sun for their owners who were currently at the medical center. Some of them sick, some healthy, visiting the patients. Some of them might already have died from some disease, or from old age, or from life itself. At the end of the eastern row, the blue Opel was waiting for me. I, too, had a piece of tin of my own, waiting only for me. Any minute, I would sit down in it and close the door. A piece of tin would separate me from the world. If I was cold, I could turn on the heater. If I was hot, I'd turn on the a/c. If silence closed over me, I could turn on the radio and listen to songs or updates regarding the decision to deport the Sudanese and Eritrean refugees to Rwanda and Uganda. I wondered what Ibastam's status was. Whether he would be deported, whether he would have time to hear the news about the tall, disheveled girl who had offered him a cigarette. The one with the red lines under the sleeves of her pink sweatshirt. As he made his way back to Africa, would he know that the girl who had smoked with him on the street was no longer here either? There's no way of knowing what form the mind takes, but sometimes you can feel its weight.

***

Two years after Eli and I got married, a bacterium came along and devoured my father. We didn't even have time to say goodbye. A tiny, invisible bacterium devoured Prof. Glover. Mom said it was an outrage. That she didn't understand it. Clara was one thing; she was old. But Dad? Why him, of all people? What did he do wrong?

The entire Israel Studies department showed up in our living room for the *shiva*,[30] and it was strange to see the parents' house fill with academia. We had gotten used to Dad's academia always being outside the house. In Tel Aviv, or in other countries. But during the *shiva*, people sat in chairs around the rug, where the beast was, and also in the kitchen, where the bread and jam was, and talked, and consoled Mom, and us, and also looked around, at our house, meaning the parents' house, meaning Mom's house, which hypothetically was his as well, especially during the *shiva*. The mourners looked at the pipe collection, and at the books, and at Greek mythology in English. And all the objects, including the kettle, which was working overtime, stood still as if they had been ordered to behave themselves, not to reveal too much, as if the spell over the house was apparent only after all the people left. It was only Mom reminding us to plug in the kettle and unplug it when it buzzed, or toggled, or danced.

All of us, Lily and Iris and Amnon and I, sat and loaned ourselves to the consoling visitors, like a group presenting its life to outside observers. *Here we are.* A family. A family that had lost something, even though it was not exactly united before. And so we sat in the living room of the parents' house without knowing what the spaces between us were made of. We gave ourselves over to the consolations and nestled into them, and other than sadness over Dad, who had been suddenly devoured with no advance notice by an invisible bacterium, we found it pleasant to be consoled. We were missing something. Lily, Iris, and I placed our head on each other's shoulders, and sometimes Amnon joined in too. We felt how the situation gave us access to something we hadn't known we wanted or needed. I had a brother, and I had sisters.

Mom sat encased in mourning, and when the visitors approached and told her that Dad had been a true scholar and a man of broad horizons, she said she knew, and that it was an outrage that he was dead. That's what she said: *an outrage*, as if someone had done something to him on purpose, perpetrated some fraud, without taking into account all his academic achievements, with no consultation, with no accountability. Mom saw no point in this death. It seemed unnecessary to her.

---

30   The *shiva* is the week-long mourning period in Judaism for first-degree relatives.

After the guests left, we seemed to hear the house heave a sigh of relief and were left to our orphaned state. "Who is missing in our little house?" we were left to ask. The space Dad left behind was odd, like something we had yet to know. Very different than the space he left behind when he was in Tel Aviv, or in other countries. It was the first time he had left through no volition of his own, and for good.

"What's going to happen now?" I heard Iris say. I realized it was the same man, the father we were mourning. The father whose absence we were investigating.

When night came, Amnon stayed to sleep in the living room. "I asked them to set up the cabin for you so you three can sleep there. No one has been living there for a long time," Mom told Lily, Iris, and me.

"You did what?" I asked her.

"The cabin, Nogilee. I asked them to fix it up for the three of you. It's been empty for years now."

And Iris added, "Noga, no drama now."

I was already thirty-three years old. I was a clinical psychologist with a graduate degree and a thesis published in *Holocaust Studies*. Married to Dr. Sarid and living with him in an apartment where all the furniture matched. But in the parents' house, Iris could tell me, "Noga, no drama now." Just like that.

The three of us left the house.

"How did we leave Amnon on his own like that?" Lily said as I found myself shuffling after my twin sisters toward the cabin. The peg was still on the deck. For more than twenty years, temporary tenants had been hanging coats or bags or umbrellas on it, making casual, daily use of this practical object that Ronnie had once installed with skilled hands. Had he somehow planned to leave something to hang on to even after he was gone? Even back then, when he drilled into the wall of the deck to install the hooks protruding like tongues toward the window of the parents' house, had he known he was made of vanishing material?

Lily took the key Mom had given her out of her pocket and the door creaked a bit, opening into the dark space. Both of them hurried in, turning on the light while I stood on the deck. This peg. This drill. The rainbow once stretching in six colors until it got stuck over the parents' house. "What's going to happen now?" Iris's words echoed through me. *What's going to happen now?* "What could happen that hasn't already happened?" Ram's words echoed from the other direction.

The air was inconceivable. The cabin was inconceivable. Lily and Iris were inconceivable. They got settled quickly, unpacking bags, moving things, chatting. "Nogi, will you sleep on the living room couch?" They added a question mark at the end of the sentence like it was up for debate, as they entered the room where my husband and my beloved had once slept, together. The room whose window I ran to in order to invite my two adopted brothers to my ninth birthday party in familial fraternity, as if I had foreseen that one day, my twin sisters would get settled there. That Mom would send the three of us to sleep in it, God knows why. Whether she had some unknown reason, or else it was one of those things that just "happened to her." An unoccupied room was needed, and there, the cabin was free, you could sleep there. No need for any unnecessary drama. You could fall fast asleep in the place where once Eli could have been Ronnie, and Ronnie could have been Eli, and Lily could have also been Iris, and Iris Lily, and any essential difference between one person and another was not necessary, and time did not have to move in only one direction. Sometimes it could also move backward, why not, or revolve around itself.

"Do you have a cigarette?" Lily asked Iris, who replied that she had not smoked for a month now, and I sniffed the room. Maybe it contained a hint of something, evidence of the life my husband had once shared with my beloved.

"Nogi, do you have a cigarette?" Lily addressed me in the most routine manner.

"I have a pipe," I answered. "Want one?" And within a second, the three of us were choking with laughter. Cracking up. We couldn't breathe, as if we had already smoked a whole pack of pipes, and every time we tried to hush each other, after all, it wasn't right, Dad was dead, we grew even wilder. It was addictive, laughing as a trio. It was hysterical. It seemed like the mother tongue had never been so uninhibited. We couldn't calm down.

"So, do you have a pipe?" Lily managed to insert words into the outburst when, immediately, another wave surged within us. "Do you or don't you?"

I produced a pack of Marlboro Golds, and the three of us sat and smoked the pipes.

"There you are," I generously offered.

"Don't let Mom and Amnon see," Iris said, and we cracked up again until we felt we were about to pee our pants.

"Smoke makes her feel bad," we continued to indulge ourselves, holding our bellies, which had already started to ache.

Gas music makes her feel bad too.

"That's not..." Iris tried to say something and couldn't complete the sentence in the brays of laughter. "It's not..." she choked.

"Well, Iris, it's not what?" We were cackling with laughter too, and she tried to go on.

"It's not men..."

"What about men?" we asked together.

"It's not mentally healthy," she screeched in one breath and the three of us were swept away once and for all in an uncontrollable wave.

"Shush," we tried to regain control of ourselves. It wasn't right, Dad was dead. It went on like that for about half an hour. More. We teared up with laughter. Until the laughter stopped, and only the tears were left.

"Do you think she's thinking about Nadav now?" Lily asked, looking at Iris.

"And you? Are you thinking about him?" Iris answered Lily with a question, and it was obvious my invitation to take part in the conversation had expired.

"Do you remember how they told her to leave the room so he could die? Do you remember when they told her that kids can't die when their mother's in the room?"

I sat in the living room across from the ashtray. The laughter had ended along with the cigarettes, or the pipes, like all things ended in our family: all at once. My twin sisters yawned, suddenly tired of the conversation, or because of something else, and retired to Eli and Ronnie's room. My dead brother's name was still flickering on my twin sisters' lips as they fixed up Eli and Ronnie's room. My dead brother's name was still flickering on my twin sisters' lips as they arranged the covers in the bed where Ronnie and Eli once slept before Eli left the kibbutz. Before Ronnie moved to the bungalow. Before Ronnie disappeared, and Eli was found, and only my body connected the two, or was torn between them.

Through the window, I could see that Mom and Amnon had already turned out the light. Good night. The Glover family was going to sleep now, almost together. Almost all of us. Almost in the same house. Some of us were already missing. Nadav. Dad wasn't here anymore. He only wrote letters to me, that's what Amnon said. He didn't need to write to the rest of them. When they were kids, he was still home, or so they said. Before Nadav got sick. Still, he wrote only to me. And the joy I'd felt when I saw the koala bears from Australia, and the Eifel Tower from France, and the long-necked women from Thailand, and the Japanese woman winking, was real joy. I hadn't imagined it. It was really there.

All night, I couldn't sleep. The figures in the next room were too crowded, and there wasn't a single feeling that could be felt all the way through without another feeling conflicting with it. I realized that the years Dad had left behind him, the ones still ahead of me, would be different than the ones I knew.

When the *shiva* was over, I told Eli I wanted to have a baby. My happy husband became even happier. "You really do?" he beamed. All those who said happiness is fleeting didn't know Eli, and as time went by, I tried not to see it as a defect. Sometimes, I could see Eli as something in his own right, with no relation to the other chaos in life, and his joy seemed legitimate to me, even if I couldn't take part in it. And when he sang loudly in the shower or when he was loading up the dishwasher or cooking or taking care of other matters in our lovely apartment that I had already learned to operate, I was grateful that my problems didn't touch him. Eli was immune to me.

"It's not the same thing," he told me with every bout of nausea I experienced in the morning, and in the afternoon, and in the evening. "It's not the same, it's normal to feel nauseous during a pregnancy," he told me daily, "it's normal," and sometimes, he would add with a wink: "Under the circumstances."

He curiously tracked my changing body, and when one morning I found my navel sticking out, I told him I thought I was about to faint, that this pregnancy was too large for me to handle. He said the pregnancy really was large; it was larger than life.

"It's not the same," I recited to myself when I felt the world assaulting me with the smell of perfume, or coffee, or cooking. "It's not the same," a voice emerged from within me when my full chest woke me up in the morning like an alarm clock. "Good morning," I tried to greet my new body, which had awakened to the world a few minutes before I did. "Good morning," I also tried to greet myself, my pale face reflecting in the window, the rounding shadow I cast on the bathroom tiles, already sending out extensions to unknown quarters, trailing under the sink, pushing its way into the notch between the windowpane and the wall like a thief trying to break out of the house. *It's not the same*, I still had time to mumble a moment before I threw up into the toilet bowl I shared with Eli, expelling roar-like sounds. What was the deal with these pregnancies, always resembling wild animals? Why couldn't you just give birth like a human being? And when I made it safely to my fourth month of pregnancy, I started to realize there might actually be all kinds of ways to lead things out of the body.

The baby born to us after nine months was covered with golden down. She was so miraculous, as if heaven had sent us a soft package enveloped in radiant light. Ram had been wrong. Sometimes, something that had never happened before does happen in life. Mom was speechless when I told her I had decided to name my baby Julie even though she had been born in August.

"She's crying because she's happy," Eli explained to me.

15.

For three whole months, Mom was hospitalized in the Orthopedic Rehab unit of Beit Rivka Geriatric Medical Center. She made friends with the medical staff, gave herself over to physiotherapy, and once, they even took her to the gym, just to check whether it was clean. "It's clean," she reported to Lily later, while I, too, was sitting in a yellow plastic chair in the unit.

Most of all, she was pleased with the food. Every morning, in addition to the salad, she ate "a whole half egg," cottage cheese, and bread with no jam. For lunch, she had "delicious food," and this was the case in the evening, too. Other than the fish and her roommate, who was "primitive," nothing at Beit Rivka was "ew." It was just too bad she was in such pain, truly hellish, and that it would take some time before she could walk. It was a really bad break, to fall headlong in the shower. How silly it was, just unbelievably silly. She said that when she was here, she felt confident. Over here, there was no such thing as leaving her alone, not even for a second.

Outside, signs of spring had begun, and a rash in the shape of half an apple appeared on my palms again, like it used to, after I had already thought I was rid of it. Spring was taunting and invasive. The ravishing blooms outside clashed with the rash blooming out from inside me and my skin became a bustling arena of collisions, with no possibility of leading the blooming in any direction, in or out.

How had she fallen exactly when I wasn't there? What was she thinking? And what was I thinking when I made that unnecessary U-turn on the road? Had I really wanted to get to Adva, or had I merely turned my blue Opel in the opposite direction from my mother? What was I thinking as I was driving on the road to the kibbutz that advanced like a saga I had learned to recite by heart, but whose meaning I had never truly figured out? What was I thinking when

I turned around at that intersection, heading for the unit, midway between Tel Aviv and the kibbutz, channeling my concern toward my adolescent patient, the one whom it had been easy for me to love, the one whose poems I waited for to wrap up the suffering in imagery and metaphors? The one who wanted to stay over and sleep on the couch in my clinic. That was what she wanted, simply to sleep over. I had driven from her to the kibbutz, to my mother, and turned back toward her in the middle of the road, until I hadn't arrived anywhere. Until the two of them ultimately brought me to the same unit, a little too late.

***

When I came into the house, I heard Eli telling me something, but I couldn't understand what it was, and what language he was speaking in. "Who was the one in Greek mythology who felt compassion for mortals?" I asked him.

"What?"

"Come on, I can't believe I can't come up with his name. The one who stole fire from the gods to bring it to mortals, in Greek mythology."

"In the Greek mythology book that you read in English?" Eli was amused, and once again, it was clear how his mood was untouched by mine. As if the house we lived in was actually two houses, on two different continents, with different weather.

"Prometheus," I remembered, bummed to discover that his questions about English had helped me remember.

"You feel like giving me a hand?" he asked as he was unpacking the bags of groceries he had just purchased, and I stood next to him, opened the bag with dairy products, and stared vacantly at it.

As punishment, Prometheus was tied to a cliff in the Caucasus Mountains, and every day, a vulture came to the cliff to peck at his liver. Zeus offered Prometheus his freedom so long as he revealed to Zeus which of his sons would kill him and usurp him. But the truth, the truth is like fire. You always need to find the right distance. You can't actually touch it.

"Is your engine stalled? What's up with you?" Eli asked me, and when I didn't answer, he added, "It'll go away soon, you'll see. Soon spring will be over, and your rash will go away. Everything passes in this world. Can you drive Tomer to practice this evening?"

***

In April, Beit Rivka commemorated Holocaust Remembrance Day.

"There's no point in you coming," Lily told me over the phone. "I'll be there."

"I'm coming," I told her.

"Mom said she couldn't bring too many people."

"I'm coming," I informed her.

"What's up, Noga? All of a sudden, it's that important to you not to miss Holocaust Remembrance Day?"

By the time I arrived, the ceremony had already begun. Most of the people in the audience, including Mom, were sitting in wheelchairs, some were in regular chairs, and others were standing. Lily was on Mom's right, Jenny on her left, and in order not to disrupt the ceremony, I stood in the back, at the end of the row. I waved to Mom to show her I had arrived, and Jenny nodded at me to indicate she had seen me and brought her finger to her lips, signaling me to keep quiet. That's what Jenny did: shushed me with her finger on her lips, so that I wouldn't interrupt. A slide was projected on the wall with the caption, "We will remember and never forget!" while Miri the social worker read out: "From year to year, there are fewer survivors still alive, firebrands spared by the flames who headed here, to persevere after the hell they've been through. Firebrands spared by the flames, left behind to tell the stories of the ones whose voices will no longer be heard. All the ones devoured in the maw of the Nazi monster. We will remember and never forget the killing pits, the crematoriums, the gas chambers, the millions of men, women, and children turned into ashes, murdered by the Nazis, may their names be obliterated, and their collaborators, solely for the sin of being Jewish."

I scanned the silently sitting audience. Mom and Lily sat erect, and Jenny, too, was attentive, even though she didn't speak Hebrew.

Miri went on to say that during the last few weeks, she had gotten the chance to listen to the unbelievable story of Ruthie Glover, née Posner, who had been smuggled from the notorious Belzec camp when she was seven years old and concealed in the home of the virtuous Julia Pepiak, Righteous Among the

Nations.[31] With exceptional resourcefulness and with indescribable physical and mental resilience, Ruthie managed to survive the conditions of being hidden away in Julia's house, the months of hunger and terror in the wheat fields and other hiding spots in the burning town. After the war, Ruthie made Aliyah, created an exceptional family, and today she was here with her daughter Lily.

Everyone's eyes turned to Mom, Lily, and Jenny, who were nobly silent.

The ceremony ended. A young singer wearing a blue dress, the granddaughter of one of the residents rehabilitating at Beit Rivka, climbed up to the stage. "*Each of us has a name,*" she sang. "*Each of us has a name, given by God, and given by our parents.*" The audience hummed along quietly. *Each of us has a name, given by our sins and given by our longing.*[32]

On the drive back home, I called Joy. For a while now, we had been meaning to reconnect, but somehow, it didn't work out, although our clinics were just a short distance away from each other.

"It was awful," I shattered into the cell phone when I heard her "Hello," as if we talked every day. As if no time had passed since we studied together in the clinical course, since we were "Joy and Nogloom," and we could just get back to updating each other on current affairs.

"What was awful?" she asked, and when I started to tell her, we both started laughing. Time had indeed gone by, but as we had already learned, it never went by equally for everything. And my mother, as Joy claimed, was after all "pretty eternal."

"Since when does my mother have an exceptional family?" I asked Joy. Maybe she could enlighten me on the matter. And after a brief silence, she replied, "It's a little like your mother's story was appropriated from you."

"Come to my clinic tomorrow," I suggested. We'd have a session.

---

31   "Righteous Among the Nations" is an honorific title used by the State of Israel to describe non-Jews who risked their lives during the Holocaust to save Jews from extermination by the Nazis for altruistic reasons.

32   From "Each of Us Has a Name," by Zelda, translated by Marcia Lee Folk. From *The Spectacular Difference*, Hebrew Union College, Cincinnati, 2004.

***

I was sitting alone in my own clinic, waiting for Joy. The windows were open and spring air wafted in from the street, but I had a hard time breathing it. As if it wasn't meant for me. I had never had a chance to think about who was responsible for air distribution. Who made sure everyone got an equal portion, who decided who needed more and who less. Who made sure that no air tycoon would suddenly arrive on the scene to take over the entire inventory, that no one was illegally trading in air or clipping some coupon.

"It's as if your mother's story has been appropriated from you," she said again, the moment she came through the door. "What does your mother's story mean to you?" That was how she chose to phrase the questions: what it meant "to me."

So, what did my mother's story mean to me? What was that faux-linear part of her, which provided meaning, or should have?

"Even though it sounds like a cliché, I'm going to say it anyway," I told Joy. "That you can take my mother out of the pit, but you can't take the pit out of my mother."

"So, your mother walks around with a pit?"

"I swear to God. And you know what the biggest problem with that pit is? That it's not even empty. It's full of my mother. It's a clogged-up pit."

"What does that mean?"

"I don't know. I feel like talking nonsense. I feel like talking in an incomprehensible language. I feel like saying my mother is the only one who doesn't fall into that pit since she's already inside it, but anything I say will sound like an image or a metaphor, right? Either I'm inarticulate, or I'm being all literary."

"When did she get out of the pit?" I felt that she was trying to help me talk in human language, that she too was trying to be linear. "I mean, when did she officially come out of it?" she asked, and I thought back to the conversations I used to have with Hani. Hani could also be linear. I'd liked it when she'd ask "when." *When did things happen? When did things start to go wrong?* After all, there was also that sort of time, a time that moved forward. A time where one thing led to another.

I wanted to accept the invitation. One day in winter, at the height of winter, snowflakes fell in Belzec. All the neighbors in Julia's street came out of their houses, meaning all the neighbors who were still alive. The ones who had been smart enough not to go near the camp just to find out what was going on there. The ones who had been bright enough not to stick their nose where it didn't belong. They went out even though it was freezing cold, in order to witness the event.

"But snow isn't unusual in Poland."

"Right, but this was different snow. It was black snow. Have you ever seen black snow?"

All the neighbors who barely left their houses in the winter emerged from their dens. Everyone's eyes were small and suspicious, as if the era dictated their features. The forehead was creased. The eyebrows barely crowded in under it, and the pale cheeks drooped down toward clenched lips. Some of the neighbors came out in pairs, leaning on each other. Maybe they were grateful that both of them were still alive in the same house. Some of the houses on the street were already abandoned and the remaining neighbors measured each other with alien gazes and darting eyes. All of them looked up to the sky, which was dropping black snow. Have you ever seen anything like black snow? Black snow falling from a black sky? Apparently, during the months when everyone had been shut up in their homes, the world had changed its laws and its colors, and now it was dropping black snow on Belzec. Within seconds, everyone began covering their nose with the flap of their coat, because the smell was unbearably weighty. Yes, that's a thing, a weighty smell.

"It's not snow," one of the neighboring women called out.

"It's not snow," the others joined in.

It wasn't snow. The camp was being burned down. Belzec was being burned down.

The neighbors stood under the black flakes piling on their heads, at their feet, upon hands reaching forward, on the roofs of the low houses, on the yards of the people who had abandoned their homes, or whose homes had been taken from them, on the road separating their street from the next one, on their embarrassed faces: *What has become of the sky? What has become of us?*

But they couldn't keep standing outside. Within seconds, the smell ran people off, back to their homes, and even there, the closed windows could not protect them from it. Clouds of smoke and soot rose over the camp, and over the street, and the neighborhood, and the town, and the smell clung to the skin as if it was one of its cells. The Germans needed to get rid of the camp lickety-split, they didn't have time, they needed to obliterate the evidence. And there was no longer anywhere to hide the bodies, so many bodies: 600,000 Jews murdered in Belzec, and several tens of thousands more Poles and Ukrainians. They burned and burned, nonstop, both the structures and the bodies, and it felt as if even if the neighbors in Belzec had managed to lock their doors upon the Jews jumping in horror from the train, they could not seal their houses off from the smell of their bodies. And from the smoke. And the ash. Since what didn't come in through the door came in later through the window. The neighbors in Belzec, the ones who were still alive, got into their beds and spread the covers over themselves, and lay there, waiting for the smell to pass.

"So, Julia came to get your mother out of the pit? Did she call someone? Did someone help her? It's not like she could move all that wood on her own."

"Hold on, be patient. That's not how it happened. It wasn't that simple."

"What do you mean?"

"It wasn't over that fast."

"Fast, huh? Not so fast."

Mom still couldn't be brought out. Everything was still extremely danger-ous, and the Germans were still there. The war was still far from over. That day, the German officers hung around in Julia's house constantly. They knew they were on their way out and they wanted to enjoy the feeling of a warm, welcoming home for a while longer. One last tribute. One last cozy treat before continuing on to Auschwitz. And to Treblinka. And to Sobibor.

"So, what did Julia do?"

What a woman in wartime does. Anything they asked her to do. It wasn't the right moment to break down, then, of all times, when they were about to leave. She did everything they asked her to do. Suddenly, though, in the middle of one of those smoky days, when the Germans were sitting in her kitchen, a groan was heard from the direction of Mom's pit. A weak one, but still a groan. Mom couldn't hold back. She felt that she was suffocating. Her pit had filled up with smoke and she couldn't breathe. She also didn't know what that smell was, the one that didn't resemble anything she knew. She felt that she was going up in flames, and that soon, in just a second, the entire stack of wood above her would go up in flames along with her, and she had nowhere to go.

"Wo?" they asked Julia. *Where? Just tell us, nicely and politely, where you're hiding her, and we won't hurt you. Germans' honor.*

Julia grew pale. Not just because she was afraid the Germans would find Mom. She grew pale because she understood that Mom was suffocating. She already knew Mom and knew that Mom never let a word out. She also knew her vocal cords had atrophied since it had been such a long time since Mom last talked. Mom only whispered. If a groan had come from the pit, Mom must be suffocating.

"Did your skin turn pale?" they asked her. "And what's with this hair standing on end?" They passed a hand along Julia's skin, from her cheek, to her chin, to her neck, down her chest. "It unbecoming to a woman to have her hair stand on end like that. It's unappealing. You have no reason to be anxious. Just tell us, nice and quiet, where you're hiding her and it will all end well. Why ruin a relationship like that?"

Julia stood petrified. She tried the same tactic that had worked the previous times. "A Jew is not a pin." She tried to imbue her voice with the same confidence that had come to her aid as she looked at the painting of the Virgin Mary carrying the baby Jesus in her arms.

"A pretty painting," one of them told her. "You love that painting, right?" He looked at her, and at Mary, and at the baby in the painting. "So, where's your baby?"

And Julia tried to go on. "A Jew is not…"

"That's very true," he interrupted her. "A Jew is not a pin. So, if you're hiding some little Jewess here, we're going to find her sooner or later."

He began to roam through the house, moving furniture, opening cabinet doors, turning over the duvets in the kitchen bed, where Julia had hidden Mom when she had just arrived, as if he was reading her mind, and Julia tried to maintain her restraint although she knew her embryo was suffocating in the pit, when suddenly, an enormous explosion sounded from the direction of the camp. A thundering coming to destroy the world. In those days, deliveries of Jews were no longer being brought to the camp, and on the tracks stood two train cars full of ammunition. Later, Julia found out that one of the partisans fighting in the area had tossed a bomb at the train cars and all the ammunition stored there went up in terrifying flames, a chariot of fire ascending swiftly to the sky, straight from hell. Everyone covered their ears with their hands. The neighbors on the street, the ones still alive, burrowed deeper under their covers. Julia and the two Germans stood there for a moment, rooted to their spots, when one of them told the other, "*Schnell*—quick, we have to go back to camp."

"We'll be back," they promised her. "Don't worry, we'll be back."

She managed to return the smile to her face and tell them her house was always open to them. "*Heil Hitler*," she saluted them, and the moment she saw their figures walking off, she did not wait that time. She hurried to Mom's pit.

"I'm burning up, Julia, get me out of here, I'm burning alive, with all the wood."

"You're not burning up," she tried to soothe her.

"Julia, get me out of here, I'm going to die here anyway," Mom begged. "I can't be here anymore."

And Julia explained to her that if she took her out, they would both die. The whole street would die. All the people in Belzec, the ones still left, would all die. She could not come out. Even if Julia wanted to, she could not do it on her own. They had to wait until it would be okay to get help from more people. Just a little more patience.

But Mom felt she couldn't stand it anymore. She started to cry. After all those months in the pit, almost without making a sound, only whispering, only when it was allowed, Mom broke down and started to cry. After all, the wood covering her was meant to be burned, and if the camp was burning so close, how would it not burn her along with the wood?

"If you cry, they'll hear you," Julia told her. "And even if they don't know where the crying is coming from, they'll kill me, and then they won't find you. Ever. We're in this together, the two of us. I can't live without you, and you can't live without me, so hold on. And don't cry. Never cry. You can't cry."

Mom grew silent. And ever since, she hasn't cried. She never cried again in her life. Not when Nadav died. And not when Dad left to work with his research assistant. Never again. Only when Julie was born. Only then.

Julia sat down on the stool and read from the New Testament. "*Blessed be the God and Father of our Lord Jesus Christ, which according to his abundant mercy hath begotten us again unto a lively hope by the resurrection of Jesus Christ from the dead.*"[33]

---

33   1 Peter 1: 3

"What's that smell?" Mom asked.

"It's the smell of fire."

"No, there's another smell inside it. What's that stench? Is it people burning? Is it humans?"

"Don't worry," Julia soothed her. "These people who are burning, they're already dead. It's only their bodies that are burning now."

Joy sat there as if turned to stone. I had never seen her like that.

"This story is supernatural," she said. "It can't be easy getting mad at your mother, after everything she's been through. And that Julia, she's mythological."

***

The rehabilitation period in Beit Rivka was the longest that the parents' house had been left alone. Once a week, Jenny came to dust and water the plants, and on other days, there was something troubling about the thought of the house waiting with its lights out and the hum of its refrigerator in the middle of the old people's neighborhood. Both of us, Eli and I, took the day off in order to check Mom out of Beit Rivka, but when I entered the unit around noon, all sweaty as the rehabbers gazed on, sitting around low tables and eating schnitzel and mashed potatoes, the nurse on duty looked at me in puzzlement.

"You weren't informed? She was released an hour ago."

"What?" I asked, and it wasn't clear if her look was pitying or accusatory, and if there had been someone here before me who was early (who?) or whether I was the one who was late. We drove to the kibbutz, accompanied by the smell of mashed potatoes the whole way.

"Your mother's something else," Eli said.

"She's something else all right," I gritted out after him. But what kind of something?

When we arrived, the parents' door opened straight into the house's private parts, with nothing to separate or mediate, and we instantly found ourselves in the living room, on the rug, with both the house and Mom already in progress. Mom sat in a wheelchair. Her eyes were staring out into space and she seemed to be succumbing to a new understanding of the situation, examining whether the house was still the same house, although she, the homeowner, was no longer the same. Jenny was walking through the rooms, emptying bags,

opening and closing drawers, exhibiting full mastery of all the mysteries of
the house, which, in her hands, looked regular and simple to operate like any
old house. It was I who was the guest in my parents' house. I who was not up
to date. Who had taken a day off in vain, and also pushed my husband down
the slippery slope of inefficiency.

"How did you get here?" I confronted Jenny and was told what a shame it
was that we had only arrived now, *such a pity*, Lily had just now left.

"Will you have some coffee?" Jenny kindly offered the two embarrassed
guests, and I replied, *No thank you*, while Eli said he would actually gladly have
a cup, and Mom said, "Oh, it hurts so much," and Jenny confirmed that she
was indeed suffering terribly, and how silly it was of my mother to let her leave
early on Christmas, *such a pity* that she didn't let Jenny stay although Jenny had
asked to wait with her until I arrived, just to be on the safe side.

"But she's stubborn, your mother, she decided she could get by on her own
and shower by herself. If she hadn't insisted, all this wouldn't have happened."
She repeated the words *such a pity* a few more times while Mom continued
to stare into the space of the house as if she saw things there that we couldn't
see, things that were beyond things and that maybe could only be discerned
from the wheelchair. The house sounds continued to demarcate all the routine
activities, the hum of the refrigerator, the ticking of the clock, and Jenny was
already pouring Eli coffee after the kettle toggled and danced when I suddenly
realized what she had just said.

"What?" I turned to her as she was in mid-pour. "What did you just say?" I
wanted to make sure I had heard correctly, but Jenny had already moved on to
a different topic. She took a chocolate cake that Becky from the Senior Citizen
Committee had baked out of the fridge, *they take such good care of Mom here
in the kibbutz, there's nothing like growing old on the kibbutz*, and I headed for
the living room and stationed myself across from Mom.

"You told Jenny to take off early on Christmas?"

She looked back at me from the depths of the wheel chair.

"*What?*" she asked me back in English, and I understood that that was it,
we'd all switched to speaking English now.

"What do you mean, '*what*'?" I asked her. "What don't you understand?"
and I repeated the question, emphasizing every syllable, "You told Jen-ny to
take off ear-ly on Christ-mas? You actually did that? And all these months I've

been walking around with the feeling that you fell because of me? Jenny offered to stay and you told her to go?"

But she didn't answer. All at once, she was overcome with fatigue, her eyelids drooped and she fell asleep in the chair.

"Let her be," Eli tried to calm me down, but I put my hand on her shoulder and started to shake her.

"I want an answer, Mom. Answer me. This is no time to fall asleep. You told Jenny to take off early on Christmas? That actually happened?"

She looked at me, frightened. Jenny walked around the house, flustered, then approached the chair in order to manually lower the brake, so that Mom or the chair wouldn't suddenly zoom off somewhere.

I started to scream, "You told Jenny to take off early on Christmas?" and just to make sure, and especially in order to exert version control, I phrased the question in English as well, in Jenny's presence, and we all waited for a response from Mom, who suddenly opened her eyes, looking at the house as if she were seeing it for the first time.

"Enough," Jenny said. "We had a long day, we should rest now," but I was already on auto-pilot. I was unstoppable.

"What exactly did you do?" I screamed at her. "Was that the plan? To ruin my life? To fall when I wasn't here?"

Eli and Jenny rushed to close the windows, so the neighbors wouldn't hear, but that didn't bother me.

"No one in this neighborhood has been able to hear anything for a while, anyway. Everyone here is old or already dead, and the ones who haven't died yet will probably die soon, right?" I screamed, looking at my mother. "Right?" I added that the question was simply how they were going to die, and how much damage they would cause in the meantime, and since when do you shower on your own when you're two-hundred years old?

"Shush," Jenny signaled me with her finger on her lips, and this time, I turned to her.

"And what exactly were you thinking? That just because my mother tells you to go, you can actually leave? What did you think was going to happen?" I realized there might have been a collaboration of sorts here, and Jenny said, *Such a pity*, and my mother stared into space and said, "My Nogilee, my pretty girl, stop it, that's enough, what's done is done, do you want some coffee?" and suddenly, everything got quiet. She had just offered me coffee, no bread and jam, and once again called me Nogilee, pretty girl, after she had disappeared from Beit Rivka an hour before I got there, and it felt as if all the rules were obliterated, no way of knowing what to expect now, anything could happen now, and "what's done is done," the mother tongue was obliterated and had begun betraying even its own rules, and I told Eli, "Right, enough really is enough, let's go. There's nothing for us here, let's go away. Forever. Jenny can go too, and my mother can shower on her own if she wants."

When I slammed the door after me I felt her eyes tracking me and from the depths of her wheelchair I heard her ask, "You'll come back, Nogilee, won't you?"

16.

The black snow also fell on the death camp, covering everyone in snow and soot. The bodies of the Jews, and the Ukrainian laborers, and the German officers. No one was immune to the smell, including *Herr Kommandant*, who was growing truly irritated, even though he was usually known as a calculated type, and in certain circumstances, even courteous. When he beat Grandma with a whip, it was because it was the right thing to do, not because he "flew off the handle," as the saying sometimes goes. But when the smell began to spread through the camp, it was unforgivable, and he doubled the number of lashes. It felt like it didn't matter how efficiently the gas chambers operated, and how efficiently the trains ran, and how eloquently the speech was recited, again and again, explaining to the Jews that they were going to shower and later would be sent to work, three times a day that speech was recited, *Ihr geht jetzt baden, nachher werdet ihr zur Arbeit geschickt!* and three times a day it managed to ignite a spark of hope in the frightened eyes that had stopped resisting, even when they were forced to run naked and shaved through the tunnel, *schnel, schnel*, fast, faster, and everything ran smoothly and as planned, and despite all the precision and the perfect execution, the smell could not be controlled. Something in Belzec had managed to veer out of control. Those Jews, even after they died, they polluted the environment, invading the cells and sucking out all the air. That's what they did: they sucked out all the air.

Herr Kommandant entered his house especially agitated and screamed at Grandma. He told her he already knew where her daughter was hiding anyway; he was just checking whether she was willing to tell him herself. If she was loyal. If she was not willing, no problem. He would go to bring her daughter back to the camp himself and would slaughter her in front of her eyes. She swore to him that she didn't know, that she missed her daughter too, that she was dying to see her, and begged him to stop whipping her, until she collapsed on the floor and fainted. But he woke her up. No fainting now; no time for that. He had an idea. Under the black sky, amongst the mists of smoke and stench, a helpful idea popped into the mind of *Herr Kommandant*. In Belzec, all the numbers were always accurate. Precisely so. *Punkt!* No deviations in either direction. If a girl had disappeared, another must be produced in her place. He tore Grandma's clothes off and did exactly what had to be done to her bleeding body. And she didn't say a word.

"That's it!" he said. "Now I truly hope, for your sake, that your body doesn't cause any problems. That we've fixed this little mishap."

The next time Grandma fainted, it wasn't because of the whip. She was weak and nauseous. *Herr Kommandant* took care of her and brought her food and didn't beat her anymore.

***

There was no point in asking Mom why she had told Jenny to leave early on Christmas and went to shower on her own when she knew I would be delayed. Just like there was no point asking her many other things. "Why" was not something you could ask Mom. Because she did all the strange things she did in the mother tongue, with rules that were known only to her. Why didn't she understand that a cigarette was not a pipe and a cat wasn't a dog and that there's a difference between psychotherapy and chemotherapy and that you don't walk around the kibbutz in a see-through nightgown even if it was suddenly very urgent to look for Varda from the Senior Citizen Committee, and it wouldn't be right to call her since it was already late at night? And why, for the love of God, why and how and where did she make Ronnie disappear to? And where had she hidden his other letters? The ones that, no matter how much I begged, she still found the strength to resist telling me about? What reason in the world could possibly explain an 'abracadabra' like that, undoubtedly carried out in a powerful, decisive move?

But this time, I felt that more than ever, she had done it to me. To me personally. Not to Lil or Iri or Amnoni. To her Nogilee, her pretty girl, the one who received postcards with clearly printed handwriting from Dad. The girl whom she would lie next to on the rug when she had a low fever, praying she wouldn't die. And when she couldn't find her for a week, she ran around hysterically through the paths of the kibbutz, yelling: *Who's seen Nogi? Maybe someone's seen Nogi? She's disappeared.* And when she found me dragging my feet and hungry after a week without food in Ronnie's bungalow, she was so happy to see me alive that she didn't care about anything else. Only that I live. That was all she demanded from me. "Nogilee, you're back," she'd whisper, as if I had been born anew every time. And when I didn't talk to her for more than two years after soaking my little tadpole into her rug, after sacrificing it, an offering to the beast lurking there on the rug, she waited patiently. Until I got my speech back. And when Julie was born, she cried. "With happiness," as Eli knew to explain to me. She did it to me, me, as if she guessed the U-turn I would make on the road, heading for someone else who needed me, a patient, the one who had already died in the ICU anyway, simply because she didn't want to live. Some people are like that; they don't want to live. Don't understand what a privilege it is. But others actually do. They cling to life and only need someone to be there with them. Maybe there's a sign like that, in the mother tongue, which points out the right way. The right direction on the road. And anyone who doesn't read the signs correctly needs to relearn the language. And Jenny, with all due respect, was after all just a foreign laborer. A paid laborer. So what if she had been willing to stay?

I hoped that at least Lily or Iris or even Amnon would understand what had happened. I hoped we could talk about it. In the mother tongue or in the usual language. I hoped we could come to visit Mom more frequently together, and not just individually. That we could say, "That was something, when Mom fell headlong, huh? How she decided to tell Jenny to leave early on Christmas until, wham bam, she collapsed in the shower? How Mom decided to sympathize with all those people who died in the showers?" I hoped we could talk in a real language, with grammatical rules and sentences that start and end with words that appear in the dictionary. That they could say to me, *Why didn't you come? Why did you run away from home when she always worried about you so much? When she wrote your school papers for you? And slept next to you on the rug?* And that I could ask Lily what the deal was with her behavior on Holocaust Remembrance Day. *Did you really think it was all my fault?* And I could remind Iris she had barely been in Israel all those years since Mom was widowed, and earlier, too. And I could ask the three of them, *Where were you?*

Where have you been all these years, when I was trapped all alone in the jaws of the beast from the rug? What did you think when Mom told you about the son she adopted, who made friends with Nogilee, and what did you think when he suddenly disappeared? And when I was hospitalized?

But Mom's latest trick left me utterly vulnerable. In fact, it left us all vulnerable, and there was no language to hide behind. Collapsing in the shower shattered our one mother into four mothers and the portion I got was the portion given to the one who was on her way there when it happened but turned around mid-way. Collapsing in the shower shattered Mom to pieces until there was no longer "our mother," and the mother tongue, too, was shattered, and instead of uniting us it began clinging to the walls of our cells like the remains of a food item that was indigestible.

"Is he a medicinal doctor?" she asked me about Dr. Weishot when I coordinated a follow-up visit for her at the hospital. "Did you bring avocada?" she asked when I came in with the bag and resignedly put its contents away in her refrigerator. "Does it have a lot of monitor value?" she asked, turning 'monetary' into one more gauge familiar to her from the medical preoccupations that had begun to take over her day: blood pressure monitor, blood sugar monitor, monitor value. And when she called me 'Lil,' I wondered if she was amusing herself with some private game that would never end, because there were no winners. When the mother tongue was cracked and I couldn't speak it with my brother and sisters anymore after "our mother" shattered into pieces that consisted of unknown children's mother parts, when the remains of the mother tongue clung to blood vessels and the tubes of the intestines and the esophagus, I felt them choking me every day, and life became a sticky, viscous goo.

Mom fell in the shower when I wasn't there, in a house smelling of mothballs and pajamas, with a door I loved to slam so many times, but who's counting. She shattered in the shower when I U-turned in the opposite direction, away from the house that had trapped me forever under its ruins, as if you could escape from a predetermined future. It's true, they weren't there either. No one was there. Other than Jenny who had been sent away early for Christmas. But she had been waiting for me. For her little girl who never wanted to be there. For her little girl who always chose to escape of her own free will, but out of all the places in the world, drowned her tadpole there and only there. Forever. In a house whose walls hummed in the middle of the old-people neighborhood, and the rug with the beast, and the kettle that danced, and the shelf with Greek mythology in English, and the shower tiles that had survived the headlong fall; all those would cling to her forever, even after her mother was no longer there. From that day on, the parents' house waited for me in the wheelchair, and in the bottles of painkillers, and in sighs of "ow" and in "such a pity" and "How silly it was." And worst of all: Mom stopped drinking coffee with bread and jam.

***

Time held me in its jaws. It was impossible to be inside it or outside of it. Mom and her chair settled in the middle of the house, and she chose to carry out all activity solely from there, until it became unclear whether it was a sort of prosthesis-chair, or, contrarily, whether she herself was part of the item of furniture, its backrest, perhaps. She would fall asleep in it at night and during the day as well. When she woke up, she resumed from wherever she had been before, as if sleep and wakefulness were not two different states but one long, ongoing continuum. In the morning, in her chair, she would eat a whole half egg with cottage cheese and a wonderful tomato, and sometimes she had the same thing for lunch, depending on when she took a break from sleep. When she felt she was "dirtful," Jenny rolled the chair to the shower, with Mom riding it, and it was obvious that the disability that had descended upon her had equipped her with new powers as she mapped the direction of the chair's progress with her hand as if moving armies: "Over there. No! No! Over there. Great, and now a little to the right, a little more to the right, and a little more, thaaat's it! Ex-ac-tly right. And now a bit to the left."

My visits became more frequent and more troubling. "How are you doing?" I asked the moment I came in, as if addressing just anyone, with a strained, ceremonial tone just before my body was assimilated into the living room and sucked into the house's private parts, and she would reply, "Everything's fine. No complaints. Other than the pain. And age. And that silly fall, headlong like that in the shower, when you weren't here. How silly. Listen to me, Nogi, sweetie, don't ever get old, it's not worth it. How does that saying go? It is not good that a man should be old. And if you are old, remember not to fall. And if you do fall, I won't be alive to see it anyway."

And so she went on and on and there was no point in answering. There was no point asking whether that was what she wished for me, that I die young. Because it really was obvious that that wasn't what she meant. God forbid, anything but that. "Not even as a joke." It was clear that as far as she was concerned, not being old didn't mean dying young. And there was no point asking what precisely her intention had been when she set Jenny free on Christmas. There was no point not only because what had been done could not be undone, but also because, regardless of all that, I really had been delayed. And I really had made a U-turn on the road while she was waiting for me. My Opel really had turned its back on the parents' house. And we all knew that. And so, I held back. I held back from answering. This was new, holding back. It was only after I held back that I realized it was new.

Gradually, it seemed as if I was beginning to understand something: my mother's collapse hadn't been random. Gradually, I began to find meaning. In the days to come, I increased my efforts at holding back. During fights with Eli. On the road. And most of all, in the way I talked to her. Sometimes, for brief moments, for split seconds, it seemed to me that I understood the mother tongue, even if I couldn't speak it. And there was that one day, just a day in the middle of the week, when I returned home in the blue Opel, turned on the radio, and settled into the driver's seat. The passing views, bringing me closer to the home I had established with Eli, reflected in the car's windshield, which, along with them, returned my holding-back figure to me.

In the next visits, I noticed that I could go see Mom willingly, "of my own free will," even if I didn't feel like it, and I never felt like it.

"Are you coming with me?" I asked Eli. "She's a little bit your mother too," I taunted him as if taking a prisoner, and when he replied that he was buried in work, I told him I'd go alone. I would recite the road to the kibbutz to myself, my Opel knew it by heart, but in the meantime, an internal road had been paved in the kibbutz, which led me straight to the old people's neighborhood. "Like a shortcut." I was frightened to think that any day now, I, too, would fit in here, next to Clara's house, may she rest in peace, and Shmul and Hilda's, may they rest in peace, and Kalman's, may he rest in peace. And that in fact, this was where I was born and raised, in the old people's neighborhood. And the old woman I would become was already waiting for me at the end of the road, had been lurking in wait for me here for quite a while. Even before I was born. She was inside me, so deep she couldn't even be channeled to the rug. And now I heard her steps fumbling slowly, advancing toward my doorstep. "Are you here, Noga? Is it you?" Now I saw her bent, wrinkled, gnarled figure, forging a path through my days. Now I felt the touch of her gripping, shaky hands. Now I greeted her.

And here was the parents' house, standing in the midst of the neighborhood, like an axiom. And once again, the familiar door, separating it from the world, opening directly into the house's private parts. And once again, "How are you doing" and once again, "Everything's fine, other than age. It is not good that a man should be old." The mother tongue had begun to grow branches that split up in new directions and arranged themselves around a different area every time. So, for example, a new topic appeared one day: makeup and perfume, and Mom said that on my birthday, she would buy me rouge. She had noticed I was pale, that I had been a bit tired lately, and she would wait for my birthday to buy me rouge to make me happy. "Don't be sad, Nogilee, it's not mentally healthy." It was true that there was still some time before my birthday, but it would be an excellent opportunity to cheer me up with rouge, which would return some color to my face. And she was sending Tomer some *eau de cologne* right now, even though it wasn't his birthday.

"He'll smell great," she promised. "Put some *eau de cologne* on him and let him know it's from Grandma. He'll be pleased, and he'll smell great."

I looked around and saw that, here and there, things had changed in the house. Photos of Lily, Iris, and Amnon had appeared on the walls, as well as photos of Iris and Lily's children. There was also a large photo of Julie in a frame that was golden, like her. And a small photo of Nadav. There was something sad and encouraging in the way family members turned into pictures. In the way you could think about people even in their absence. At least about some of the family members. In the gap formed on the wall between the person and his or her photo. And I was already thinking that I was the only one missing in all the photos, that I was the only one with no gap between my presence and absence, and therefore there could be nothing between me and my mother. Either I was inside her, or she was inside me, or we were nothing to each other. But that thing, that "between us," was not there. Until, next to her bed, I found a photo of my father lifting a three-year-old girl with golden hair in the air. All at once, the longing crested within me. That was how it crested:

all at once, and I understood why longing was talked about in terms of waves. A wave filling the entire body with heat, and immediately after it crashes in the chest, another one arrives. Warm like the body's temperature, blowing like the wind assaulting from the outside. That was how I felt across from the two figures in the photo while waves of longing washed over me, and I couldn't tell which of the two in the photo I missed more.

> Long ago, I had a little girl
> and two braids down her back fell.
> When she undid those two thick braids
> my heart came undone as well. [34]

***

Four months had passed since Mom fell headlong in the shower. Four months since Adva sealed her fate with a well-sharpened pencil. Four months that had accrued all of the world's big time, as if they were a distilled capsule of a different time, larger and more primal, trapped on the road within a reckless U-turn, and now it was stuck with me like a rat in an experiment. Perhaps that was why Ariella Appel's name, suddenly flickering on my phone's screen, looked like the closest thing to motion. She heard the hesitation in my voice when she called to invite me to her home and was apparently prepared for it when she said, "Bring your husband along."

"It happens, you know," Eli told me on the way. "It would be a little presumptuous of you to think you could have saved her."

Outside, it was already hot. The winter that had been here not that long ago had not left any sort of trace behind. This year too, as always, there had not been enough rainfall here. The rain in this country went on strike along with every other institution. "It should tell us what it wants in order to come down, and we'll provide it," we would joke, but, in fact, we were worried. We felt the sky was betraying us. That with a sky like that, we didn't need external enemies, although we still had them.

When we arrived, we met the front door as if meeting an old acquaintance.

---

34   From the poem "The Girl with the Braids," by Gershon Franski.

It was heavy and opaque, but I remembered that I had opened it before, into the grieving home. I already knew how to do it, I reminded myself. I had already entered this foyer, I had already crossed past the black-and-white notice, I had already been here.

It would be a little presumptuous of you to think you could have saved her, I recited Eli's statement to myself, but when I saw Ariella standing there, in a gray housedress, with no makeup, with a photo of Adva, smiling at the world, propped up on a bookcase beside her, Ariella and I both started crying. Four months, and it was only now that we could cry together.

"Sometimes I can't bear the pain," she told me.

"I can imagine," I said, and tried to imagine. Tried to imagine someone else's pain, even when she wasn't my patient. The pain of the mother of a patient who could no longer be saved.

"What did she want?" Ariella asked herself, or me, or someone. "If I could only understand what she wanted. After all, it couldn't have been because of that motorcycle we wouldn't let her have."

"Maybe she didn't want anything," I answered. "Maybe she just didn't want to live. It was too painful for her. It was too much of a burden. Maybe she hoped you could agree to that. And maybe we just don't know what really happened. Maybe there are things we don't understand."

I parted from Ariella with a hug, and when she asked, "Will you be in touch?" I felt that I was grateful for that generous offer.

"Sure," I replied.

On the way home, Eli drove and I opened the window and allowed the wind to do whatever it wanted to with my hair. It did whatever it wanted anyway, but now I let it.

"You want to know something?" I said to Eli. "It's ungraspable, the more I think about it. It's inconceivable."

"Her suicide?" he asked.

"No. I actually meant my mother. It's inconceivable that she hung in there in that pit for so long. I wouldn't last a week in there."

"No doubt," he replied. "Your mother is supernatural."

***

For one of our anniversaries, Eli bought me Erich Neumann's book *Amor and Psyche*. "*Noga my love,*" he wrote me on the first page. "*This time in Hebrew,*" and signed it "*Yours forever.*"

He gave me the book with a smile when we were sitting in bed in the bedroom. A breeze coming in through the window ruffled his hair, exposing his contemplative forehead. My contemplative husband bought me a book about Greek mythology, this time in Hebrew.

"Isn't it simpler this way?" he asked and rose to start tidying up the room. He never liked a messy room. He neatly folded my purple knit, which was sprawled out on the floor in exhaustion, straightening out the wrinkles in the fabric with his hands. "Isn't it a shame?" he looked straight at me. Then he walked over to the plastic hamper in which we brought the clean laundry into the room and began folding the clothes. I looked at his busy body, at his measured motions. Eli was a man who knew what he was doing. He constantly knew what he was doing. He was simple and open and easy to operate. Unlike Cupid, who was hidden from Psyche's eyes while she dwelled in his palace. "If you see me, you shall no longer see me," that's what he told her. And she, who could not bear her blindness, violated the command. She illuminated him with the light of a lantern, and fell in love with him even more, a moment before being banished from his palace.

"It's interesting," jealous Aphrodite told her maliciously. "I wonder how an ugly handmaiden like yourself will manage to carry out all the tasks in order to be reunited with him."

"It's interesting," Eli continued talking while folding the laundry. "I wonder how Erich Neumann explains the fact that Psyche failed at her mission and opened the ointment of eternal beauty although she knew it would kill her."

"Are you really interested in that?"

"I've learned to take an interest in these things. You see? People change. So, did she fail because humans can't take something that belongs to the gods?"

"No, it's exactly the opposite," I explained to my law-oriented husband who had begun to take an interest in mythology. "She actually failed precisely because she was human. She wanted to look beautiful for her reunion with Cupid."

"But she was already the most beautiful among women, wasn't she?" he insisted on circumstantial evidence.

"Right, but before that, it wasn't for him. She was just born that way."

"I get it," he said. "So actually, before, it was just blind love."

"Just?"

"Yeah. It's not that she was really willing to make such an effort before."

"I don't understand," I told my law-oriented husband. "I can't understand what happened with Ronnie. Did you ever come across anything like that?"

"The truth is I haven't," he said, almost distracted, folding my underwear and placing them tidily in the drawer. Then he folded the comforter and stretched out the bed cover. "That's better, right?"

"Eli," I said.

"What?"

"Thank you."

17.

In honor of the dizzying success of the Belzec extermination machine, which, despite several mishaps, managed to raise the quota of the exterminated to impressive numbers, *Herr Kommandant* received a promotion and was appointed to supervise all the death camps established as part of Operation Reinhard. His housekeeper helped him pack his things and left his residence spotless for his replacement, *Hauptsturmführer* Gottlieb Herring, who arrived in order to supervise the shutdown of the camp and was happy to find such a tidy residence with well-organized files. All the employees at the camp were certain that *Herr Kommandant* would send his housekeeper to the gas chamber before he left, or find some other way to get rid of her. Therefore, everyone was surprised to find the skinny woman in the back seat of the Volkswagen, between the boxes; her whip marks had yet to fade, although in recent days, he had stopped whipping her.

In order to get rid of the mass quantities of bodies, the camp employed 600 Jewish prisoners. One prisoner for every thousand bodies. They opened the mass graves, took out the bodies, and began to burn them in a special incineration facility built from the rails of the iron tracks. They worked around the clock: opening the graves, taking out the bodies, or the body parts, whatever they found, and burning, and burning. But it never ended. The bodies emerged from the ground, more and more, inconceivable quantities. When did all this happen? When had a whole world been created here underground? A world now overflowing from the netherworld and once again flooding the Belzec camp with masses of people that had seemingly already disappeared from it. Arms with beckoning fingers extended from the soil, eye sockets gaped from hundreds of thousands of skulls, the sight of the bony skeletons stabbed at the eyes of the digging prisoners, and you could see how, when the bodies melded with one another underground, clinging to each other with the solidarity of those who were once people, with names, and history, and had now become remains of skin and bones belonging to the ghosts blowing through the Belzec sky, the bodies had grown powerful and their gaping mouths shocked the camp with a horrific unheard cry.

The prisoners dug, and dug, and burned, and burned, to the sound of whips cracking and the barking of dogs, *schnel, schnel—faster, there's no time, we have to hide the evidence; everything that happened here, in this camp, never happened.* The bones they did not have time to burn were pulverized into bits. Then they returned the ashes of the bodies that had been burned, along with the fragments of bone, into the pits, and buried them again, and covered them again. Day and night, until the moment when the mouths gaping in a frozen scream would finally be shut, the eye sockets would close, and the ground would stop moving. And peace would return to the pastoral camp of Belzec.

Trees were planted over the pits, interspersed with plants that were commanded to bloom despite the smoke and the soot. To join the national effort, since when it came to war, everyone was required to pitch in.

Herr Kommandant 's housekeeper didn't know where the Volkswagen was going. Her body had developed a new kind of weakness with which she was unfamiliar and she wondered how it even still existed after all the lashing that had come from outside, and the pregnancy lashing at her from inside. There was no relief in leaving Belzec since, although she did not know where her daughter was, and whether she was still alive, she had a feeling someone was taking care of her. That she was somewhere close, perhaps even very close. Sometimes it seemed like she could actually hear her, and feel her. That she was still in Belzec, where she was born, and after all, the people, where they were born, that's where they'll find help. Therefore, when *Herr Kommandant* prodded her to get into the car, she had to forcefully command her feet to move, since she was afraid he would recognize her hesitation and once again interrogate her to find out where her daughter was. She was afraid he would recognize her gut feeling, the one reserved for mothers, and would realize on his own that her daughter was somewhere truly close. When she told him, "I have no idea, I wish I knew where she is," he would stare at her and say: *There's no such thing. We both know that mothers always know.*

But *Herr Kommandant* didn't ask anything else about her daughter. After he found a way to sort out the numbers, he never talked about it again. And she knew she had to go with him, wherever he went. That if she gave in to the urge to flatten herself against the electric fence now, to join the bodies piling up on the ground, and her brother who had gone mad after saving her daughter, and her parents, whom she had seen getting off the train with her own eyes, and all the people who had grown up in the village with her, if she did that, who knew what would become of her daughter. And she had a feeling that so long as she held on, and so long as this terrible pregnancy held on, her daughter would hold on as well. After all, the *Kommandant* had said explicitly: a girl for a girl. And so, she survived her pregnancy, which lashed at her from the inside harder than the lashing of any whip, and more painfully. Simply because the lashing of the whip would sometimes pass. It included reprieves and time to recover. But there was no reprieve in her pregnancy. Every day, and every hour and minute, it honed in inside her, carving an indelible sign in the body. A discordant, nauseating tattoo.

From the day she left Belzec, she lost any interest in geography and had no idea where she was. *Herr Kommandant* 's life became more dynamic, and he would roam between Sobibor and Treblinka, sometimes also traveling to provide consultation services in Auschwitz. His reputation as an expert on murder with gas preceded him, and he was honored everywhere. But all the places seemed identical to her. All of them stood on ground that was trembling with bodies, under a black, smoky sky, engulfed with sooty air into which she would expel the embryo that was driving her mad from inside, and she waited for the moment when she could get rid of this pregnancy, but was equally terrified of it. She became frantic. Her thoughts were in one place only: Belzec. She knew a girl was waiting there. That she could not have been smuggled too far away. And she waited for the day when she could come and get her. And prayed she would hold on. That if there was a God in heaven after all, He would protect her girl.

***

Life at the parents' house assumed a new routine. I made sure to come at least once a week, and on other days, I would call.

"Nogilee, my pretty girl, sweetie, is that you?"

"Yes, Mom. It's me. How are you?"

"What can I tell you. As they say, it is not good that a man should be old."

"That's probably true. But what's the alternative?"

"What did you say, Nogi?"

"I said it is what it is. I'll come visit you tomorrow."

"At four?"

"I don't know. I'll come over when I can."

"Okay, Nogilee. Have I ever told you how much I love you?"

I powered off my cell phone. Twilight was flickering outside, and the sky began to expose its stars, as if it had decided the time had come to reveal some of its cards. I watched the light blending with the dark, which is in fact hiding the light. After all, there's no such thing as darkness. I remembered a statement Hani would frequently say to me when I came to her for counseling: "If you want to be a better person, you can. It's only up to you. You know, Noga, these things aren't pie in the sky."

Mom lost her appetite. She was gradually shrinking in the chair, and from one visit to the next, looked more and more reduced, as if she were a Russian Matryoshka doll, with a smaller, more wizened version of her emerging in every visit. She remembered she had once loved coffee with bread and jam, as well as "avocada," and "I scream," but she couldn't remember why.

"Do you remember, Nogi, how we'd once drink coffee together and eat bread and jam together?"

"Sure," I took pity on her. "I remember."

To her, life resembled the leftovers of something she had to finish, cleaning her plate, although she no longer had any appetite. Occasionally, memories stirred inside her like chicks hatching from the egg for a second time to fly nowhere, and she would randomly bring up moments and events from various periods in her life, which all blended together.

"I always loved being pregnant so much," she said. "I'd have had more kids but Dad didn't have the energy. If it was up to me I'd have had more and more kids," she said, looking at me. "After Nadav died, I wanted to have another child too, but Dad said he didn't have the energy. And besides, you were little. You were only three years old and I wanted to take care of you."

I looked at her body, which was shrinking away, gradually nestling into itself. This body from which, so they say, I had once emerged into the world.

If it continued to shrink into itself like this, it might yet reach the place where Mom met herself. I remembered my three pregnancies. Julie, who emerged into the world golden, a moment before Mom cried for the first and only time. Tomer, with whom I was laid out for three months of bed rest after making such great efforts to get pregnant, and Eli would serve me water and food in bed. And my little tadpole, absorbed into the rug on which Mom and I were sitting now.

"Mom," I turned to her.

"What, Nogilee?"

"What's the story with Ronnie?"

"Oh, Ronnie," she sighed. "You know, Nogilee, in the years when I was a social worker, I got the chance to see all kinds of people. There were those broken homes, and the parents who got divorced and the ones who couldn't get along at work, and all kinds of others as well, you know, there's no lack of stories. But there was something beautiful about the faces of those who had no idea what was going on around them."

"Come on, Mom…"

"That's it, Nogilee. I'm already a little tired," she said and fell asleep. Her head dropped onto her shoulder, her body sank deeper into the chair, and she began snoring.

***

The *Kommandant*'s housekeeper began to experience contractions the night before he left for a visit in Treblinka, to observe how his innovative methods, surely the result of experience and creativity, were being put into practice. Thus, for example, the idea of weaving pine branches into the strands of barbed wire in order to obscure what was going on in the camp had been his. As the idea had worked so effectively in Belzec, it was only natural to implement it in Sobibor and Treblinka as well. Misdirection. That was the keyword. The idea of building the gas chambers in the form of showers had also been his. In fact, most creative ideas within the misdirection effort were his, including the false signage system, which made the train platform look like a way station by hanging up false signs seemingly directing passengers to other platforms, to a waiting room, to a diner, to the ticket office, and also to the "hospital," where the elderly, the sick, and the disabled were shot in the back of the head. But now, when he was more experienced and had a proven track record, *Herr Kommandant*'s creativity was growing more and more sophisticated. While in Belzec, the Jews had been crammed into the chambers in whatever position suited them, in Treblinka they were led into the chambers with their hands raised above their heads, so that the process of cramming them in was more efficient and the chambers could contain a larger number of Jews, with the children also tossed over their heads for full utilization of the available space. *Herr Kommandant* liked maximal utilization in every situation and had zero patience for any kind of tomfoolery or waste. That was what he was: efficient. Efficient and creative. Therefore, the contractions, which had appeared the night before, with perfect timing, aligned wonderfully with his plans, and he had the option of driving the housekeeper to the home of midwife Gerda Braunsteiner, who had been clearly ordered to carry out her duties without asking questions.

"This is it!" he told his housekeeper. "*Endlich*—finally."

The time had come to complete the last part of their collaboration and to extract from her body the girl who was to replace the one who had disappeared. She didn't understand what he meant when he said "This is it," and hoped that on this matter, at least, they were in agreement and that if the previous girl hadn't been meant to live anyway, perhaps he would kill this one as well. In her stead. He left her at Gerda's house and returned to his lodgings to get ready.

The contractions were incontrollable and sneaky. They started in her back and seemed to be advancing upwards, toward her head, until she thought she was about to vomit her embryo out, through the mouth, and smear it on Gerda Braunsteiner's white sheets. But mid-way, in her upper back toward the head, the ascending contractions encountered a different kind of contractions, ones coming from above and exerting an immense, unbearable pressure downwards, and all night long, while *Herr Kommandant* was fast asleep in preparation for his visit to Treblinka, while the instructions in preparation for his arrival had already been placed on the tidy desk of camp commander Franz Stangl, the housekeeper's body struggled, squeezed between two kinds of contractions: the ones trying to vomit out the embryo and the ones trying to release it into the world in the conventional manner. This pregnancy, which had been lashing at her from the inside for several months now, decided to escalate its final lashings as if she herself had swallowed *Herr Kommandant*'s whip, which now obeyed him even in his absence. And, based on Gerda Braunsteiner's gaping eyes and her appalled expression, the housekeeper realized how terrible these long hours were, and that there was no point in waiting for them to be over, and they did indeed go on, and on, and when *Herr Kommandant* entered his Volkswagen in the morning on his way to Treblinka, she was still tormented by her contractions, and even as he stepped into the ten new gas chambers that had been built since the original three no longer sufficed, she was still being torn out of herself, feeling how this embryo was not emerging from one place, but rather was evacuating itself through each one of her cells, emerging from every orifice, not skipping any area in her body until, among her screams, which had begun to fill Gerda Braunsteiner's room, a different, alien scream was heard, the scream of a strange, alien creature, perhaps a monster.

"That's not my voice." The housekeeper managed to identify the discordance, and while *Herr Kommandant* was shaking Franz Stengl's hand and praising him for his impressive achievements, Gerda told her: *That's it. It's over.*

A moment before she fainted, the housekeeper managed to briefly see the two blazing eyes of the creature that had erupted from her body gazing at her.

"What a cute baby girl," Gerda said.

And the housekeeper just had time to mumble, "I have to get to Belzec."

***

"Julie, you get it," I yelled from the shower since I was waiting for a call from Eli. We had tickets to see the play "The House of Bernarda Alba," and I was trying to get ready quickly.

"It's someone named Carmel. She wants to talk to you." Julie brought me the cordless phone. I quickly wrapped my body in a towel.

"Carmel, what a surprise."

"Yeah, the truth is I just felt like hearing your voice. How are you?"

"I'm fine, all in all," I replied, and heard the words playing out from inside me: *You know what they say, it is not good that a man should be old.*

While officially I was not old yet, in recent months, since my mother had slipped, the old woman in me would emerge at all kinds of unexpected hours, staring back at me through the mirror, lurking in wait for me in the corners of the house, under the covers, waking up from her sleep before I did, trailing me into my dream, revealing herself in the shape of unwanted veins that had appeared on my legs, new splotches on my face, flashes of gray hair, as if playing a game of "scavenger hunt" with me, concealing clues along the path until she fully revealed herself to me.

"And how are you?"

"I'm okay too, you know, a lot going on. I thought about the fact that next year we'll be fifty. What do you say, should we organize something, some kind of reunion?"

"Fifty, huh? That's unbelievable." And in a second, time contracted as, on the other end of the line, I heard my forty-nine-year-old friend reducing, along with me, the time that had always been sucked into those years, as if the years were piling up on one another on a slope, with all the memories always draining to the bedrock of time. To the paths of the kibbutz, to the mulberry tree and the silkworms. To Palm Tree Preschool.

"Remember Blackie, how we celebrated her first birthday with a ribbon and a bell?"

"Sure I do." Carmel's voice trembled a little, and although I couldn't see her, I imagined how the old woman inside her was also already playing scavenger hunt with her, lurking in wait for her through the mirror, hiding in her lower belly. "You bet I remember. And I remember Nadav the rabbit, too, and the ant farm, and Polynesia, and the letter we sent Dr. Dolittle. I'm sure you heard Sigal is very ill."

"Sigal?"

"Yes, our preschool teacher."

Our preschool teacher? We cracked up. We were on the verge of turning fifty and were still saying "Our preschool teacher" to each other. Somewhere in Palm Tree Preschool, the girls we were once were still concealed, still waiting for a trip to the sea, to see the place where the water blended into the sky. Still thrilled to see the night-blooming jasmine blossoming in white on the wall of Wheat Preschool. Still having the dream about the old man who grabbed kids and threw them into the deep end of the pool. The memories washed over us, flowing steadily. *Remember that? And that?* And even though we had plenty of things in the present to catch up on, talking about the past was addictive. Its power was sweeping and irresistible. Stronger than the two old ladies who had already begun to bud within us, uniting against us and defeating us in the "race against time." A childhood friend keeps you in time. Her body signals to you what you look like and how much you've changed. Her skin wrinkles on your face, too. The clothes she wore in high school and in her twenties and thirties were tossed out of your closet, too. A childhood friend is an ally and a confidante, keeping the memories along with you in joint custody. A childhood friend will always be a sense of longing, even when she's right there.

"So, who do you keep in touch with?" I couldn't help but ask, although I knew Eli was about to arrive and pick me up for the play, and might not be cool with the woman-in-a-towel look. "I come to the kibbutz about once a week, to see my mother, so I get a chance to see some people here and there, but there's hardly anyone left from our class."

"Right. Other than Ram, of course. There was an incident a little while ago, maybe you heard. Someone told me he was running on the path surrounding the dining hall, still going on about that idea that there's no such thing as an axiom. He was running and yelling at the top of his voice that two parallel lines actually will meet, and that more than a single line can pass through two points."

"Imagine if it actually turned out to be true?"

"What do you mean?"

"I don't know. Sometimes I just get to thinking. Even though Ram is ill, maybe he sees something we don't. Maybe somewhere, at some point in infinity, even parallel lines can meet."

***

I loved my patients. From the window looking out on Shimon HaTarsi Street, I saw them as their steps approached the session. I saw their figures cast a shadow on the access path, one that grew so long at certain hours that it reached me before they did. I saw the anticipation in their body, in their gaze, I could almost hear their heartbeats a moment before the door opened and we said "hi." Sometimes, the clock was less frightening. I let the minutes go by at their own pace, which could never be predicted. Over the years, some understanding nevertheless developed that if the minutes went by, there was no reason to resist them. I could let them take me with them. Wherever they went. There was no reason to stay in the armchair without them. To isolate myself in a sealed capsule, to freeze within a beautiful face that "had no idea what was going on around it," as my mother would say. Time passed over all of us, and we all passed with it, wondering anew each time as we discovered its tracks: "How did a whole year go by?" "What the hell?"

Many of my patients were busy seeking the truth. Where it was. When would we finally understand what had really happened. They would replace each other in their spot on the couch, emptying the supply of time at their disposal into it, searching for the truth. I, too, sought it. I, too, sought the optimal distance from it. Sometimes I imagined it as a big, lame bird hovering between us, suspended in the air, landing occasionally in some unexpected region when it ran out of stamina on its way onward to other lands, crashing into the ground in mid-journey as if it had no legs. Sometimes I felt it truly close to me, at high noon, circling above me as clear as the sun, or in the middle of the night, revealed in a dream. Age brought the aches of time with it, and the unexpected awakenings at night. The dream I would once dream, back when I shared the bungalow with Ronnie, returned to me. About the bald baby talking to me in adult language. Once again, I complained to him: *I don't understand, I don't understand what you're saying, speak clearly!*

I kept Adva's photo in the corner of my desk. Ariella brought it to me, encased in a thin frame, and at the end of every workday, I found myself looking at it. "So, what have you got to offer me?" I could hear her say in a taunting voice. "Seriously, sis, that's the best you can do? Awesome."

At the end of each day, I closed the blinds and went out to the street. During the summer months, the sun had yet to set as I walked to the car. My long shadow crossed the road, crushed under the wheels of passing cars, when from the depths of my purse, my cell phone would ring with a ringtone reserved for one woman only, the one sitting in a wheelchair and dialing.

One day when I came to visit, she gave herself over to reminiscing, as if she had started packing up the stories of her life and was sorting them by topic.

"You know what's strange, Nogilee?"

"What's strange?" I asked, as if strange in her life, in our life, was the exception to the rule.

"What's strange is that when I think back to the little girl I was inside the pit, I can't grasp that it really happened to me. It's like it happened to someone else. I don't understand: how didn't I scream? How didn't I go crazy?"

At such moments, I'd sit down in a chair next to her.

"So, really, how didn't you scream? How did you hold back?"

"I had a kind of quiet whistle. I'd go *foo-foo-foo* to myself, silently. No one heard."

Mom once again entered her linear time, and I would listen.

And this was how it went down: One day, Julia informed her that the Russians were on their way. It was no longer a rumor; the entire town knew—the Russians were on their way.

"So, can I come out?" Mom asked.

But Julia said they still had to be very careful. Anti-Semitic terrorists were walking the streets, aiming to finish what Hitler hadn't had time to do, and determined to slaughter every Jew they found. This was the summer of 1944. Mom's birthday was approaching, and Julia said she hoped her birthday could be celebrated outside the pit, beneath the skies, the vault of heaven. The death camp had been burned down a long time ago, replaced by a forest planted on soil that had stopped moving. Outside, it was already possible to hear the neighbors, meaning the ones who had survived, coming out of their homes.

"How are you?"

"And how are you?"

"Who's still around in your family?"

"What do you know about the others?"

"And you? Do you know something?"

And Mom could hear all that from the pit. People were talking a little louder. The sound of their steps on the ground was a bit less mistrustful. In the morning hours, the chirping of birds was now audible. It seemed as if life was beginning to return to Belzec.

And then came the longest day in Mom's life. Why the longest? Because in the morning, Julia told her that in the evening, they would get her out. And Mom couldn't wait. Not even a minute. She wanted to know what this thing called "the vault of heaven" was. The small opening in the pit revealed the ground, but nothing above it.

"Can I come out yet?" Mom asked every hour, and Julia told her: *In a little while, be patient.*

"How about now? Can I?" Mom asked, and Julia replied: *In a little while, be patient.*

And so it went on until the evening. Mom didn't understand how time would pass. How she would hold on until the evening. But evening finally arrived, and in the evening, the neighbors came. Each of them picked up a log, and they began to take the pile apart. Mom heard the wood moving. She couldn't wait any longer. Her body began to tremble and she couldn't stop it. Another log was removed from the pile, and another, and the neighbors marveled over when Julia had managed to stack this entire pile over Mom, and where was this girl that she claimed was hiding here. Some time, it's unclear how much, went by like that until all the wood was removed, and on the ground, a little girl was revealed. Although she was already nine years old, she weighed maybe twenty-two pounds and was lying curled up on a rag, with an empty food bowl and the New Testament next to her.

Julia couldn't hold back her tears. For two years, she hadn't seen the girl that God had sent her from heaven, only heard her barely whispering, and now that girl was lying before her eyes, for real. She was small, but was a whole girl, with all her limbs; God really had watched over her.

"You can come out," she whispered to her. "Come on, you're allowed."

But Mom didn't move.

"It's okay, you can do it," Julia continued whispering, and the neighbors, too, nodded and confirmed that it was okay, it was allowed now.

But Mom didn't move. She couldn't get up. Her legs were paralyzed, and so was her right arm after she hadn't moved for two years. Her left arm, the one that would hand Julia the bowl, was the only one that could move. She wanted to come out and couldn't. Now, when she was allowed to move, she couldn't do it. She had imagined this moment for so long, and now it was here, and she was letting it down.

Meanwhile, night had fallen outside, and Mom still hadn't moved, until one of the neighbors walked over and carried her in his arms. He lifted her out of the pit and stood under the sky, in the open air. All the neighbors stood and watched the girl whom he carried in his arms look at the sky. This entire time, when they had been ensconced in their homes, under the white snow, and the black snow, and the burning summer, and the smoky days, there had been a girl here, under the firewood. This entire time, while they were carefully locking their doors and the windows so that no Jew who had jumped off the train would invade their yards, this entire time when German officers were living in Julia's home, there had been a girl here. Under their noses. They looked at each other, then looked down, and mostly stared in amazement at the little girl, who was, it was true, nine years old, but weighed as much as a baby. How had Julia managed to do it? Where did she find the courage?

But Mom wasn't looking at them. Her eyes were fixed only on one thing.

"What's that?" she asked, looking up.

"What's what?" the neighbors asked.

"That." She directed her eyes upward and pointed with her left hand. *What are those shiny things up there?*

But they didn't answer her. Julia and all of the neighbors were standing and crying.

"What is that?" Mom continued to ask, while they stood and cried.

***

Darkness was falling on the kibbutz as well, and I wanted to go home. Tomer had a history test tomorrow and needed help preparing for it, but I couldn't move, either. I felt that I had to hear more.

Julia hugged Mom carefully so as not to squash her. *Ladna dziewczynka— my lovely girl,* she mumbled through her tears. *My precious, lovely girl, I knew you would make it.* And Mom wanted to cry along with her, but she couldn't. She wanted to hug her back, but she couldn't. She could barely hug with one arm. She wanted to thank her, and couldn't. Thank her for what? For saving her life? For risking her own life, and that of her family, and the lives of all the neighbors now standing around her and crying? For telling the German officers, for two years, that a Jew was not a pin? For sitting next to the pit for two years and reading to her from the New Testament so that she could hold on? How do you thank someone for all of that? Where do you start?

During the first few days, Julia allowed Mom to look at the sun only from inside the house, through the window, so that she wouldn't be blinded. She didn't let anyone go near her when she wasn't there so that they wouldn't give her the wrong kind of food by mistake, so that they wouldn't suffocate her, so that they wouldn't ruin her girl. She milked the cow and spoon-fed Mom. She touched her a little each time, carefully, stroking her with soft fingers, constantly singing and crying, and when she felt that it was safe to wash her, she took the washtub, filled it with lukewarm water with a little soap, and

THE LOST GIRL FROM BELZEC | 199

washed her hair, marveling at the gleaming gold that began to emerge from the grime. Pure gold. *My girl, my lovely, golden girl, my courageous girl, I knew you would make it.*

Some time later, the neighbors summoned a doctor who lived in a nearby town, and he said she was suffering from degeneration from which it was probably impossible to recover. But Julia said there was no such thing. That this was no ordinary girl. That it was true she wasn't a doctor, but it was obvious to her that some things were outside the doctors' sphere of knowledge. That if she had held on the way she had, she would also be able to walk. And so Julia took care of her for a few more weeks before they took her to the hospital. She carried her in her arms from one place to another, and sang songs to her, and couldn't stop crying all day: *My girl, my lovely girl, I knew, I prayed constantly, and I believed, that you would live.*

This entire time, Mom wasn't waiting for her mother to come get her. If she hadn't come for so long, why think she would show up at any point? After all, she had been truly close when Mom hid in the crypt in the cemetery, and she hadn't come. She hadn't come at night when Mom had shivered with cold on the surface on which bodies were prepared for burial. She hadn't come in the mornings, when Mom hid in the wheat fields, eating grains and drinking rain. From within the fields, Mom could see the camp's fences. She had known her mother was there, truly close, and that she hadn't come to look for her. She hadn't come to save her. Even when she was starving. And she hadn't looked for her even once during the two years when Mom was in Julia's pit. Not even when she had nearly been burned alive. So Mom wasn't waiting for her anymore. She thought that either her mother was already dead herself, or else she had simply abandoned her. There was no other explanation.

She had no idea about the deal her mother had made: a girl for a girl. She had no idea that during the course of the last winter, *Herr Kommandant* had decided to put an end to Operation Reinhard and eliminate the Jews still left in Lublin District and in the camps, once and for all. Forty-three thousand Jews were killed in this operation, called "Harvest Festival," and once it was over, the entire staff of the camps was transferred to the Trieste region, on the border between Italy and Slovenia, in order to fight the Jewish partisans. *Herr Kommandant*, who was later killed in Yugoslavia in a partisan ambush, had no interest in taking his housekeeper with him and ordered that she be sent to

Bergen Belsen. As far as he was concerned, her role had come to an end. However, a moment before sending her there, he spun on his heels and returned to his lodging again. Anyone standing there, looking from the sidelines, could see him dragging out her girl as he left. Meaning the new girl, who, hypothetically, was the girl replacing her old one, who had disappeared. She was already a year old but had never made a sound, which was a good thing. He instructed that she be brought to Gerda Braunsteiner's house and then took off. Her mother, too, took off. For Bergen-Belsen. But Mom didn't know all that. She didn't know how, every day, as the other prisoners in the women's camp died of typhus, her mother prayed not to get sick, anything but typhus, and waited for the day the war would end, and she would go to Belzec to look for her girl. She didn't know about that day when a storm blew away the tent that was housing the women's camp, and they were forced to stand all night in the snow. There was no need to shoot them. They died on their own. One by one. And only her mother stood and remembered she had a girl in Belzec. But Mom didn't know all of that. Including about the day when the British liberated Bergen-Belsen, and when they began to clear out the mountains of bodies and the survivors, her mother said there was only one place where she was going.

It happened on Sunday afternoon, when Julia came back from church and was preparing a meal in the kitchen. Mom was sitting in the yard of Julia's house. She still couldn't walk, or stand, but when she leaned against the wall, she could assume a posture that resembled sitting. This was the position she was in when she saw a silhouette from afar, gradually coming closer. All the neighbors came out of their houses. They knew something new was happening on the street. There were rumors. Someone had already seen the emaciated woman at the end of the street, and although he didn't recognize her, she recognized him. She told him she was from here, from Belzec. Someone else had already heard her inquiring whether there was a nine-year-old girl there, with golden hair. "Maybe you've seen her? Maybe you've heard? A little girl?" She kept on asking questions like that and walked until she came to Julia's yard. And Mom saw her. And didn't move. Both because she couldn't move, and because she didn't know what to do now, with this woman, who had disappeared for so long, who she had thought might have actually died. But there she was, she had survived, and despite surviving, had not come to look for her all that time. Had abandoned her. And what to do with her now, as she stood like that, at the edge of the yard, emaciated and stilted? And where would she live, this woman? Did she want to live in Julia's little house, too? Maybe she wanted to sleep where the German officers had slept?

Don't come any closer, she silently prayed. *Don't come any closer, walk away, go back to wherever you came from,* she prayed soundlessly.

But the emaciated woman didn't walk away. All the neighbors stood and waited to see what would happen next. Her mother also stopped at the other end of the yard and didn't move. She saw her: it really was her girl. Small and skinny, as if she had frozen in time, as if she had stayed six years old, but smaller, and more shriveled. As if time hadn't passed. But time had passed. It did pass. It passed without her. The neighbors couldn't take their eyes off the figures of the woman and the girl looking at each other from either end of the yard. They didn't dare move, or blink. They just stood, as if turned to stone, just like the woman and the girl on either end of the yard, until they saw the emaciated woman extend both her arms. What was she thinking? That her girl would run to her? What was she thinking? That her girl could even walk? What did she think had happened to her girl throughout that time?

And, indeed, her girl didn't move. She sat there, leaning against the wall and not making a sound. Her gaze was frozen in response to those two arms extended stiltedly into the air, reaching for her. Now she came? Where were those arms when she was lying in the cemetery during the cold nights? Where were they when the Germans' jeep almost caught her when she fell asleep at the edge of the wheat field? Where were those arms when the Germans were searching Julia's house, kicking with their boots, turning over the furniture, scaring Julia while she was lying with the mice in the pit? She looked at her and didn't move. Only the neighbors cried. At first, they only wiped away a tear, quietly, then another. Until the tears flowed down and they all cried together. They keened. All the neighbors stood in their yards and keened. For all those years, the terrible ones, for the houses on the street that had remained orphaned. For what had become of this world. They cried for themselves. And for one woman, and one girl, now poised, frozen, on either side of the yard. Until Julia came to the threshold of the house. She had an apron around her waist, and was clearly in the midst of household tasks. For a few moments, she, too, stood as if petrified. She knew this moment would come, but had preferred not to think about it. There were more urgent things to take care of.

There was a girl here who needed to be saved under the entire pile of wood.

The entire street froze in its place. The arms of the *Kommandant*'s house-keeper remained in the air, between heaven and earth, gesturing in a motion of invitation. *Come to me, my girl*, they might be trying to say. *Come to me, I came to you from Bergen-Belsen, I stayed alive for you, I survived the lashing of the whip, and the freezing snow, I left another girl with* Herr Kommandant *in your place, so that he wouldn't come looking for you.* But the motion was stilted, awkward, unconvincing, it had been a while since she used it, and now she was raising her arms in the air like a spasm in front of all the neighbors standing and watching the scene.

Until Julia placed her hands on Mom's shoulder and told her, "This is your mother. She's come to take you. You have to let her take you."

But Mom didn't want anyone to take her away. She wanted to stay with Julia. How could she leave Julia?

"This is your mother. She'll take you, and I'll keep you here in my heart, my lovely, courageous girl," Julia said, and her mother approached, and didn't say a single word to Julia. What could she say? *Thank you? Thank you for saving my girl while I couldn't even ask where she was?* Or maybe, *pardon me? Pardon me for taking away the girl that God sent you from heaven? The one who came to replace your dead child?*

And that was the last time in her life that Mom saw Julia.

$$***$$

Time continued being bothersome and haunted. Sometimes it blew into the house like a draft. Mom gradually diminished into her chair, until it seemed like she would soon return to the size of the small pit in which she was hidden. She continued to sort through her memories and pack them away by subject, and it was clear that she was preparing to say goodbye. From her place in the wheelchair, impaled at the center of the rug like a mark of Cain, she began to close up shop, "wrapping up her workday here," and I realized this thing called "Mom," this phenomenon that loved me endlessly from the heart of the rug, loved me from the deep like a pit loves the fruit, could one day simply disappear. Disappear as if there was no reason not to leave things the way they were, undeciphered, sparkling in the dark in front of the beautiful faces of those who had no idea what was going on around them. Sometimes she held her cane while she sat in the chair, and by raising her scepter, would signal Jenny what to bring her. "That," she pointed the scepter at her shawl when she was cold. "That," she pointed the scepter at the air-conditioner remote when she was hot. And the objects would obey her with some slight encouragement from Jenny. Now, when she wanted nothing from life, she felt she could bully it. From her seat in the chair, she also gave out instructions on how to proceed after her death.

"Don't forget to unplug everything," she said. "So the whole house here doesn't burn down. Nogilee, this is important. Don't forget, the entire neighborhood could burn down. And return the chair to the organization we got it from. There's no one to use it, it's a waste, some other old lady might need it and there's no point in it rotting here in the middle of the living room. And make sure Jenny vacuums the rug before the *shiva*, and after it, too. You never know what kind of dirt people who come to console others track in with them sometimes. I remember it from Dad's *shiva*, all the scum of the world was brought in here. Ew. And make sure Jenny cleans the pipe collection, too. Don't think that just because I can't see, I don't care. And then each of you should take a few pipes, so you have them."

There were only a few times when Lily and Iris and Amnon and I would come to the parents' house together. Mom's last collapse in the shower embarrassed us so much that we couldn't stand the sight of our figures that had been absent that day in the winter, at four p.m., and on all the other days. Our guilt increased when we reflected in each other's eyes, as if gazing at a thousand mirrors. And she said, "It's nothing. Everything's fine. It was already a long time ago when I fell headlong." And I held back from correcting her: *It was already a long time ago when you told Jenny she could leave.* I held back since I knew it didn't matter. That it was already a long time ago when I didn't want to come here.

On her eighty-third birthday, the three of us, Lily, Amnon, and I, came and set up chairs on the rug, next to Mom's chair, and were sad. Lily's phone rang, and Iris spoke from inside it, calling to say congratulations. Lily had Iris, I thought, and Iris had Lily. And Amnon had had Nadav. Our gifts to her were a toaster and an espresso machine to replace the dancing kettle, and she said, "Those are great gifts, right? Are you happy?" And then she added, "You know my mother never celebrated my birthday? Back then, those kinds of things just didn't happen."

"Well, Mom, you weren't really speaking to her," Lily reminded her.

"What do you mean, I wasn't speaking to her? It's not that I wasn't speaking to her. It's just that I didn't really have anything to talk to her about. We'd said everything that needed to be said. And that was that."

"Mom didn't speak to Grandma?" I asked.

"You didn't know?" Lily and Amnon looked at me.

I'd never thought about it. Grandma had died a long time ago, when I was little, and I didn't notice whether they talked or not.

"What else don't I know?" I asked into the space of the room.

"Who wants cake?" Mom asked, and Amnon asked which cake, and Jenny replied that there was no cake.

"But there are wonderful grapes. Anyone want some?"

"Who wants bread and jam?" I asked, and no one laughed.

The birthday celebration continued like that for another two hours or so, and when we rose, to leave, Mom said, "It's not that I wasn't speaking to her. She's the one who told me not to ask anything. That it's better not to ask. That it's better not to know."

And when the three of us were standing in the doorway, she looked up at us.

"You'll come back, Nogilee, won't you?"

18.

Mom passed away shortly after the birthday celebration just as tensions in Gaza were rising, and 7,000 protesters there embarked on a "Great March of Return" as part of the events of Nakba Day.[35] The news reported thousands of protesters gathering outside the wall between Israel and the Palestinian National Authority, burning tires and casting stones at IDF forces. But I decided to disengage from the news for a bit and focus on the clinic. It would never be quiet in this country anyway, I remembered my father saying. So it was better if everyone did what they did best. And this was what I had learned to do best: to make things mentally healthy. And even if I didn't always succeed, it was the only thing I had ever learned how to do, although I never really understood how I did it, and how it worked, and what really happened during those hours at the clinic, those holy hours, when my phone was off and I was utterly engaged in a mode that could not be recreated during any other moment. A mode where no one outside the room could get hold of me.

That day, twenty-five people were killed when a volcano erupted in Chile. At that same time, the Israeli prime minister met the German chancellor in order to discuss the Iranian threat in view of President Trump's decision to withdraw from the nuclear treaty. *It's amazing*, the prime minister claimed during the discussion, *that even today, there's a threat to exterminate millions of Jews*. That's what he said: *It's amazing that there's a threat to exterminate millions of Jews*. He thanked the chancellor for her personal commitment to Israel's security and promised her that "our hands are extended in peace." On

---

35   Nakba Day, observed by Palestinians on May 15, is an annual day of commemoration of the displacement that preceded and followed the Israeli Declaration of Independence in 1948.

that same day, Bill Clinton stated that even today, in the "Me Too" era, he would not have resigned due to the exposure of his affair with Monica Lewinsky. And the sports journalists were reporting on the cancellation of a visit to Israel by the Argentinian national team, headed by Lionel Messi, due to threats from the Palestinians.

I saw it all when I powered on my cell phone during my break and almost failed to notice six unanswered calls from Eli, from Lily, from Iris, from Amnon, from Varda from the Senior Citizen Committee, and from another, unidentified number. *So what happened, did she fall in the shower again?* I thought when I saw that they were truly looking for me. I tried to figure out whether I had once again promised to come over and failed to do so, whether I had screwed up again, like back then, like always, whether I had drifted away from her again. *So, does she learn nothing from experience?* I felt the rage mounting within me again and checked my weekly planner and grew utterly convinced I had not informed anyone that I was coming over today. Not at four p.m. or at any other time. The weekly planner didn't lie. If someone was waiting for me anyway, that was entirely her problem. Eli was on the other line when I called. So, who should I call back first? Definitely not Lily. Or Iris, of course. She wasn't even in Israel, so how exactly was I accountable to her? Not Amnon, either. I felt myself rating my siblings based on my degree of distance from them. My mother's words rang out: *And did you call Lil yet? No? Not Iri either? What about Amnoni? Not him, either? Okay, it's not that bad, maybe you'll call later.*

Obviously, obviously it wasn't that bad. Obviously, everything was fine, and I could call later. After all, we weren't having any problems. And if we were, there was no need to talk about it. Not everything had to be talked about, and remember the beauty of the faces of those who had no idea what was going on around them. All the ones who didn't distinguish between psychotherapy and chemotherapy, or between a dog and a cat. I called Varda from the Senior Citizen Committee.

"Nogi, it's a good thing you got back to me. I'm sure you've already heard from your siblings."

"Heard what?"

"You didn't hear?" she asked, surprised, and kept on talking, and elaborating, *this morning, it happened just this morning*, and as we talked, I watched the prime minister's speech on the cell phone's screen, still on Ynet news, *how amazing that even today, just like back in the day, some still aspire to exterminate millions of Jews*, and he went on to say that this was us, this was our nation, a nation that was still quintessentially orphaned, and the next story reported an increase in the death toll of the volcanic eruption in Chile, up to thirty-seven, even more, forty-two, and the Palestinians in Gaza continued to burn tires next to the wall, and I felt that during each additional moment when I talked to Varda, things were happening in the world, and perhaps this conversation was troubling in some way. *What did you say happened this morning? What? What did you say?* Varda said, *Nogi, I know you loved her in your own way*, and slowly, it became clear to me that the rage that had surged within me in the last few minutes, meaning the rage that had always been there and was now erupting again like the volcano in Chile, was rage at a woman who was no longer there, who had not been there since that morning, that when the prime minister talked about millions of Jews who needed to be protected, she was no longer among them, and when I dropped the phone on the couch without disconnecting, I still heard Varda saying all kinds of things, I loved her in my own way, she knew, everyone knew, everyone had already heard, only I hadn't heard.

So, who to call now? I asked myself and thought that maybe more than anything, I'd like to return to the unidentified call. *Hello*, I could say into the receiver, *it's me, you were looking for me*, and from the other end of the line, the unidentified voice would answer me, *How are you*, he would ask, or she would ask, inquiring how I was doing, and I could reply that I was doing well, other than what wasn't well, meaning *how I'm doing is unidentified, like you*, and meanwhile the phone rang and Eli said, "I'm on my way to you."

***

Shiva at the parents' house. Jenny vacuumed the rug like Mom had ordered and cleaned all the pipes in the collection, one by one. The house smelled of bleach and other more or less friendly detergents that managed to confine the smell of mothballs and pajamas to the inside of the cabinets. "Mom must be pleased," Amnon said, and I checked that everything was unplugged. Jenny served the guests espresso from the new machine we had just bought, for her birthday, and the four of us were spread out over the house like we were on patrol, trying to make it look natural and normal. After all, we were all ordinary people, normal under the circumstances. *Shiva* at the parents' house, in the middle of the old people's neighborhood, where no old person had lived for a long time. Mom had been the last of the old ladies to live there, while all of the other houses were home to families with children, who'd never known Hilda and Shmul and Clara and the bats splitting loquat peels on the walls of Kalman's house. Families with children who never knew the old cabin and the drill.

The consolers arrive one by one. What a well-oiled machine the *shiva* is. How quickly everyone knows how to transition to a new state. How obvious the "new state" is, having waited patiently for years, and now, when its time has come, it fills the house with banal naturalness. Mom is no longer here. *So sorry for your loss. My deepest condolences.* The words emerge all ready from the mouth, prepacked for the *shiva. It hasn't been easy lately. She didn't have an easy life in general, your mother, but what a unique woman, the way she always took care of you*, and the consolers come and go, one shift replacing another. Lily's friends, and Iris's, and Amnon's, and mine too. My entire class is here: Carmel, and Einav, and Tamir, and Liat, all the kids from Palm Tree Preschool and Oleander Class. Some of them have put on weight, a few of them have gone bald, while others are clearly displaying the weight of the years on their shoulders, some of them gracefully diminishing the panic of time, but all of them have remained the kids from preschool and from class, children with serious faces, submissively advancing toward their silently waiting decrepitude, and now I, too, am a girl again, the girl who wrote Storio the Elf, an orphaned middle-aged girl, sitting in a parents' house in which there are no longer any parents, just a house, an army with no commander, the house where I had never dared invite a friend over, and the entire house is in motion, not just the kettle, the rug is teeming as if the ground is moving beneath it, the wheelchair is gleaming at the corner of the living room, it seems as if any minute, it will roll into the shower, soon the doors of the cabinets will open and the smell of mothballs and pajamas will burst out, and the consolers come and go, even the ones who didn't know Mom, they come for me, they want to console me, they're sorry for my loss, for my mourning, draped upon me like a garment that someone else sewed for me, and I fit the fabric to my body. Here are Lior and Nitzan and Arbel who went to high school with me. *Noga, it's been years, you had that boyfriend, Ronnie, you'd run off to see him all the time, are you still with him? No? Well, it's been so long, we've all changed, we've all had other loves since, but we remember how you couldn't breathe without him, how we'd make fun of you for coming to school wearing his underwear, so who are you married to? His buddy? Are you serious? Sometimes life is funny.* And the consolers come and go, they look at the walls of the house, at the photos, it's actually a regular house, with regular furniture, and regular customs. From the sidelines you couldn't tell that the coffee's gone crazy, or that the K300 bug spray wallops, and here come Tal and Ophir from my bachelor's degree, *it was obvious you'd end up as a clinical psychologist, it was just you informing us every day that you were quitting school, it actually suits you to a T, although during your bachelor's degree you were a little weird*, and here are Gil, and Noa, and Ohad, from the rental apartment era, they're not only here for me, they're here for Eli, *we knew you'd get married, from the second we saw you meeting at the Iguana Pub back then, when you told us your brother had died, we had a bet going who would find out about your wedding first, us or you. So this is your parents' house? Are there any photos of your mom? Or of you when you were little?* And here's Joy, of the binary opposition comprised of Joy and Nogloom, *wow, you're dressed so nice, you look so good, remember back when you had nothing to wear to the psychiatric unit? When you got stuck behind the dressing room curtain in the store and nothing fit right?* And here are Shai and Aviram, I hug them, it was so long ago when we paid rent while the three of us were sleeping in the sleep lab. When we were tending to the potted plants that were wilting in our place, it was so long ago when I came down with dysentery a night before the delegation left for Poland after writing the paper about literary devices in autobiographies of Holocaust survivors. *So, have you gone to Poland since then? You never went?* It was so long ago when they came to see me at the kibbutz, right here, in the parents' house, "the scene of the event," when I opened up the collection of postcards from Dad. When the letter from Ronnie fell on me. "My most Rabbit in the world," they heard me mumbling again and again when we drove away from here, before that night when I stood at the window till morning, trying to identify the point from which the light emerges and illuminates the objects on the street. And the consolers keep coming, replacing each other like the sun and the moon, their shadow occasionally falling upon the bookshelf, on

Greek mythology in English. I remember the day when Mom bought me the book. *Are you happy?* she asked when she gave it to me along with the wooden recorder the day I came from the cabin and didn't dare ask how someone was living there, someone young, suddenly moving into the old people's neighborhood. *Are you happy? Are you pleased? Don't be sad, Nogilee, it's not mentally healthy, and you don't have to talk to me if you don't want to,* that's what she said on the day I fled from the cabin at the sound of her calling me, when Eli and Ronnie asked whether that was my mother and I said it wasn't. That's not my mother, and I don't have to talk to her if I don't want to. She's just the one who will always lie next to me on the rug when I'm sick. When my fever is "sky-high." Who will write my school papers by the murky light of the kitchen bulb. Who will hide letters that are not mentally healthy for me. Who will fake other letters for me, from France, from Thailand, from Japan. And now Ram is entering the parents' house, and I start to cry.

"So, have you already made some new discoveries?"

"What do you mean?"

"You know what the *shiva*'s always like. You suddenly make new discoveries. All kinds of letters, photos, clues. Maybe you'll find out something about that boyfriend of yours, the one your mother made disappear."

"But how? Now that she's dead, there's no one to ask anymore."

"Oh, come on, Noga. Don't tell me you buy all that bullshit they're always feeding us. That after a person dies, you can't ask them anything anymore. I'm constantly talking to the dead." Then he approached me in that weird way he sometimes had, and whispered in my ear, "It's true that I'm in and out of the hospital, but I'm still not willing to buy the bullshit."

That's what he said: that he was in and out of the hospital. That's the way he suddenly said it. In exactly the same way Eli had talked about Ronnie's mother. She, too, was in and out of hospitals.

"What just happened?" he asked. He had noticed something.

"You tell me, Ram. Tell me, what would you do if, this entire time when you were in and out of the hospital, you had to raise a kid? What would you do?"

He yawned loudly and said he was dead tired. I was afraid that within a second, he would return to that state in which it was impossible to talk to him, and the conversation would be over. But he actually replied lucidly, "I'd ask my mom to take care of him, or else I wouldn't even have to ask. That's what she would do anyway. It's instinct, right?"

"Sure. Sure." I hugged him. It was instinct. *I love you so much, Ram.*

"But I have to go," he said and got up suddenly, with no warning. "I'm dead tired. What do I look like more to you, dead or tired? The medication's killing me. And yet I still don't sleep at night. And look how fat I've gotten," he said, and once again retreated into his floating gaze, and within a second, I saw that he was no longer with me. But I, too, was already elsewhere. There had to be clues in this house. There had to be something. The rug didn't just move for no reason. The kettle didn't just dance. The K300 bug spray didn't just wallop, and the coffee didn't just go crazy. And the shadow, of course. The shadow didn't just cruise from the floor to the walls, and to the ceiling, and back. There had to be clues here.

***

As night approached, the consolers left the parents' house alone. Eli took Julie and Tomer home, Yossi, Ilan, and Iris's kids left to sleep in Amnon's apartment in Tel Aviv. Nadav, Gilly, and Roy also dispersed to all kinds of places and the four of us were left to our orphaned state. Just the four of us. Mom had no siblings or relatives. No uncles or cousins. And the ones she'd once had, she never met, other than the uncle who'd carried her for fleeting moments in the bread basket. We were her family. We held up the walls of the house from the inside. We now protected the parents' house from something, or protected ourselves from it, so that we would not collapse under its burden, so that we would not burn in the fire that might break out if we didn't remember to unplug everything. We were the ones striving to endow it with that same cozy scent that houses have. This was the house from which we'd always liked fleeing. Slamming the door behind us. Feeling Mom's eyes stabbing into our back: *You'll come back, Nogilee, won't you?* This was the house where Dad would come visit on weekends. This was the house to which he sent his postcards. This was the house of *foo-foo-foo*, of *there you are* and *you deserve it.* This was the house where Nadav died.

We sat in the living room together and looked at the objects around us, which continued to exist with their own independent existence. How strange, how strange it was that objects survived people. The refrigerator kept on humming as if it had a few more things to convey to us, a few more instructions Mom didn't have time for. Mom's dressing gown was folded up next to the bed, ready for use. Her shawl had already been returned to the closet. *Does anyone want it? No one wants it?* Dad's pipes curled in dandyish poses. Countless times, Mom had cleaned them, rubbing their long necks, running a rag over their exhaling mouths, polishing them in preparation for his arrival in one of her races against time. *Are you pleased, Dad? Do you like our clean house?* And the cabinets. The cabinets. When would I really dare open all the drawers in all the cabinets? After all, there must be more letters waiting for me there. Crammed into the smell of mothballs and pajamas. Letters hidden from me, God knows why.

Darkness descended on the parents' house, and the four of us huddled together in the living room as if orphanhood were a blanket that was supposed to cover us all. When had we ever sat like that? Were we ever really together?

"Why didn't Mom speak to Grandma?"

"She was mad at her."

"But when she grew up she must have understood at some point that Grandma couldn't have come to her."

"She was mad at her because Grandma had promised Julia she would write to her, but she never sent her a letter."

Amnon rose to smoke a cigarette. "Noga, why do you keep messing with all that your whole life? You can't mess with it your entire life. Aren't you sick of it?"

"And Julia never wrote herself?"

"Never. Grandma asked her not to write. She promised that she herself would write, and she never did."

"Enough, Noga, aren't you sick of this?"

"But Mom's not exactly disabled either," I said, startling and correcting myself. "I mean, she wasn't disabled for most of her life. She could have found Julia at some point. After all, Mom can move mountains when she wants to."

"Noga, don't you get it? You don't get it, do you? It wasn't just Mom who didn't speak to Grandma. It was impossible to talk to Grandma. She was always saying that you don't talk about this, and you don't talk about that, and you have to focus on what's important. That none of us had too much time to waste."

"She's right," Amnon said. "Life is for living. Not just for talking about the past. Life isn't just all about shrinks, Noga."

"Excuse me?"

"What do you mean, 'excuse me'? What do you want to be excused for? For the fact that ever since you were born, you've been wallowing in all kinds of things that can't be changed? You think it always helps, wallowing like that? We've already seen how much it helped all of us here, how much it helped that patient of yours who cut herself exactly when you decided not to come see Mom," he said, and we were all silent.

Until Lily said, "Amnon, that's kind of a low blow."

"Maybe it is. But she always wants the truth, Noga. Right? So maybe the truth is sometimes a low blow."

Amnon's face flushed, and he said he needed another cigarette. He went outside, and Lily hurried out after him. Iris and I stayed in the living room. Once again, the four of us had dispersed. The blanket of orphanhood could not cover all of us together. I looked at Iris; maybe she would say something. Maybe she had some stance on what Amnon had said. But she got up and followed Lily out. Through the window, I saw the three of them standing outside the house and smoking.

Now it was just me again. Me and the house. Me and the space my brother and sisters had left behind. I remained sitting next to the rug, thinking about what Amnon had said. Life wasn't just all about shrinks. Maybe it was actually the other way around. Shrinks should be all about life. And it was true, he was right. It didn't always work out. But at least Amnon had spoken out. He said something. At long last, he had said something. I got up and went out to them.

"That's it? You're planning to stay outside?" And they were silent. Amnon's speech was over. All out. There was a fixed quota, and he had already made use of it.

Until Iris said, "You're not happy in this house? Well, get used to it. It's ours now."

I looked at my brother and sisters standing and smoking. They were within arm's reach. I could almost touch them.

What would we do with this house now, a house that could not be sold or rented out, but only lived in? And what was with that "get used to it" from Iris?

"What do you want from me? What's your problem with me?" I asked Iris suddenly. She looked at me in disbelief, and I couldn't believe it either. Whose mouth had just said those words?

"Maybe I'm sick and tired of your drama?" she answered. "Maybe I've had enough of the mess you've been making your whole life. And of the fact that one day you decided to stop speaking to Mom. And then later, I'm not sure exactly when and why and how, you two started speaking again. Until one day, you just didn't show up to take care of her, when it was your turn."

I didn't answer. I thought maybe Lily would tell Iris, too, that that was a low blow. But Lily was silent. Lily would never tell Iris anything of the kind. And maybe Iris was right, not just Amnon. And in some way, in spite of everything, I wanted Iris to keep talking. I wanted Amnon to keep talking. I wanted us to talk.

"I want to talk to you guys. I want us to be able to talk about all kinds of things. I want to be with you more. I've missed you all these years," I said, and couldn't believe I'd said it. I've said so many things to people in all my years as a therapist, and it was only with my brother and sisters that I never could. And they were silent, but I went on. "I want to look for things in the drawers and the cabinets tomorrow. I know Mom hid Ronnie's letters. Will you help me?" And they were silent. And I kept going. "Is there a chance you'll help me?"

"Tomorrow," Lily said. "It's late now."

We went to bed. This time, Mom hadn't reserved the cabin for us, like she did during Dad's *shiva*. Through the window, I could see that whoever was living there had gone to bed a while ago. The cabin was asleep. Lily and Iris went to sleep in the parents' bed. Amnon made up the living room couch for himself.

"I'm leaving you Jenny's bed."

I rested my head on the pillow of the woman who had taken care of Mom in her last years. For about two hours, I tossed and turned, trying to find out what it felt like to sleep in the bed of someone who truly took care of people, meaning taking care of their body, not their mind. Washing them, and feeding them, not just talking to them. And so I tossed and turned until I fell asleep, but in the morning, I woke to a buzz. At first, the buzz mingled with the dream, as if the dream had grown wings and begun floating through the room, but gradually, the buzz turned more realistic. It was unclear what kind of buzz it was, a fly or some other flying creature, until I thought I recognized Lily's voice, immersed in a rustling of paper, a new sound emerging from the depths of the cabinets and drawers she was sorting through.

Oh my God, I heard her muttering. *Oh my God.* Lily shook her hands as if trying to get rid of some vile creature, dropping an old, yellowing letter, in English, on the rug.

What happened?

Oh my God. She sat down on the floor, shivering, pointing with one hand at the drawer in which Mom kept all the documents. "It was in here." She was shaking, pointing at a drawer with a false bottom. "God save us. God save us, all of us."

***

2.5.1976

To Ruthie Glover,

I didn't mean to write to you. I don't know if our mother, or actually your mother, told you about me. If you know that in recent years, the kibbutz has transferred part of her reparation payments to me. At her request, of course. I wouldn't ask for it for myself. For myself, I don't need anything. I've never had, won't have, and don't have a life. But my son can't stay at the boarding school anymore. Next year he'll be seventeen. Please. I'm not asking for anything for myself. But please take him in. He has no one here. No one in the world. I'm not in touch with his father. And about his grandfather, damn his name and memory, he, of course, knows nothing. And he won't. Take him in.

Vera

***

4.8.1976

Ruthie,

Thanks for getting back to me. You don't have to believe me. Just take him in. Our mother, yours, actually, said that after she died, I could send him to the kibbutz.

Vera

גֶשֶׁם

6.10.1976

Dear Ruthie,

Thank you for your answer. I don't blame you for not believing me.
There are some things that are unbelievable. Sometimes I don't believe
myself either. Just take my boy in. He's a good boy. A little sad, but good.
He wants to make Aliyah to Israel, he wants to serve in the army. You
don't have to tell him that you're his aunt. He doesn't know he has any
family. Just, please, pay attention to what's going on with him. Make
sure he's okay. It's the little your mother could have done for him.

Vera

***

9.13.1976

Hello Ruthie,

I'm speechless. Tell me what arrangements need to be made.

Vera

***

7.22.1977

Hello Ruthie,

I'm sorry I didn't write for a few months, and maybe it's better that
way. Ronnie wrote me that he was very pleased. That he has a nice
roommate. That they're studying Hebrew in an ulpan[36] and that they
live in a cabin next to a social worker who takes care of him. I understand that you made sure he would be close to you, and I thank you
with all my heart. Don't worry, I won't tell him. This terrible secret
will be buried with the two of us. He tells me you have a nice big
family, and also one little daughter who has made friends with him.
I hope he knows happiness.

Vera

---

36   An *ulpan* is an institute for the intensive study of Hebrew.

***

6.19.1978

Hello Ruthie,

You might have heard. I'm not doing well. Please forgive me if I don't write. Please take care of Ronnie. I'll pray for him. Who knows, maybe one day we'll meet.

Vera

***

8.26.1989

Dear Ruthie,

I'm so sorry about what happened when we met. For years, I thought about what would happen if we would meet. For years, I imagined the conversation that would take place after she, your mother, would die. Who could have ever imagined that this would happen. He wrote to me that they were close. I thought that maybe in some way, they sensed that they were cousins. Even though the circumstances are horrific. When he wrote that she was pregnant, I didn't know what to answer. What could I do other than tell you? What a terrible mistake I made when I didn't tell him in the first place. But how could I? Please don't cast him out. He has nowhere to go. We've been cast out enough in our lives.

Vera

***

December 1989

My most Rabbit,

If you don't find me, it's not because I wanted to disappear. Your mother has been good to me all those years. More than my mother was, I'm sorry to say. I don't know what happened to her suddenly. But something did. Did you know our mothers met? Maybe one day, at some point, maybe we'll meet again too.

Your Tortoise

The four of us sat and shivered. Outside was a noontime sun, illuminating all the paths and lawns of the kibbutz. From the parents' kitchen window, we could see a handful of people crossing through the old people's neighborhood. Some on foot, some on bikes, going down the path adjacent to the cabin. The cabin with the deck, and the peg, and the drill. Once, a new immigrant had lived there, with dimples and white teeth. He held the drill, plugged it in, held the handle, and pressed one button that made lots of noise until the entire neighborhood was shaking and it seemed like any minute now, even Kalman would leave his house. The light coming in from outside illuminated the four of us, and if we had dared look at ourselves, we would have seen how pale we were. Iris's teeth were chattering. Lily covered her face with her hands. The objects in the house stood silent; only the wheelchair moved, just a little, as if reacting to the very slow movement of the Earth. The refrigerator hummed quietly. The kettle was silent.

"I feel sick," Amnon mumbled, and Iris got up and said she was going to go throw up in Mom's bathroom.

"Irisssss," I heard myself screaming in horror. "Move away from the rug quick. Move, quick, you're stepping on him!!!"

19.

A month after the funeral, we gathered in the kibbutz dining hall. For a month, we hadn't talked among ourselves, the four of us. Each of us, brother or sister, carried back to his or her home the shivers that had grabbed hold of us when we pulled our hands away from Mom's drawer, as if we were on fire. Words stirred within me in a muddle. *It's instinct*, Ram had said. It was instinct for a grandmother to take care of her grandson if his parent was in and out of hospitals. *What are you worried about, Noga*, Ram would always say. *What could happen that hasn't already happened? We've all changed*, Arbel and Nitzan and Lior had said. *We've all had other loves since, but we remember how you couldn't breathe without him. So who are you married to? Sometimes life is funny*, that's what they said: funny. And I really couldn't breathe without him, simply because my gills were on his skin, simply because we shared the same skin, with the same cells.

And on the cell phone, I found a WhatsApp message from Hani. She had just gotten my message now, she hadn't been able to make it to the *shiva*, since she was having some health issues, too. *How are you? How are you dealing with the loss? It must be complicated. When would be a convenient time for me to come over?* And I didn't answer Hani. Some things are outside the bounds of psychology. What would I tell Hani? That anything is normal under the circumstances? "Over my dead body," that's what I had told Nathaniel Hazon back when he invited me to join his study on the autobiographies of Holocaust survivors. *Over my dead body*. And Aviram had said I might actually be wrong, that maybe it was in fact determinism, that there was no free choice there, and Amnon had said, *how much can you wallow, aren't you sick of it? We've already seen how much it helped, your patient died, killed herself, a girl for a girl, and Grandma's right that you can't talk about everything, that none of us have too much time to waste.* And Eli opened the door for me when I came home and asked, *what happened, why are you shaking,* and I opened my mouth a little as if I was actually trying to say something, something about the adopted brother we shared, "we've been cast out enough," his mother had written, meaning my aunt, that's how she had written to my mother, meaning his aunt. Where had she made him disappear? And Eli said, *Noga, should I call an ambulance?* And I looked at him. *An ambulance for whom, for me? I'm not the point here, I'm mentally healthy, having me was mentally healthy, look what a mentally healthy effect I have.* "Call Ronnie," my mother had told me back then, when I disappeared on her. "He's looking for you all over the kibbutz." *I'm losing my mind,* she said, *I'm losing my mind, where has Noga disappeared to?* That's how she always wanted to keep me safe, so that I wouldn't get sick, so that I wouldn't die, so that I wouldn't get suspended from school, so that I wouldn't think my father had abandoned me. He didn't abandon me; I was the only one he wrote letters to after his son died. *It's an outrage, it's an outrage that Dad died,* that's what Mom had said. She always wanted to keep me safe, and yet hadn't managed to keep me safe from this, of all things. And Eli said, *Noga, I'm calling an ambulance,* and I told him, *no, Eli, we don't need an ambulance, nothing new has happened that hasn't happened a long time ago.* "But you're shaking," he said, and I answered that I wasn't the one who was shaking, it wasn't me, it had never been me, it was life that was shaking. *Can't you feel it? It's been shaking all the time, for years now, I'm just displaying the shaking. But now I'll stop for a moment, here, see, I've gotten tired. I'll lie down in bed now, and I'll lose my mind like I know how to do, and later, at some point, I'll find my mind again, I know how to do that too, and you'll bring me water and I'll tell you everything.*

A month after the funeral, we gathered in the kibbutz dining hall. For a month, we hadn't talked among ourselves, but we could feel how the blanket of orphanhood, the one that could not quite cover us, was gradually falling apart between us. How its threads, which had never been woven correctly, were gradually loosening their faint grip on the fabric, melting and being absorbed within the days and the hours, exposing the thin, undone fibers, the ones that were always hidden within the effortful labor of warp and woof. There, the weave was falling apart between us; there, the undone fibers were touching skin; there, the nerves between us were being exposed; there we were.

"I didn't know, Nogi, I didn't know any of it," Lily had told me back then, when she came from the Golan Heights to bring me back home after my hospitalization in the psychiatric unit. "How nice that you two keep in close touch," Dad had said before our family trip to the Golan Heights, before Mom suggested that I invite Ronnie to join us, "after all, he's family," and *what a beautiful day, what a wonderful trip, are you happy?* And Eli said, "It was just blind love," and Lily said, "God save us, all of us."

"That's one hell of a story," Eli sighed. "Life really is shaking." He started to tidy up the room, putting things in their place. "Are you okay?"

"No."

"Obviously."

"It's normal, under the circumstances," I tried to laugh and he hugged me, and I cried. In front of my eyes, the river of blood I'd spilled on the parents' rug mounted. My little tadpole, God save us from it, had managed to wiggle out of me; perhaps it knew there was no room for it among us, "we've been cast out enough," and Julie knocked on our bedroom door; tomorrow she was going back to the army, and meanwhile, how about if she made dinner for all of us?

A month after the funeral, we gathered in the kibbutz dining hall. Varda from the Senior Citizen Committee eulogized Mom. *An extraordinary woman. A true survivor. How much strength and faith are required to keep going. And here are her four children, and her grandchildren, and now there are great-grandchildren, too,* gazing with a smile at Nadav's new twins, *the family line continues, the family line has a power that is unstoppable, the family line is the proof that we cannot be destroyed, and although you don't live here,* and Varda looked over to the four of us, standing next to each other, holding on to our shared secret the way you hold on to explosives, carefully, so that we wouldn't make a wrong move, *although you don't live here,* Varda continued, *the kibbutz will always be your home.* On the table stood a large photo of Mom on the day she returned from her trip to Washington to speak to an audience of Jewish American youths. She stood smiling with a bouquet of flowers in her hand. Next to the photo was another bouquet, with a memorial candle next to it. *May Ruthie Glover rest in peace.*

A moment before we turned away, heading for the parents' house, I felt a soft hand resting on my shoulder. Grandma Lily gave me a hug.

"Thank you, Nogi," she told me.

***

The path leading from the dining hall to the parents' house hasn't changed, although so many years have passed. It hasn't grown old and hasn't learned from experience, for better or for worse. The blue jacaranda and the flame tree and the coral tree bloomed on either side of it, with oleander bushes rioting in pink and white, vines growing wild as if this was their natural climate, and pansies planted between the bushes with a loving hand. The four of us walked along the path. We walked side by side, and behind us strode Ilan, Yossi, and Eli, with the grandchildren and the new great-grandchildren in a stroller. The paths of the kibbutz, without Mom. People greeted us, asked how we were, and congratulated Lily on the new grandchildren. "Sometimes good news comes in pairs," they joked with her, and she said it was great to be a grandmother. The same love, the same rejuvenation, but without having to get up at night.

The door of the parents' house opened straight into the living room. It had been a month since we'd touched it, and we hurried to open all the windows, to air out the house, which had stood shuttered, and now, we could hear it letting out some kind of sigh, expelling air, letting the toxins loose. Gradually, air infiltrated the house and we turned on the lights and sat down in the living room, around the rug.

"I don't want this house," I told my brother and sisters. "But we can't sell it either, right? So until they change the rules in the kibbutz, what are we going to do with this house? Don't you ever feel like starting life over?"

They were silent for a while, until Iris said, "We don't have a choice. It's ours. What do we do? Donate it to some charity?"

And once again, we were silent.

And Amnon said, "You can't get rid of everything."

And once again, we were silent.

And I asked, "Do you want us to come up with some kind of idea? And in the meantime, it'll belong to all of us? We could meet here sometimes. Our kids could come here when they wanted to."

And once again, we were silent. All of our photos were displayed on the walls. There we were, a family. A family line. A family line that persisted, with "a power that is unstoppable."

Yossi got up to make himself a cup of espresso from the machine. "Does anyone want espresso? Everyone?" And the four of us exchanged looks. How do you exchange looks? How does that work? A look for a look? In any case, we exchanged looks. We verified very carefully that we understood what the looks were saying, that we could, that it was allowed, and then we all said, nearly simultaneously, "And who wants bread and jam?"

The mother tongue. Our mother tongue. Come back to us, don't leave us now, of all times. We have a few more things to look into in this world. Our labor here is not yet completed. Here we are, our eyes nearly wide open. We agree to bread and jam. Even if it's impossible to swallow. And we also agree to a whole half egg. After all, you should look at the half-full half, right? And also a wonderful tomato. And *I scream*. Return to us, mother tongue, tell us, once again, *there you are, you deserve it, are you happy?* After all, that was what you wanted, wasn't it? For us to be happy. Come back to us and the four of us will speak you. And remember, in you, our Nadav. And our father. Return to us, mother tongue, and, in you, we'll remember you, as well.

We sat and drank espresso from the new machine. *Does anyone want the old kettle? It's not necessary anymore. We'll leave the refrigerator here. The furniture too. And what about the rug?* I asked, and all at once we cracked up. How mother had wanted to "freshen up" the house, how she hadn't managed to pass on the rug to anyone. We laughed, and we cried, too. Together. *What do we do with the rug? What did you just say, Amnon? That there are some things you can't get rid of? So what do we do, leave it here?* I looked at it. I searched for the beast within its rhomboids, but I didn't see it. Maybe it was hiding. Maybe it had returned to its own land. To the forest.

"We'll vacuum it," Lily suggested. Vacuum it, and clean it, and leave it in the house. I could think of at least one person who might be happy to live here.

Dear Vera,

We hope this letter finds you well. Our mother, your sister, passed away. We didn't know. We never knew, although we might have sensed it. We want you to know that for a period that wasn't quite brief, Ronnie was part of us. We'd be happy to know where he is and what his address is. We'll be happy if he wants to live in our house in the kibbutz.

Warmly,

Lily, Iris, Amnon and Noga

***

My brother and sisters agreed to the letter. After all, even back in Palm Tree Preschool, I knew how to phrase good letters, although Dr. Dolittle never came to our preschool. Polynesia got sick and died, and so did Nadav the rabbit. Not everyone can be saved.

***

"It's not pie in the sky," Hani said. "If you want to be a better person, you can. It's not pie in the sky." No, it wasn't pie in the sky. Psyche, too, came down from heaven after illuminating her beloved with the light of the lantern. And all the neighbors stood and cried. *Have you ever seen anything like it? A girl who doesn't remember the sky?* And Mom looked for God. After all, Julia had told her that there was a God in heaven, that he was watching over her, and Mom said that if this was the heavens, then where was God? She needed to ask him a few questions. And all the neighbors raised their eyes to the sky.

"Oh, come on," I once said to Hani. "It's not like you can really put your mind somewhere." And she smiled and said I was right. That sometimes, ridiculous statements came out of her mouth.

"Let's open the window," I suggested. "Let's open the window and look at the sky." Like I'd looked at it back then, with Ronnie, with my solitary Tortoise, when we clung to each other on the bed before he opened the blinds. Before the first time he opened them since I had settled into his bungalow, and a screen of stars burst into the room, looking as if it had waited in the sky until the sky overflowed and shattered into our bungalow.

***

Two months after Julie concluded her military service, we all traveled to Poland. Lily and Ilan, Yossi and Iris, Amnon, Eli and I, with all the kids and grandkids. Eli filled up the suitcase with medication of all kinds, "can't hurt," and I sat in the living room and looked at the man I had married, my beloved's roommate, the only friend my cousin might have had, putting on his glasses and carefully examining all the expiration dates. "It's still good," he said about the pack of antihistamines, "and so is this," and shoved a box of daytime and nighttime cold medicine into the suitcase, and prescription eye ointment, *can't hurt*, and anti-nausea pills, most important of all. And so we all drove to the airport with our luggage.

"Did you take the bag with the medication?"

"Yes, I took it."

"And the sweater?"

"Yeah, yeah."

"I didn't know you had a Jewish mother for a husband," Iris teased me, and I had time to shoot back that it wasn't true. "We're the Jewish mothers, remember?"

Four hours of flight separated our skies from the skies of Poland. Four hours of skies. What's four hours? It's nothing.

"Kitchen duty," Amnon said.

"A shift in the cotton fields," Lily added.

"Night milking in the dairy," Iris cracked up, and all of our children looked at us in concern, at their parents who had suddenly become children. The kind of children who ask, "Are we in Warsaw yet?" Four sessions at the clinic, I thought, poring over the meaning of this item of information, whether it even mattered that Poland was equivalent to four sessions.

And now came the landing on Polish soil at an early hour of the morning. Poland woke to a sunny day while we walked through the jet bridge. And there was the line for Passport Control. The clerks leafed through the pages suspiciously. Some turned them while suppressing a yawn. The Israeli passports were okay; we got through. In the Warsaw Airport, we rented a minibus from a Polish clerk with glasses (how old was he? How old were his parents? What were they up to during the war?) and began to make our way toward Belzec on the roads passing through the wheat fields.

"It's the annual field trip," Lily and Iris laughed. *Should we sing the song about the boiled chick? What's the deal with that song anyway? Did you ever think about the lyrics?* We had, but then all the songs we sang in the kibbutz were surreal. *Remember "A Camp Is a Useful Thing"?* We looked at each other, but we didn't laugh.

Anyone driving down the broad roads of the land of large planes, and, for hours, seeing the stork nests resting in the tops of the trees by the sides of the road like cradles, understands why the stork is said to deliver babies. Year after year, the stork returns to the same nest, and upon its return, renovates and expands it, so that the nest gradually grows over the years. Anyone who sees the cradles built by the stork realizes that babies can grow in all kinds of places. In houses. In treetops. Under the ground.

We parked the minibus in the lot outside the camp, among the trees, and came in through the gate.

"So that's where it was, huh? There is such a place as Belzec. This is where Grandma went, of her own free will."

The sky was blue and the wind was blowing. You could hear the birds and us. Other than us, there was not a single living soul there. The sound of our steps echoed as we walked down the path between the lawns toward the monument. On our left, abandoned, stood the cement chambers. They could not be burned down. There was no way to make them disappear. Nothing helped. This is where Grandma went. Of her own free will. This is where she was born, and after all, the people, where they were born, that's where they'll find help. Perhaps 500 yards away, Julia's house still stands. Julia must be gone for ages now, but 500 yards away, the house to which Mom's uncle's horse galloped might still be standing. "Here," he brought her the cradle of bread. *Here, it just came. Straight from heaven.* Five-hundred yards away, the house might still be standing, with the bed in the middle of the kitchen, covered with duvets. The painting of the Virgin Mary carrying the baby Jesus in her arms might still be hanging there. The house near the wheat fields, and the cemetery, and the crypt. The house with the barn and the pigs. And the little pit Julia dug with her hands and a stool next to it. The house illuminated like a little firefly within an endless darkness. The house standing 500 yards away. Maybe right here, where our feet were stepping, Grandma watched over Mom. A girl for a girl. Maybe right here, the shadow of a new girl who was born was cast.

The museum was open and a short, smiley woman greeted us. There were many photos hanging on the walls. We already knew some of them, from the internet. From the Yad Vashem Holocaust Museum. Some of the documents were there, too. And the meticulously drawn blueprints of the camp. And letters. We had heard so much about Belzec. Much too much to believe it really existed. We asked the smiley woman to see the list of survivors.

"Survivors?" she wondered. "Don't you know? Belzec wasn't a labor camp.

Don't look for survival stories here, like in Auschwitz or Sobibor. Belzec was a death camp. Three survivors. That's all." She showed us the printed letters on the page. Our grandmother, and two other survivors.

"That's not all of them," we told her.

"What do you mean?"

"There was someone else here, a girl. Would you believe it? A girl survived here."

Made in the USA
Middletown, DE
07 March 2022

62246815R00129